Arcadia Snips and the Steamwork Consortium

Being A Wholly Accurate Historical Account Concerning Matters Of Steam, Skullduggery, And The Irresponsible Application Of Reckless Mathematics In The 19th Century

Robert C. Rodgers

Published by Steam-Powered Press
PO Box 11532
Takoma Park, MD 20913

On the Internet at www.steam-poweredpress.com

This book is printed on recycled paper

All characters in the following narrative are fictional; any resemblance to actual persons, real or dead, is purely coincidental.

ISBN: 978-0-984129-00-3

To my grandfather, the sorriest, surliest bastard to ever put pen to paper. For every word that follows, blame him.

ACT 1

~*~

"In yet another example of tragically misapplied genius, the mysterious anarchist who calls himself Professor Hemlock has done it again—several of the Eastern Aberwick Bank's calculation engines have been crippled through the irresponsible application of reckless mathematics. The rogue chaotician claimed responsibility for the financial disaster in a letter delivered to the Isle Gazette (see page 9a), citing the company's cutthroat business tactics, support of imperialism, and rude bank tellers as justification. Authorities continue to investigate the anarchist's activities while urging all citizens to behave no differently during this time of fiscal duress. Meanwhile, one question lingers upon the lips of every man, woman, and child: Who is Professor Hemlock?"

—Front page of the Isle Gazette, 'PROFESSOR HEMLOCK STRIKES AGAIN'

~*~

CHAPTER 1: A BRIEF INTRODUCTION TO OUR TALE OCCURRING 20 YEARS PRIOR, WHEREIN PIGS TAKE FLIGHT, FOOLS TAKE NOTE, AND A GRAND PARTNERSHIP IS PROPOSED

~*~

"Dear Madame," the letter read. "Although we remain appreciative of your continued attempts to bring a feminine touch to the world of aeronautics, the Royal Society of Aviation regrets to inform you that your design shall fly only once swine have taken to the skies."

The letter was framed and mounted on the dining room wall.

The room had become a workshop. An exquisitely crafted flame maple table that had once been its centerpiece was now pressed against the far wall, its rich and vibrant texture smothered beneath greased tools and blueprints pinned under various bits of silver cutlery. Nuts and bolts were organized by size and dumped into teacups along the table; at its edge sat a battered mechanics book smudged with oiled fingerprints.

The woman who studied the book was fiercely handsome, possessing the allure of an ominous storm. Her dark, thick eyebrows grated against each other like cogs in some vast and terrible engine, trembling beneath the pressure of her thought. A pair of aviator goggles dangled just below her delicate jaw and over her pale throat. It added to the contradictions of her appearance—the grease stains upon her fine evening gown, the grime beneath her well-trimmed nails, and the sweat above her elegant brow.

Abigail Parsley drew her attention away from the tome and turned to the contraption that occupied the middle of her dining room. Its main body was a canoe, with a chair fastened down inside it; a complex knot of ropes, pulleys, levers, and beams connected it to an immense woolen sack that draped over its side and across the floor. Though the machine had been built from spare

Abigail inspects her marvelous contraption.

parts and plundered ideas, its overall design remained her own. She knew every inch of it - every screw, every fastener, and every fold.

She took her seat in the cradle of her invention and pulled the goggles up over her eyes. She now found herself facing the letter that had spurred her to action; taking in a slow breath, she read the last line to herself:

Your design shall fly only once swine have taken to the skies.

"Very well," she said, and then she turned the machine on.

The frame shuddered. Valves hissed. Wood creaked and sheepskin bags groaned.

"Soar," Abigail whispered.

The woolen sack was soon flushed with gases, rising up over her in a cigar-shaped lump. As it grew bloated and buoyant, Abigail was struck by a peculiar dizziness; the vessel was gradually leaving the earth, its skids sliding across the tiled floor. It bobbed, sluggishly rising toward the dining room's open glass portal.

Abigail held the controls steady. The edge of the vessel's balloon came precariously close to the opening's squared edges - she instinctively held her breath as she felt a metal corner scrape across the bag, denting the fabric. But in only a moment, the airship had cleared the gap and floated out into the brisk day's air.

She waited until her estate sank far beneath her feet. Then, biting down on her bottom lip, she twisted the levers and dragged the ship's nose down.

It groaned before lunging into a dive over the fields of the village.

Abigail eased the levers back, allowing the ship time to regain its altitude. Then, wearing a supremely satisfied grin, she reached up and unraveled the rope that kept the canopy over the balloon in place. When the cover slid off, it exposed her personal touch to the design.

Abigail laughed and steered the first unpowered dirigible towards the sun.

~*~

Some considerable distance away, the author of the missive that spurred Abigail to action was enjoying his afternoon tea with friends among the ivy-drenched gardens of the Royal Society of Aviation's chapter-house. The setting was splendid, with lush foliage weaving its way through the ivory lattice fences and the friendly shade of a tall willow tree supplying respite from the afternoon heat.

"The very premise is preposterous," said Mr. Twine. "Preposterous!" He would often shout this at the slightest provocation; it was a word that suited him well. Mr. Twine's mind suffered from a surplus of opinions in much in the same way that a person's looks might suffer from a surplus of face; all but the mightiest features disappeared beneath the tyrannical enormity of the whole.

"Of course, of course," agreed Mr. Elle, who was prone to getting lost in city streets as a result of following strangers who looked as if they might know the way. "Absolutely. Ah, but I do not think Mr. Cork heard you when you said exactly which part of the premise was so preposterous. Might you explain it, merely for his sake?"

"A letter that arrived at our fine establishment only a month ago. Penned by a woman, its very premise was preposterous. Preposterous!"

"Preposterous, you say?" said Mr. Cork, a rotund dirigible pilot who had been responsible for so many airship disasters that his name now appeared on the government's annual military budget. He had just awoken from a brief nap, and sleepily joined the conversation. "Howso?"

"Why, the whole thing!" Mr. Twine said. "A navigable unpowered dirigible? One which sails the skies much like a ship sails the seas? Ridiculous. Everyone knows that an engine is required for any true degree of control."

"And a skilled navigator," Mr. Cork lazily added.

"And a skilled navigator," Mr. Twine agreed. "But just imagine—some fussy filly thinking she could understand the nuanced complexities of flight."

"Er," Mr. Elle said, looking up. "Did it suddenly get a bit

cloudier?"

"So, of course, I told her that we were quite sorry, but penmanship does not count..."

"Er," Mr. Cork said, following Mr. Elle's gaze. "I beg your pardon, Mr. Twine."

"—and that her invention would fly—"

"Mr. Twine!" Mr. Elle and Mr. Cork spoke in unison.

"—only once swine took to flight. What?" Mr. Twine snapped, scowling.

"Look up."

Mr. Twine did.

And stared with slack-jawed shock.

The dirigible had been painted into the likeness of a pig, with gaily colored wings drawn upon either of its sides; its front wore the visage of a cheerful porcine grin, complete with stubby nose. Sitting in the gondola tucked beneath it was a young comely woman wearing a formal dress, a scarf, goggles, and an aviator's cap.

"Good afternoon, gentlemen." Abigail said, wrenching the controls forward to bring the dirigible down gracefully in the center of the chapter-house's garden. "Are you having tea? How delightful. Might I join you?"

~*~

Exhausted and exhilarated after a day spent making her peers look like fools, Abigail returned home to find two men of dubious character waiting for her in the smoking lounge.

Both were young and well dressed, but after that, all comparisons between the two failed. One was dark and calm, sitting in a comfortable arm-chair as he enjoyed a freshly lit pipe; the other was blond and fidgety, wearing down her expensive carpet with the soles of his expensive shoes. Abigail's eyes flashed with fury at these two men and their unannounced intrusion.

"I do not know who you two are," she told them, retrieving the fire poker from her hearth. "But as I remember telling the servants to allow no one in, I can only assume you have arrived through some means of mischief—"

"Mischief," the dark haired one said, laughing. "Yes, you could certainly make that claim, Miss Parsley."

At once, the other turned to her, glaring at the poker in her grip. "I still think this is a mistake, Nigel."

"Oh, quiet down. She's exactly what we're looking for."

"Explain yourselves at once, or I will send someone to fetch the constable," Abigail said, pointing the poker at the blond.

"We apologize for our crude manner," Nigel replied, moving to stand and bow. "We gained entry by convincing your servants that this is a matter of the utmost importance. Do not think poorly of them; we are quite persuasive when we wish to be. I am Professor Arcanum, and this is my associate, Mr. Daffodil."

The iron poker wavered in her grip, its tip beginning to sink toward the carpet. "Arcanum? Daffodil?"

"Yes," Jeremiah said. "We're very important people, you know."

"Yes, yes. I recognize your names," Abigail replied. "I know you, Nigel—the famous naturalist and mathematician. And you," she added, glaring at Jeremiah, "the equally infamous mad scientist and administrator of the Steamwork. I read that last paper of yours."

"Oh?" Jeremiah asked, the scowl melting into something cheerful and bright. "Did you?"

"Yes," she said. "Absolute rubbish. You had no clue what you were babbling about."

Jeremiah blanched.

Nigel laughed. "Oh yes," he said. "You are most certainly what we need."

"I've read your work as well," she told Nigel. "You, at least, seem to have some fundamental grasp over your field." She now held the iron poker out in front of her as if it were a sword, still watching the men warily. "Nevertheless, I fail to understand what matter requires you to intrude in my home at such a late hour without so much as sending a letter of introduction first."

"Secrecy, Miss Parsley." Nigel said, then tapped the bell of his pipe to spill the loose ash into a tray. "We require your assistance. Jeremiah and I are working on a remarkable project."

"A project?" Abigail's eyes narrowed. "Oh yes, let me guess. You are working on some sort of ground-breaking research; some immensely important and grand experiment. But just one problem—you have yet to find some means to fund your wondrous project."

"Well," Nigel said, "Funding is always a problem, yes—"

"And so you've read a little bit about me, found out that I'm a very rich and unmarried woman who is very keen about matters of mathematics and engineering?"

"Well, yes, something like that—"

"And so you think, 'Oh, of course she'll sponsor our wonderful experiment!'," Abigail finished. She swept the poker up and pointed to the exit. "Out."

"You've got it all wrong," Jeremiah began, but Nigel cut him off.

"Of course. We shall leave at once," he told her. "We apologize for bothering you with this trifling matter. Would you care to perhaps show us to the door?"

Abigail glared. "The faster you are out of my home, the better." She gestured for the gentlemen to follow; it was then that she noticed both were carrying umbrellas with peculiar stylized hilts. "Are you daft? There isn't a cloud in the sky."

"Isn't there?" Nigel asked, then shrugged.

This gave Abigail pause, but she was quick to brush it aside. She led them both to the exit, opening the door and stepping aside to let them leave. Before she could slam the door shut, both had turned to face her.

"Mr. Daffodil?" Nigel said. "Time, please."

Jeremiah removed a gold pocket watch from his coat, checking it. "Forty five seconds."

"Madame, if I may just mention, before we go—one of the reasons we came to you was because of a paper you wrote. 'The Impossibility of Weather Prediction', I believe."

Abigail's hand rested against the doorknob. "Yes? What of it?"

"Even my compatriot acknowledged it as a brilliant

summary of what makes accurate weather prediction absurd," Nigel said. "You describe the difficulties of understanding incredibly complex systems elegantly. We were particularly smitten with your example of how, over time and through a chain of countless events, the stroke of a sparrow's wings can change the course of a hurricane."

"Yes, yes," Abigail said irritably, although she flushed beneath the presence of the compliment. "Well, then, I'll bid you both a good night."

"Time, Mr. Daffodil?"

"Twenty seconds."

"You were correct, of course. Predicting weather with our standard model of mathematics is impossible," Nigel said. "The best we can do is attempt a somewhat educated guess."

"I'm aware," she snapped. "I wrote the paper. Now, as I was saying, good night—"

"Mark," said Jeremiah.

Both gentlemen lifted their umbrellas skyward and opened them with a pop. At that exact instant, thunder roared over their heads. A shower of rain dropped down over Abigail's estate like a curtain on the stage.

Abigail stared up into the sky with an expression of bewilderment.

"Well, then," Nigel said, turning back to the road. "I suppose we'll bid you a good night as well, Madame. Again, we apologize for bothering you with this insignificant matter." He and Jeremiah began to walk away, umbrellas held high.

It took Abigail a moment to find her voice. When she at last did, it was burdened with a hoarse croak: "W—wait."

Jeremiah and Nigel stopped, looking over their shoulders. Abigail ran out into the rain. When she reached them, she was soaked through and through.

"Perhaps my original assessment was hasty. If you gentlemen might need someone to look over your notes—"

"We are uninterested in a secretary," Nigel said.

"And we are certainly not looking for a sponsor," Jeremiah said.

"But," Nigel added with a swiftly growing smile, "we are in the market for a partner."

~*~

Nigel Arcanum and Jeremiah Daffodil propose a grand partnership.

CHAPTER 2: IN WHICH TWENTY YEARS HAVE SINCE PASSED, WE DISCOVER MUCH CLAMOR IS AFOOT, AND OUR TITULAR PROTAGONIST IS AT LAST INTRODUCED

~*~

A river of gold flowed through a steam-powered city.

It was carried upon the greased rails of human ingenuity, ferried from one civilization to the next along a massive trumbling track that speared its way through air and soil. Every day, its trains pumped prosperity and corruption in equal parts through the city's brass-lined veins. And every day, its trains ran on time.

The city of Aberwick was a topographical nightmare wrested from the laudanum-fueled fever dreams of half-mad cartographers. It was cradled in a yawning canyon of volcanic rock, with communities swelling up into massive heaps of brick and timber; the trains flowed aside, above, and even through these mounds.

If the train rails were Aberwick's veins, then under Aberwick was its steam-powered heart. Beneath the crusty topsoil and the jigsaw puzzle of slums was a maze of tunnels and caverns where ancient boilers harvested the burning expulsions of geothermal vents, providing heat and power to the urban sprawl above. A tangle of pipes tied in mad knots of right and wrong angles slurped the volcanic gas like a thousand straws, drawing it up to the slums and the extravagant villas that lay high above. But despite all of this, it was the trains that had become the symbol of Aberwick: ceaseless, endless, and punctual.

Count Orwick watched the city through his office window as the trains outside plunged into tunnels and emerged across bridges, forming a tangled knot complex enough to give even Alexander's sword pause. Powerful locomotives weaved their way through the web, their conductors following Orwick's calculated directions—directions so divorced from common sense that calamity seemed inevitable. Yet like a magician poring over archaic alchemical formulae, he snatched success from the jaws of failure again and again.

His office was extravagant yet tasteful. Sets of exquisitely crafted maple chairs inlaid with floral patterns and padded with matching damask cushions gathered around his marble-topped desk. Ornate brass fixtures capped with glass spheres provided light along the walls, with coils of gas burning brilliantly within.

The elegance was lost upon Mr. Eddington as he marched in; for him, it was all the useless trimmings of a noble busy-body. The rail-thin administrator of the Steamwork was the sort of man whose face had been designed explicitly for the purpose of expressing outrage. There was never a moment when he lacked either a cause for indignation or the indiscretion necessary to express it.

He was accompanied by a gentleman who clutched a pile of documents to his chest as if it were a crucifix and he had just blundered into a den of nosferatu after wading through a pool of blood mixed with steak sauce. Mr. Tweedle was the chief administrator of all six of Aberwick's banks, and yet he was so boring in appearance that we shall waste no more words to describe him, save to note that he sometimes wore a very uninteresting hat.

"Count Orwick!" Mr. Eddington cried, the force of his voice causing Mr. Tweedle to cower. "I demand an explanation!"

Count Orwick tore himself away from the window with great reluctance. He observed the gentlemen as an alley cat might observe a pair of exotic birds kept safe in a cage; interesting, but ultimately inconsequential.

"For what do you demand an explanation?" Count Orwick asked.

"For this!" Mr. Eddington slapped the newspaper down onto the desk.

"That," Orwick said, "is a newspaper. I believe it may, on occasion, contain news."

"Sometimes crossword puzzles," Mr. Tweedle said, before sinking under Mr. Eddington's withering glare.

"Not the paper, Count Orwick. The article on the front

page." Mr. Eddington's finger stabbed at the title. It read: STEAMWORK UNDER INVESTIGATION.

"Oh, that," Orwick said. "It should be of little concern to such law-abiding men as yourselves."

"My associates and I brought our business to this fair city under the assurances of non-interference at the hands of the government."

"And so you have received it. And so you will continue to receive it. Her Majesty has made clear her desire for your sovereignty over personal affairs," Count Orwick said.

"Then what is this talk of an investigation? Why were we not informed?"

"I planned on scheduling a meeting with you this afternoon to discuss the matter," Orwick said. "Her Majesty has requested your full compliance in a government investigation of your facilities. She is concerned about the recent rash of attacks against our banks, and what it might mean should your inventions at the Steamwork fall into the wrong hands."

"Our security is second-to-none," Mr. Eddington said. "I will not have your men interfering with my work, blundering about in my workshops and disturbing my machines. We can carry out our own investigation, thank you very much."

"And what have you unearthed concerning the recent demise of your research assistant, Mr. Copper?"

"A tragedy, to be certain, but a wholly inevitable one," Mr. Eddington said. "Mr. Copper's research was highly dangerous. He ignored safety protocols time and time again."

"Her Majesty has reason to believe it may be part of an anarchist plot," Orwick said. "She wishes for the case to be re-opened and investigated."

Mr. Eddington's scowl deepened. "I have no desire to see your 'agents' in my house of business, Orwick."

"Please, Mr. Eddington. Agents? In my employ?" Orwick brought a narrow hand to his chest, as if fending off violence. "I have no such thing. I am merely a humble instrument of the Queen's will."

"In that case," Mr. Eddington said, stepping backward and

folding his arms over his chest. "I demand the investigation be carried out by a third party, unrelated to you or your government."

"Such a strange request," Orwick said. "Do you think us as little more than a motley collection of spies and thieves?"

"I think that history speaks for itself, Count Orwick."

"Very well. Hire any investigative agency you would like, so long as it is clear that they are impartial to the matter. I only ask that a government consultant be allowed to join the investigation, to ensure that our concerns are addressed."

Mr. Eddington's eyes narrowed into a stare that could slit open stone. "One consultant," he said.

"Only one," Orwick agreed, and then he smiled. Both Eddington and Tweedle instinctively recoiled; Orwick's smile was a vicious thing, full of malice and sharp edges. Nary a friendly flat-topped tooth lay in sight.

~*~

Beneath Arcadia Snips' derby hat and short black curls was the face of a silver-fanged cherub—a mocha-toned angel with enough charm to sell a pack of matches to a man doused in lamp-oil. But whenever she grinned, the very tip of that silver fang would tuck over the edge of her bottom tooth. It gave her a savage, frightful look.

Snips squirmed in the grip of the prison's complimentary straitjacket and accompanying chains, left hanging by her feet from the musty cell's ceiling. The nearby locksmith rattled off items from his list, scoring checkmarks as he went.

"Straitjacket, check."

Beside the locksmith stood Morgrim Prison's warden. The man resembled an old goat with all the mental flexibility of a chalk brick. Recent months had taken their toll on him; his once proud uniform fit him like a glove fitted a foot, and his eyes had sunk into deep craters.

"You see, Miss Snips," the warden began, "I want you to be extra comfortable. I've realized why you keep escaping. It's because we just haven't taken that extra step for you. We haven't been giving you the special attention you deserve."

"Manacles, check. Padlock on manacles, check."

"Really, I feel this whole sordid affair has been my own fault. But don't you worry. We're going to take every step possible to make sure you are comfortable." The warden twitched. "In fact, once we're through, I'm sure you'll never want to leave Morgrim again."

"Suspension cords, check. Padlock on suspension cords, check."

"Twice now," and here the warden's voice trembled, much like the plucked note of a cello string wound a quarter of an inch too tight, "you have vanished from your cell without apparent explanation or effort. Twice now, you have soiled my reputation as a capable jailer. I *will* earn my reputation back, Miss Snips. There will not be a third occasion."

"Reinforced triple padlocked deadbolts on the door, check. We're finished here, sir," the locksmith said.

Snips smiled.

"Oh, do you have something to say, Miss Snips? Perhaps some sort of amusing quip? A clever parting word?"

Rather than reply, Snips just kept on smiling.

"All for the better. Rest assured; there is nothing on the tip of your tongue that can change the fact that you will die here, alone and in the dark."

The warden spun about on the heel of his boot, stomping out of the room with the locksmith in tow. The door slammed shut, followed by the clamor of many, many locks snapping into place. Once the sound of their footsteps put them at the far end of the hall, Snips stuck out her tongue.

On its tip was the warden's key.

Snips pulled the key back into her mouth and began to writhe with great violence, rocking from side to side. Every minute would end with a rattle of metal or cloth as she threw down yet another implement of bondage. After five minutes of this, she had shed her bindings much like a snake might shed its skin. She unlocked the chain that held her feet in the air and tumbled to the floor, now clad only in her prison arrows and beloved hat.

She didn't get far out of the cell before stepping out in front of someone.

"Now what do we 'ave here," asked the towering guard. He was swarthy and broad, with palms large enough to seize skulls and arms strong enough to crack them. When he spoke, it was with barking alacrity—as if he found the language somehow distasteful to his tongue, and was glad to have it off. "Still tryin' to drive the warden mad, eh?"

"Morning, Agrippa," Snips said, unflinching. "And, yeah. You got a mind to try and stop me?"

Agrippa laughed; it was a short and violent noise that sounded like something he had caught from a fellow who had died of it. "Maybe," he said. "You think y'could take me?"

"Probably not," Snips admitted, meeting his smile with one of her own. "But I'd charge you an eyeball for the right." She wiggled her thumb.

For a moment, there was silence. Then Agrippa chuckled.

"Give me a strike to th'back of th'head," the guard said. "Make it look good, eh?"

Snips searched the room until she found a crowbar. She advanced toward Agrippa, who obligingly turned his back.

"Some world, eh?" Agrippa said. "You can't even trust your own kin not to turn you in for a nickel."

"It's always been like that," Snips said. "Besides, the only two things I've ever trusted were myself and a sturdy crowbar. And I ain't too sure about that first thing."

"Well, I think—"

She brought the makeshift bludgeon down with a brutal blow.

~*~

CHAPTER 3: IN WHICH OUR TITULAR PROTAGONIST MEETS, GREETS, AND FLEES FROM HER NEW EMPLOYERS

~*~

It was always the smell of the Rookery that hit Snips first—like a flaming freight train filled with manure. The stench stabbed its way to the back of the brain, signing a signature at the top of your spine. It was a smell you could always recognize but never quite pin down.

The Rookery was several hundred tight knots of vendors, carts, and houses tied along a crooked and winding length of road. The looming brick walls drew so close in some places that no more than two people could pass at a time—and the way they tilted toward the street implied an imminent avalanche of mortar and wood.

To the right, an immense mechanical spider picked its way up and over the crowd, its delicate bronze legs scraping across cobblestone while while its smokestack belched thick ribbons of steam and soot. A gondola containing a mobile smithy sat on top, filled to the brim with metalworkers who diligently reinforced buildings that showed signs of wear and potential collapse. Valves along the machine's belly hissed and released great clouds of vapor, thoroughly drenching any unfortunates below. Street urchins in war paint dashed in between the pincer-like feet to snatch up pieces of metal that tumbled down from the workers' hands. Sometimes, a coveted lump of coal would fall, inciting the children into a frantic scrabble.

To the left, a crowd of spectators laughed at a mechanical puppet show made of metal and timber. Its automated clockwork cast went through the same motions they did every day; a hook-nosed jester with a nasal voice sang a jaunty song as he clubbed his wife and infant with a steady series of thwacks, drawing whooping laughter from the crowd.

Above, restaurants kept afloat by sheepskin balloons

inflated with hot gas catered to the whims of those on balconies and airships, who enjoyed their lunch while watching the going-ons from a lofty perch. A few of the nastier customers dumped their finished meals onto the people below, or even relieved themselves on some poor sod's head. Snips ducked through an opening to avoid the aerial flotsam and stepped into Dead Beat Alley.

No one there would give her a second glance. It didn't matter that she was still wearing a prison uniform; the people of Dead Beat Alley didn't much believe in the law. It was an imaginary thing that applied to fictitious people—something you paid a penny to read about in cheap news rags not fit to clean the ground with.

The buildings here were frightful affairs conceived by daredevils and madmen. The sky above was blotted out by a quilted canopy stretched across the rooftops, giving the alley a feeling of perpetual gloom. Here, gold-toothed hags tried to sell Snips bottles bubbling with strange new experiences—narrow-bodied men with sinister smiles offered her discount back-alley surgery to add, augment, or replace limbs—and pamphlets on the ground promising a hot meal and regular pay in the Isle's army cushioned her every step.

Snips shoved her way through a narrow door located near the back. In the dim light, she could see the outline of her apartment; a wide and open room with a cluttered, cramped second floor overlooking the first. Furniture here was made up mostly of books; one table was nothing but dusty tomes, arranged in four piles with a massive copy of the popular penny dreadful, <u>Professor Von Grimskull and the Zombie Sky-Pirates</u>, balanced on top. Snips lit a candle on a shelf to the side and then headed upstairs via the ladder.

A barrel half full of alcohol was stashed in a corner. Snips swiped a glass beaker she had filched a week ago from a local alchemist and took a swig. She grimaced as the stuff burned on its way down—the rotgut doubled as floor cleaner.

She grabbed a change of clothes and slipped behind a faded scarlet curtain, trading her prison attire for something a bit more respectable. When she emerged, she looked at herself in the broken and rusty mirror she had hammered to the far wall. She had left the off-yellow jail shirt on, but subdued its presence with a tattered black coat and her beloved derby hat.

She tilted the hat to the side, then laughed and curtsied to her own reflection. "A pleasure to meet you, Lady Snips."

"The pleasure is mine."

A pistol barrel hovered several inches from the reflection of her tanned nose.

It was held by a one-eyed thug who had to hunch over to fit inside the upstairs quarters. He and his companion had emerged from behind a bookcase; both were built from a wide variety of large-bodied ruffians and animals—in fact, the stitches still looked quite fresh. The one with the gun had been cobbled together from parts of an ape, and wore a tiny red fez on his head. The other one had a wide-brimmed hat and the head of a jawless jackal, his tongue dangling out from the base of his muzzle. They were dressed in very sharp and high-class suits; a pair of metal bolts jutted from the sides of their necks.

But the one who spoke was directly behind them—he was a gentleman in an expensive cream-colored vest, charcoal black dress coat, and matching top hat. His eyes could quiet jovial laughter with but a glance, and his muttonchops were thick enough to qualify as tusks.

"Oh Lord," Snips said, staring at the pistol with her eyes crossed. "Is it Tuesday already?"

The bearded man presented a most unpleasant smile. "My name is Charles Peabody. The gentleman with the pistol—I apologize for the implicit threat—is Mr. Cheek. His companion is Mr. Tongue."

"Pleasure to meet you," Snips tipped her hat up with the rim of the beaker.

Mr. Cheek grunted. Mr. Tongue gurgled.

"You don't say," Snips replied.

"Now that we have completed the pleasantries," Mr. Peabody said, stepping forward. "My employer wishes to speak with you."

"Is this about the duck?" Snips asked.

Peabody tilted his head. "Duck?"

"Duck? Did I say duck? I didn't mention any duck," Snips said. "Why do you keep bringing up ducks?"

Mr. Peabody scowled. "Enough of this. Miss Snips."

"Hey," Snips said, turning to Mr. Cheek. "Did you know that rotgut can cause blindness?"

Mr. Cheek blinked his eye. "Eh?"

"Oh, yeah. Especially when applied directly."

In one smooth motion, Snips slapped the pistol to the side and threw the contents of the beaker into his face. Mr. Cheek roared, dropped the gun, and ground a pair of meaty mismatched fists into his eye sockets. Snips hurled the glass at Mr. Peabody and sprang out the back window.

Peabody swatted the glass aside, cursing. "Get her!"

Snips slapped her palms against the next building's wall, pushing herself off and diving into a roll that left her crouched in the alley. She flew to her feet and ran down the narrow street, heading for the heart of Dead Beat Alley.

As Snips moved, she unraveled a length of twine from her leftmost pocket and looped it over her hat, tying it down. "Soar," she whispered.

And then she sprang into the chaos of the Rookery.

The front door to her apartment exploded from the inside. Mr. Cheek emerged with his fists swinging like sledgehammers, his eye as red as an overripe strawberry. The wolfish Mr. Tongue soon followed. He threw his head back and sniffed at the air, then dragged Mr. Cheek on after Snips' scent. Mr. Peabody soon ran out behind them, disappearing down the street.

With a twist of her shoulders, Snips flowed through the crowd like a pebble through a stream; she sprang over the head of a thieving ragamuffin (busy picking the pocket of a plump fruit-mongerer) and brought her hands down on the shoulders of the victim, shoving hard and vaulting herself to a windowsill. As her feet met the mantle, she kicked back and landed on the roof of the clockwork puppet show. Below her, its hook-nosed mascot had moved on to beating a policeman until the officer's head popped

"That's the way you do it!"

off with a comical boing, spurring the audience to applause.

Mr. Cheek hit the morning crowd like a rolling boulder smashing into a heap of Christmas pudding. People rolled out of his path, desperately sweeping aside as he swatted away anyone dim enough to stand still. His eye was starting to clear up, and locked on Snips—who even now was leaping from the puppet show to the leg-joint of the passing mechanical spider, swinging up and clambering into the gondola.

"Stop!" Mr. Cheek roared, stepping straight into the giant machine's path. "Halt!"

The spider's vents hissed as the vehicle ambled forward, its foot nearly squashing Mr. Cheek flat. The thug cursed and jumped back just as its leg slammed into the ground. Inside the gondola, engineers were yelling and waving their tools at Snips, who was now on top of the furnace that powered the device—watching the balcony of an approaching apartment.

In the meantime, Mr. Tongue had managed to hug one of the mechanical spider's back legs and was slowly inching his way up towards the first joint with each step it took. Mr. Cheek followed the machine, batting people out of his way and engaging in a shouting match with the engineers above.

Snips counted the feet between her and the balcony. Sixteen feet, fifteen, fourteen...

"Stop the machine!" Mr. Cheek roared.

Thirteen.

The spider came to a lurching halt; Snips leapt.

Her belly and knees smacked across the wall—but her fingers brushed up against the balcony's rim. Curling her hands into tight fists, she pulled herself up.

A small group of spectators had been drawn away from the puppet show by Snips' antics, and were now cheering the thief on. Snips dragged herself up to the railing and perched on it like a cat on a fence; she threw a grinning shrug at the crowd and turned to the door.

Charles Peabody stepped out from the doorway, pistol in hand.

"An excellent display of your craft, Miss Snips. But

ultimately futile. Now, if you will come with me—"

Snips sprang back on the railing, landing in a crouch.

Peabody sighed. "Really, Miss Snips. Now you're just being childish."

She looked over her shoulder; the mechanical spider was lumbering out of reach. But one of the airship vendors had been coaxed over by the cheering, and was swinging in for a closer look.

Mr. Peabody followed her eyes. His disapproving stare melted into an outright scowl. "Don't be an idiot."

It was too high for her to reach, but one of the anchor cords was dangling low. It was fourteen, maybe fifteen feet away. If she could get the right angle, maybe she could grab it.

"Miss Snips. Please." Mr. Peabody now sounded frustrated. "If you cooperate, I assure you that no harm will come—"

That clinched it. Snips gave him a silver-toothed grin. And then, with every last bit of force she could muster, she turned and leapt over the heads of the people below, reaching for the dangling strip of hemp.

She almost made it.

~*~

CHAPTER 4: IN WHICH WE MEET THE SCION OF THE DAFFODIL LEGACY, LEARN THE TRUTH CONCERNING NEGATONS, AND DISCOVER JUST WHO IT IS WHO ENSURES THE TRAINS RUN ON TIME

~*~

William Daffodil resembled what you would get if you dressed up a scarecrow and taught it to act polite; he wore his clothes as if they were an ill-fitting burden. Though he was very quick on his toes, the young mathematician had the sneaking suspicion that one day he'd visit Napsbury Asylum only to discover that they weren't going to let him leave.

The institution remained one of the few mental health facilities that actually had a success record. This was credited in large part to the ground-breaking theories of its founder, Louis Napsbury. One of these theories centered around the existence of invisible, soundless, and scentless clouds of evil impulses known as 'Negatons'. Having studied the Negaton menace for quite some time, Napsbury perfected his three step program to their complete annihilation. This program included:

1) A healthy diet of fruits, vegetables, and meats. There was very little a Negaton disliked more than a well-fed victim.

2) Regular exercise. Negatons, Napsbury explained, absolutely hated exercise. It was like nails on chalkboard to them.

3) Most important of all, routine salt baths. Negatons loathed salt baths with every last unseeable molecule in their being, and would run screaming (silently) into the night at the first whiff of salt in water.

As none of these steps were any more invasive than a hot meal followed by a dip into a sodium enriched tub, the asylum had a certain appeal for William. He had much preferred *their* crazy-talk to the crazy-talk of the places that wanted to drill holes in his grandmother's skull and see what would happen.

William arrived in the lobby of the criminally insane wing;

here, male and female patients were occasionally allowed to mingle under the watchful eye of several thick-shouldered orderlies. The room had the look of a sterilized prison; furniture had been stripped of everything that could feasibly be used as a weapon or fashioned into some manner of doomsday machine, leaving everything with a look of sparse functionality.

Sitting in one of the chairs was one of his grandmother's fellow patients, Mr. Brown. His obscenely thick spectacles and long flaring eyebrows gave him the appearance of a very confused owl. When William saw him, he immediately stepped back in expectation of the worst.

"I seem to have invented something by accident again," Mr. Brown said, looking rather dejected. He glanced down at the large and innocuous brass box that sat on the table in front of him. On top of it was a bright cherry-red button with a note scrawled in grease-pen above it: PUSH ME. "I'm not quite sure what it does."

"I understand, sir," William said, although the young mathematician certainly did not. He looked about for one of the asylum's orderlies, but could find none in sight. "Have you considered trying to disassemble it?"

"Oh, yes, I could do that," Mr. Brown agreed. "That's a very good idea."

"Definitely."

"...unless I thought of that while I was building it, and equipped it with some manner of trap."

William gave Mr. Brown a blank look. It was quite a bit of time before he could properly enunciate his reaction: "What?"

"I've been fairly depressed lately," Mr. Brown reasoned in a surprisingly affable tone. "I think that my subconscious might be trying to kill me."

William blinked. He had not come prepared for this level of madness. "I—I beg your pardon, sir?"

"Well, you see, it's all quite simple. My therapist explained it to me in detail," Mr. Brown said. "Apparently, I have a deep and desperate need to do unspeakable things to my mother, while simultaneously hating my father. And thusly, I subconsciously hate myself." He sighed, shaking his head. "What a ghastly affair."

"Oh, Mr. Brown, do stop trying to scare the poor boy," Gertrude Daffodil said, rolling in behind William on her wheelchair. William's grandmother had a short curly mop of iron-gray hair and a quilt that seemed to miraculously manifest in her lap regardless of where she was or what she was doing. She glared at Mr. Brown as she took her place besides William.

"I'll probably just put it with the others," Mr. Brown said.

"Come on, William. Take me for a walk, would you?"

William was happy to do just that; he pushed his · grandmother out of the lobby and into the hallway. As they walked, he began telling her all about what was happening at the Steamwork and the big important project he was now working on.

"That's all very nice William," Mrs. Daffodil agreed. "I've been working on sewing myself, you know. I even stitched you a little something in my last class." She reached beneath her quilt, withdrawing a lump of misshapen twine. William took it, trying to reason out what it was for. It had three sleeves and two necks.

"It's, erm, very lovely," William said, placing it across the back of her chair. "I'll try it on when I get home, most certainly."

"Wouldn't you wear it next time you come? I'd love to see how it looks on you."

"I, uh, of course," William said. He quickly aimed to change the subject. "I'm glad to see you're trying to distract yourself from your, uh, condition."

"I wish you wouldn't call it a 'condition'," she replied, crinkling her eyebrows together in consternation. "What I have is a gift, William. Your grandfather had it, along with your father. You have it, too."

William sighed. He had been through this before, and wasn't interested in renewing the argument. "I'd rather just stick to maths, you know. Much safer."

"But much less interesting!"

"Well, it depends on your perspective. Mathematics can get quite dangerous, you know. Why, just the other day, while calculating a polynomial, I almost stabbed myself with a pencil!"

Mrs. Daffodil looked back up at William.

William smiled sheepishly: "Uh, you know. Lead

poisoning."

"Right," she said. "But come now. When was the last time someone was horribly maimed by Pi?"

"You might be surprised." William's voice dropped off. "Grandmother, what is this?"

"Eh? Oh," she said, following William's eyes down to the base of her seat. A crude battery produced from inserting two metal strips into a potato was stashed away under her chair. It even had a small gauge jammed into the side of it, apparently to measure power output. "That's just, you know. Something to keep me busy."

"I thought we talked about this," William said, trying to sound as stern as he could manage. "None of this nonsense. It's why they won't let me take you home."

"It's just a potato," Mrs. Daffodil said with a disdainful sniff.

"Oh, yes, just a potato," William agreed, frowning. "It always starts small, doesn't it? Today, just a potato, tomorrow, a lemon. And then before you know it you're riding an armored dirigible and threatening to disintegrate half the city with your death-ray—*again.*"

"Well, I asked you what you wanted for your birthday, and you said you wished that awful boarding school you attended would burn down," Mrs. Daffodil responded huffily. "Don't blame me for wanting to spoil my only grandchild."

"I was fourteen years old! Grandmother, please. This is the sort of thing that's made it so hard for me to get an ordinary job. Everyone hears my last name and they instantly think, 'oh no, we can't hire him, he'll likely wall himself up in his office and emerge a week later in a steam-powered suit made from spare paperclips'."

"Well, it would be nice if you showed some interest in the family tradition, you know," Mrs. Daffodil said. "Just a little bit. I mean, after all, you owe your life to it!" She reached up, tapping right above his heart with meaningful ire.

William gently pushed her hand aside. "I'm a mathematician, grandmother, not a mad scientist. Why can't you just accept that?"

Mrs. Daffodil sighed. "I can, I can. It's just that I sometimes get the feeling that you're fighting who you really are, William."

William shook his head. "I have to go. There's a lot of work to do at the Steamwork; Mr. Eddington wants me to finish inputting the new figures into the engine later this evening. I need to get a head start on the final touches."

"All right, dear. Will you come and see me in a few days? It will be Mr. Wanewright's birthday soon, and he so wants to meet you again."

"Is he the one with—" William twitched. "—the cats?"

"Yes, he quite fancies cats," Mrs. Daffodil agreed.

"That man is terrifying."

"Please, William? I promise not to bring up the subject of science at all," Mrs. Daffodil said.

"Of course. But I'm keeping the potato."

~*~

"You are quite lucky to be alive," Count Orwick said from across his desk. "How fortunate that Mr. Cheek broke your fall."

"He could have been softer," Snips replied. She was seated in an obscenely comfortable chair in the middle of Orwick's rather expensive office, trying to wriggle her way out of a pair of manacles. They consisted of no more than two solid chunks of iron fused together at the wrists; she wasn't sure how they came off. She wasn't sure they were *supposed* to. "Why am I here?"

Count Orwick smiled. "I have pulled several considerable favors. You have been placed in my custody."

"Wonderful. But just so you know, I don't do windows. It's a phobia I've had since childhood. A wild pack of 'em killed my mother." Snips narrowed her eyes, glaring at the window behind Orwick. "Horrible things, windows."

Orwick's fingers steepled together. "Do you know who I am, Miss Snips?"

"Hm. Are you Susan? You look kind of like a Susan. Do you mind if I call you Susan, Susan?"

"I am the man responsible for making the trains run on time."

"Fascinating," Snips said. "Hey. Listen, Susan. This is fun and all, but why don't you take these cuffs off me and send me back to Morgrim? Better yet, just cut me loose. I'm sure I can find my way back."

"In addition to the trains, some problem of general governance that has defied conventional solutions will occasionally find its way to my desk. I solve these problems."

"See, they've got these rocks there, and if I want to be reformed, they tell me that it's critical that I move these rocks from one side of the prison yard to the other." Snips switched from trying to wriggle out of the manacles to gnawing on them.

"In my search for 'unconventional' solutions, I sometimes employ men and women of 'unconventional' qualities. You are such a woman, Miss Snips. In exchange for your services, I offer reasonable pay. Quite likely the easiest money you'll ever earn."

Snips paused in mid-chomp. "This is cutting into my rock-moving time. I could have moved a rock in all the time it took for you to tell me this. That'd bring me one rock closer to legitimacy."

"It will also be the perfect opportunity for you to lay low until this other matter comes to a close."

Snips paused, lifting her head. "What 'other' matter?"

"Oh, you know," Orwick said, as if distracted. "The pardon."

"Pardon?"

"Oh, you mean you haven't heard? You're scheduled to receive a full pardon for your various excesses. Signed by Her Majesty herself."

Snips sprang to her feet. "What?"

"Why yes." He slid the notice across the desk for Snips to inspect. "See for yourself."

Snips' eyes scurried down the document. Her? Pardoned? It was too good to be true; in an instant, all of her indiscretions were forgiven and forgotten. It meant a perfectly clean slate—it meant she was out of prison. It meant she could tell the Count to build a set of rails straight up to his posterior and send the trains down the line at full steam. It was a public notice; everyone could see—

Near the end was the list of crimes Snips was being

pardoned of.

Snips stammered. "You—y-you—"

"You'll be free as a bird, Miss Snips."

"You p-published—"

"You've made it crystal clear that our prison system isn't for you. And we've heard you, Miss Snips. We wouldn't dream of putting you back behind bars. Even if you begged."

"You put down their names!" Snips' voice rose to quivering yelp. "The people I've been stealing from! Do you have any idea what they'll do to me?!"

Orwick's expression resembled a smile in the same way that the light of an oncoming locomotive resembled a tunnel's exit. "*Especially* if you begged."

Snips slumped back to her seat, head spinning. The Count could have held anything over her head—execution, jail-time, the wanton slaughter of puppies—and Snips would have wriggled free. Escaping was her specialty. But with a stroke of the pen, Orwick could turn Aberwick itself into her prison. Except this one had no locks to foil and no doors to open. And it would be filled to the brim with all the two-bit murderers, thieves, and ne'er-do-wells, who—until now—had been unaware that Arcadia Snips had been cheerfully robbing them blind.

Morgrim was suddenly looking extraordinarily comfortable.

"At least you don't know about the duck," Snips said.

"Check the back side."

Snips flipped the document over. "Oh."

"I hear Jake 'The Beak' Montgomery still shrieks like a little girl when he hears a quack."

Snips relented. "What do you want from me?"

"For you to solve a murder."

For a while, Snips let silence speak for her.

"I'm sorry. Come again?"

"Are you familiar with the Steamwork?"

"Big, noisy place. They build things there," Snips said. "Like, uh, I don't know. Steam-powered butter knives or some such nonsense."

"I have reason to believe that their level of technological sophistication is far greater than what they have been reporting on their tax forms," Orwick said, leaning forward. "A gentleman under their employment sent word recently that he wished to speak to me about a very important matter."

"Breakthrough in steam-powered butter? To go with the knives," Snips said.

Orwick ignored the thief's speculations. "But before I could schedule a meeting, he met with his untimely demise."

"Oh, that's a shame. Let me guess—died in a horrible automated cutlery accident."

"He was killed in an explosion," Orwick explained. "His burning corpse was propelled out of his workshop and into the ocean."

Snips grimaced. "Ouch."

"And you will be aiding in the investigation of his death."

"Uh, I don't know if you've noticed, but I'm not exactly the investigator type."

"You do not need to be. The Steamwork has hired a detective agency to look into the matter. You will be accompanying them as a government consultant. It will be their task to provide the cover of an investigation into Basil Copper's demise, allowing you an opportunity to—"

"—be a sneaky little fink and find out what he wanted to tell you and why someone decided to put a stop to it?"

"Exactly."

"I don't understand. I'm no government agent," Snips said. "I'm not even government material. I'm a con artist. Why me?"

"Precisely because you are a con artist, Miss Snips, and precisely because you are not a government agent. As I have stated: your methods are unconventional. They may work where other methods have failed."

Snips snorted. "You're a nut. A salty, roasted nut."

"All I ask is that you take your position seriously. Through hook or crook, Miss Snips, get to the heart of the matter. In exchange for your services, I will see to the disposal of this—" Orwick gestured to the pardon notice, as if its mere presence offended him. "—odious document."

Snips' eyebrow twitched. "And what happens if I don't?"

"Then, Miss Snips, I think it would be wise for you to consider another profession. Before your colleagues decide to consult with you."

~*~

Shortly after Snips left, Mr. Peabody entered with a bundle of paperwork.

"If I may, sir," Mr. Peabody began, setting the pile down on top of Orwick's desk. "I would like to inquire as to what you are hoping to accomplish by assigning Miss Snips to this affair."

Count Orwick looked amused. "Are you questioning my judgment, Peabody?"

The assistant immediately grew pale, stepping back. "Ah, not at all, sir."

"Calm yourself." Orwick turned to stare through the window, watching the railway. "I assigned Miss Snips to this matter for two reasons."

"The first, sir?"

"An adequate solution that fails to accommodate for the unknown is neither adequate nor a solution. Miss Snips may solve the matter; she may not. She may serve to do nothing more than provide a useful clue—a clue without which those better trained than herself could never succeed. But any solution that constrains itself to the boundaries of merely that which we predict will happen is a solution doomed to stagnation and failure."

"She's a mongrel, sir, and self-destructive," Mr. Peabody noted. "It is likely that she'll die."

"Yes," Orwick said. "In which case, we come to my second reason. Should she die in her service as a government agent, I will have every right to investigate the Steamwork at my leisure—for suspicion in the murder of an official operative."

Mr. Peabody smiled. "She succeeds, you win. She fails, you win. Very good, sir."

"The only way I can lose is if she manages to do nothing.

And considering Miss Snips' history, I find that possibility to be the least likely of them all."

~*~

CHAPTER 5: IN WHICH WE RETURN TO THE PAST IN ORDER TO INVESTIGATE GOINGS-ON CONCERNING RAINSTORMS, SECRET SOCIETIES, AND BUTTERFLY WINGS

~*~

An engine growled beneath Aberwick's streets.

The machine occupied a hundred feet of space; it was a geometric puzzle of precisely arranged gears and cogs, gnawing at mathematical enigmas presented to it by means of a series of levers. It was powered by a crank, which Jeremiah now turned; each revolution brought it one step closer to a problem's inevitable solution.

"Incredible," Abigail said.

"Jeremiah called the original design a 'calculation engine'," Nigel explained. "A machine capable of performing all manner of mathematical formulae, removing any element of human error."

"And it works?"

"It does."

"I hope to replace this portion with a steam engine," Jeremiah commented, panting. He finished with the crank, stepping away and wiping his sweat-soaked palms off on his trousers.

"It is a fascinating machine, and surely deserving of attention," Abigail said. "But it does not explain how you predicted the rain."

"When Jeremiah finished the machine, he showed it to me. I realized at once that its applications extended far beyond matters of simple maths," Nigel said. "With modification, it could perform incredibly complex calculations—processes that could predict nature itself. A sort of 'probability engine'."

"But that is not feasible," Abigail said. "As my paper showed, even the slightest change in atmospheric pressure—"

"—disrupts the most precise predictions," Nigel agreed. "We discovered this on our own, independently; we were quite surprised when you discovered it without the aid of our probability engine."

Jeremiah stepped to a basin of water, splashing his face. "The problem was that there were too many variables," he said. "To be successful, any system of prediction had to account for them all."

Abigail hesitated. "You found a way."

Jeremiah dried his face with a towel. "We did. Our equations were perfect—too perfect. We needed an agent of chaos; an element of imperfection. We needed something that made our engine's calculations fallible."

"We experimented with sub-systems—mechanisms in the engine that would create inaccurate results. And in the process, we blundered upon something very interesting," Nigel said.

"The larger and more unpredictable a system was, the more accurate our flawed predictions became," Jeremiah said. "Predicting the weather became child's play. Yet predicting something as simple as the rate of speed at which a feather should fall was impossible."

"Your findings are remarkable," Abigail said. "Why have you not submitted them to the Academy? Why have you kept them secret?"

"Because we haven't told you the whole story," Nigel said.

"We didn't predict the rain," Jeremiah said. "We made it happen."

Abigail stared at Jeremiah as if he had just confessed to secretly being a monkey in a person-suit. "I beg your pardon?"

"The flapping of a butterfly's wings half way across the world can cause a thunderstorm over our heads," Nigel said. "We discovered that, with the right calculations, we could become the butterfly."

"We predicted what action would be necessary to attain the results we wanted," Jeremiah said. "And then we took that action. Whether it be the flapping of a butterfly's wings or breaking a teacup on the floor, we discovered how to identify the first domino in a chain that could lead to any result we desired."

"That's—that's absolutely impossible," Abigail stuttered,

leaning forward to hear more.

"There are limits," Nigel confessed. "The system must be large, and ultimately of an unpredictable nature; such as the weather, or a civilization. In addition, changes must happen slowly over time. The more rapid of a change we propose, the more powerful the initial catalyst must be."

Jeremiah nodded. "If you attempted to make it rain tomorrow rather than next week—"

"You would have to find an awfully large butterfly," Nigel finished.

"I still don't understand. Why keep this silent?" Abigail asked. "Why, we could control the weather—end droughts! Prevent famines! Circumvent floods!"

"I thought much the same at first," Nigel said. "Jeremiah revealed to me the error of my ways."

"In your defense," Jeremiah said, grinning, "neither of you were raised by mad scientists."

"I do not understand," Abigail replied. "What error am I making?"

"You're assuming these equations would be employed for the better good," Jeremiah said. "You look at this and see an end to famine; I look at it and see a way to inflict it. You see a way to bring about peace; I see a way to strangle nations and topple governments."

Abigail hesitated, staring at the probability engine. "Then you wish to keep your discovery away from those who would abuse it," she said.

"Yes," Nigel replied. "But the possibilities it offers are far too great for us to ignore. We must understand it, but resist the temptation for its abuse."

"Such as creating unnecessary rainstorms to impress a lady," Abigail snapped, but then quickly abandoned her indignation. "I understand all this, but—why me? Certainly, I am an exceptional mathematician and engineer, but there must be others who are more qualified than myself."

"You are a brilliant mathematician," Nigel said. "But you are also a woman."

Abigail blanched.

"Please do not be offended, Miss Parsley. I feared that whomever we came to would turn about and reveal our discovery."

Abigail stiffened in realization. "No one would believe me if I did."

"Indeed," Nigel agreed. "Were you to betray us, you would be dismissed as merely another 'hysterical damsel'."

"How shrewd. Your mind must be a frightful place," Abigail said, her voice dry.

"Perhaps so, Madame. But do you not understand our need for duplicity? For secrecy? Do you not see what is at stake?" Nigel asked.

Abigail hesitated, allowing the silence to speak for her. When she at long last grew tired of what it had to say, she reluctantly nodded. "Yes, I do. But Professor Arcanum—"

"Yes?"

"To what end shall we ultimately put this machine?"

Jeremiah and Nigel exchanged glances; they looked back at Abigail, who regarded them with absolute disbelief.

"You have no idea, do you?" she said.

"Well—" Jeremiah began.

"Our primary concern has been to prevent its misuse, while simultaneously investigating its feasibility," Nigel said. "As for what we shall do with it—that has yet to be decided."

"And have you determined how you will finance this research?" Abigail asked. "I have no small fortune at my mercy, but I am unconvinced that it will be enough."

"We're still working on—" Jeremiah started again, but Nigel soon cut him off.

"Yes, actually—I have formulated a plan that should serve our purposes quite adequately. Both to fund our research and insulate it against the curiosity of those who might misuse it," he said. "We will create a secret society. One with an intriguing name; perhaps 'The Society of Distinguished Gentlemen'?"

Both Abigail and Jeremiah stared at him. It was Abigail who spoke first:

"So your solution to the matter of money is to construct

some sort of secret boy's club?" Abigail asked. "Shall you have secret handshakes, and meet in a hidden tree-house?"

"Yes, actually," Nigel replied.

"I, uh. Beg your pardon?" Jeremiah asked.

Nigel laughed. "People thrive on mystery. They'll happily donate money to any organization that provides them with an opportunity to add a sense of enigma to themselves."

"But I don't understand. To what end, Nigel?" Jeremiah pressed on. "Why create some secret society? The whole notion seems so silly."

"It most certainly is silly," Nigel agreed. "However, we cannot accomplish our research without additional funding; your profits from the Steamwork and Abigail's considerable fortune are not sufficient. We require sponsorship—and simultaneously must refrain from allowing the scientific community to learn of what we have discovered."

"At the very least we should think of a better name," Abigail complained.

"What's wrong with the one Nigel proposed?"

"Really, now," Abigail said. "The Society of Distinguished Gentlemen? What a wholly boorish title."

"Oh, come off it," Jeremiah said. "Don't tell me you're going to get on Nigel's case about the 'gentleman' thing, Abigail. There are bigger concerns to be addressed here."

"I am one of the founding members of this little group of yours, am I not?" Abigail reasoned. "And I am certainly no gentleman. The name will have to be changed."

"To what? 'The Society of Distinguished People'? It makes it sound like some sort of book-of-the-month club," Jeremiah said. "The Society of Distinguished Gentlemen rolls off the tongue. It is clearly the superior name."

"It is an exclusionary name," Abigail snapped. "Why can a lady not be distinguished, hm?"

"I agree with Abigail," Nigel said.

"Exactly, Nigel, thank you very mu—wait, what?!" Jeremiah spluttered.

"Her point is valid, Jeremiah. We are in the 19th century,

yes? We must be modern in our mindset," Nigel explained. "Language is important, and as Abigail's work has demonstrated, exclusionary practices are outdated relics of the past."

"And yet here we are discussing the creation of an exclusionary social club," Jeremiah pointed out.

"We'll only be selling exclusiveness, not practicing it," Nigel said.

"But certainly, people would eventually realize it's all a sham," Abigail said. "You can't just make mysterious societies appear out of thin air."

"Why not?" Nigel asked. "We need only insinuate that the Society has existed throughout antiquity. People are drawn to mysteries without answers—references and symbols without meaning. Given the opportunity, they shall construct the meaning for you. In addition, by maintaining this 'air of mystery', we shall insure that the scientifically minded avoid our work."

"I have asked you before, and neither of you could provide sufficient answer. So I ask again: What is our ultimate goal, here?" Abigail said. "What is it that we seek to accomplish?"

Jeremiah thought on it for a moment, and then said: "To build a more powerful probability engine, and perhaps to use it for some small good."

Nigel hesitated. "And yet we have used the engine frivolously, Jeremiah. Abigail was quite correct when she criticized us for employing it to impress her with a rain storm. It is never a large step from benevolence to despotism."

Abigail nodded. "Then from now on, we shall refrain from using it frivolously."

"Let us set a rule," Jeremiah said. "No change may be wrought through this means by any one of us without the consent of all three of us."

"Yes," Abigail said after thinking it over for a moment. "I find that to be a most agreeable solution."

Nigel thought it over the longest; after a minute, he reluctantly nodded his head.

~*~

CHAPTER 6: IN WHICH WE ARE INTRODUCED TO RECKLESS MATHEMATICS AND AN ASSASSIN MOST FOUL

~*~

"How I loathe intrusive little weasels," Mr. Eddington said, his hands clenched into bundles of frustration. "How I despise nosy finks!"

He stepped into Daffodil's workshop. William was currently scribbling away at a blackboard with a long stick of chalk. The young man's work was a labyrinth of geometric shapes and equations; it was steadily filling the wall's entire surface. At only a glance, any sane mathematician would have instantly declared them to be meaningless gibberish. He hadn't limited himself to dividing by zero; he had divided zero by zero. When he had been feeling particularly sadistic, he subtracted by cat and multiplied by dog.

But beneath the fanciful whimsy and frolicking chaos was an underlying structure that no one could quite comprehend. Real numbers choked on their irrational counterparts only to spit out imaginary ones. Formulae appeared out of nowhere, treated the other equations rudely, then ate and ran without paying the tab. Brief and spurious flashes of precision emerged from the madness —and each time William found such a point, he stopped to meticulously write down everything that had lead up to it in his notebook.

Mr. Eddington cleared his throat. The mathematician jumped, turned, and politely smiled.

"Good afternoon, Mr. Eddington."

"Mr. Daffodil," Mr. Eddington said, glaring. "Am I to understand, then, that you have once again wasted company time on this fanciful whimsy of yours?"

"Oh, merely more preventative measures, sir. I want to ensure that our calculation engine can sustain every feasible manner of attack," William quickly explained. "There may still remain several possible ways to disable it—"

"I understand your desires, Mr. Daffodil, but must I remind you once again of the dangers of reckless mathematics?" Mr. Eddington said. He stepped up to the board, glaring at the equations. "This is absolute drivel—pure madness. Incomprehensible babble. Are you *attempting* to follow in the footsteps of your parents, Mr. Daffodil?"

William nearly became a statue; only his eyebrow moved, twitching in a steady rhythm. "No. Of course not. Not at all," he said, his voice sliced open and drained of its strength.

"Because I would hope that you, of all people, would know the disastrous consequences inherent in practicing mad mathematics, Mr. Daffodil. After all, it is only a small step from mad maths to mad *science*."

William cleared his throat. "With your indulgence, sir, we must first understand the enemy if we are to defeat him."

Mr. Eddington sighed. "How does your work on the engine go?"

"Very well," William said. "We're nearly complete. We just need the data from the banks and we'll be ready to make a test run of it."

"Mr. Tweedle is seeing to it that it is shipped here tonight across the pipes," Mr. Eddington said. "In the meanwhile, Mr. Daffodil, please return to your work. And see to it that this—" he pointed at the wall of equations. "—is erased immediately."

William's left eyebrow twitched yet again. Regardless, he obediently nodded. Mr. Eddington turned and headed back to his office.

Shortly after the administrator had left, William fetched a damp rag with which to obliterate his work. But as he lifted it up to his equations, the mathematician paused—he was struck by the sudden silence. The constant chatter outside was absent; the steady hum of the calculation engine next door had inexplicably stopped. William pinched his eyebrows together and sat the rag down, poking his head out of the workshop.

No one was present. William frowned, walking out. "Um. Hullo?"

His voice echoed through the lobby.

"That is odd," he said, and then he noticed the clock mounted above the lobby's exit.

It seemed to be broken. The second hand struggled valiantly to usher in the next moment, but could not get past the three. Instead, it would tremble with effort before snapping back to the point where it had rested an instant prior.

William watched, perplexed, as the hand fought to move forward. It gave another spasm, and then sprang a second backwards.

"Mr. Daffodil?"

William nearly jumped out of his clothes. At once, the world was precisely as it should be; he was swimming in noise, surrounded by researchers going about their daily business. The engine rumbled beneath his feet, and one of his fellow engineers stood beside him. The clock's second hand was ticking merrily along, having long left the three behind.

"Is something wrong, Mr. Daffodil?"

Fearing he might be going mad, William shook his head. "No. Not at all. Nothing is wrong. Everything is perfectly rational and fine," he said, and then he marched right back into his office and locked the door.

~*~

Mr. Tweedle was waiting for Eddington in the Steamwork administrator's office.

"This is a disaster," Mr. Tweedle said, pacing back and forth over the expensive rug. "A catastrophe! He'll discover what we're up to. And then we'll go to prison!"

"We're not going to prison," Mr. Eddington said.

"I hope that they give me a cell with a nice view," Mr. Tweedle said, worrying away at the corners of his boring hat. "Perhaps with a tree. Do you think they have trees in prison? I hope they have trees."

"Be quiet," Mr. Eddington snapped. "No one is going to prison."

Mr. Tweedle grew quiet, watching Mr. Eddington with a look of desperation. The administrator sighed and reached into the bottom of his desk for a flask of spirits.

"Let us assume that, for the sake of argument, that you and I are engaged in some... 'questionable' activity. Merely for the sake of argument," Mr. Eddington continued, pouring out shots for Mr. Tweedle and himself. "Whatever that activity might be, it is not the target of the Count's investigation."

Mr. Tweedle was so eager to drench his worries in alcohol that he slopped the liquor over the front of his coat. It was not long before he was thrusting the glass out for a second helping. "But they'll blunder upon it, no doubt. You would have to be incompetent *not* to see what it is we're up to."

Mr. Eddington supplied the refill with a smile. "Yes," he said. "You would, wouldn't you?"

"Who on earth would be—"

"Are you familiar with a detective by the name of Mr. Watts, Mr. Tweedle?"

Mr. Tweedle was given a start. "Jerome Watts? The mad inspector? The one with the pigeons?"

"I think he would make an exceptional investigator for this case, don't you?"

Realization hit Mr. Tweedle with a start. "I see! But still, it seems all so delicate, Mr. Eddington. I'm just worried—"

"Leave the worrying to me, Mr. Tweedle," Mr. Eddington said, suppressing the desire to roll his eyes. "So long as you abide by my instructions, everything shall go according to plan."

"But what of that 'government consultant' fellow? That sounds a bit troubling, doesn't it?" He almost sounded hopeful; as if the thought of having it all found out brought the man some degree of comfort.

"Oh, yes, that," Mr. Eddington said, chuckling derisively. "I have every bit of confidence that the matter of this consultant will be solved swiftly and decisively."

~*~

The government bureaucrat's waiting room had long since passed ostentatious, strolled beyond elegant, and waded through a pile of money back to ostentatious again. Long rows of books with impressive titles threatened to crush the many shelves beneath their weight. The upper walls were choked beneath framed diplomas and awards all clambering over one another to heap countless honorifics upon their owner, while the lower walls were crowded with extravagant panel moldings of flora and fauna. The area was illuminated by a gilt-covered gasolier and several windows lurking high out of reach, as if placed in a direct attempt to prevent the room's occupants from escaping.

Present were four figures of note:

Kronan the Butcher; a solid block of muscle wrapped in a cheap suit and topped off with a battered cap. He was known both for his affinity for violence and his artistic sensitivity; his most recent work had received rave reviews. Entitled 'Corpse Poetry', it was a method of expressive corpse arrangement, allowing the artist to convey a variety of emotions and concepts. When he wrote a rather conservative piece using several critics who had treated his previous work harshly, the art community as a whole suddenly discovered a newfound respect for his unappreciated genius. He sat upon a comfortable armchair, remaining perfectly still.

Taz the Burr; a contortionist with a constant smile fixed to his face and an affinity for aggressive property redistribution. He had reportedly broke into the Royal Treasury with nothing more than a rusty nail and his cheerful grin, then slipped on out the front door—tipping the guard on his way. He sat upon a lovely side chair, remaining perfectly still.

Durden the Knife; a mysterious foreigner who wore a hooded robe that sharply contradicted the stuffy coats and jackets of his contemporaries. He preferred the pearl-lined hilts of his razor-edged scimitars to the cool grip of a pistol; according to the rumors, he had once dodged a bullet. He sat in an open cot, remaining perfectly still.

And finally, the man in black. He possessed all the lethargic grace of a long-toothed alley cat, with the scars to match—and his head was shaved as smooth as glass. He wore a pitch-black long coat and stood at the back of the room, rolling a cigarette. His nose was made of bronze and hooked like a vulture's, attached to his face by glue and several crude looking bolts.

The door opened. A slender gentleman with over-sized spectacles stepped in, reading off a clipboard. "Now, I believe we're ready to discuss the matter of your payment, gentlemen—"

Something was wrong. He leaned forward, inspecting the scene. There was far too much perfect stillness. Reaching for the nearby gasolier valve, he turned it up and bathed the room in an orange glow.

Kronan the Butcher was currently slouched back over his chair, a dozen knives emerging from his ribcage like the back ends of tacks stuck through a notice. His jaw had dropped, his eyes wide and glazed.

Taz the Burr was still smiling, but his head was all that was left of him. He had been smoothly decapitated and pinned to the chair with a knife through his hair; there was no sign of the body.

Durden the Knife had been shot in the mouth; fresh trails of smoke trailed up from his nostrils. Someone had taken the additional liberty of breaking his scimitars and forcibly jamming the hilts down his smoldering throat.

"Excuse me," the official began, stifling an uncomfortable cough. "Might I ask what has transpired here?"

"Cancer," said the man in black.

"Cancer?" This took the official by surprise.

"It's a silent killer."

"You are telling me that your fellow assassins died from cancer?"

"Can't beat cancer, can you?"

"Can you explain, then, why they look as if they have been victims of violence? I do believe that one's body is, in fact, missing."

The man with the metal nose finished rolling his cigarette and lit it with a flick of flint and steel. The tip unraveled into threads of fragrant smoke. "Very *dire* cancer."

Absolute silence.

"Huh. I suppose that means there's only the matter of your

payment, then."

"Funny thing. They left explicit instructions for their share to be given to me in the unlikely event of their deaths," the man announced. He drew a rolled up contract out of his coat and tossed it the official's way.

The official snagged the document and unrolled it, looking it over critically. "All three of them, while dying—"

"From cancer," the man in black reminded him.

"—found the time to write out and sign a document bequeathing their portion of the reward to you."

"Heroes to the last." He drew a deep and hungry breath, soaking his lungs in the smoke's bitter tang. "Examples to us all."

"I see. Well, then."

"Well?"

The official smiled meekly. "Everything looks to be in order. This way, please."

~*~

"I must admit. I've never met an assassin as—as—"

"Pay me."

"As direct about things," Bartleby confessed.

The bureaucrat's office was a typhoon of paperwork, books, gifts, trophies, and other meaningless detritus that had apparently gathered around him not through any conscious work but merely by his sheer magnetism when it came to useless junk. The assassin was sure that if he spent hours digging through the piles of self-important knick-knacks that surrounded him, he'd never find so much as a functional bottle-opener.

The assassin relished his cigarette like others might enjoy a fine meal, allowing the smoke to languish across his tongue and throat. When he spoke, he was sluggish and calm, but beneath every drugged syllable lay the threat of cold steel.

"Speaking of direct. Pay me."

"Oh, yes. Your payment. My employee told me you'll be accepting the shares of your companions. They died? Very tragic."

"I'll send flowers. Pay me."

"Of course, of course." Bartleby swelled up to his feet,

wobbling about. The man wasn't just overweight. He had long
flown past the boundaries of polite obesity on a rocket-propelled
sled, making a rude gesture on the way. The man was an
amorphous blob. He waddled to the far side of the room, shoving
aside a few trophies to get at the safe. "I must admit, it's been an
exceptional thrill to have a legend working for me."

The man in black amused himself by imagining how
Bartleby would look as he tumbled out of his own office window.
"Oh? You've heard of me?"

"Of course I've heard of you! Who hasn't? You're a
downright legend around these parts, sir!"

"Good to know."

"In fact," Bartleby continued, fiddling with the safe's lock.
"I have all your books. I must say, they're quite good. Do you write
them yourself, or does someone else write them for you?"

"Books?" The man's eye twitched. His mouth began to
spasm. *Oh, God. Please, no,* he thought to himself. *Please make
him shut up. Make him shut up right now.*

"Yes. I've read them all. I'm quite the fan. Although I
always I thought you'd be taller, in all honesty..."

The assassin turned around in his chair, staring at Bartleby's
back. If the city bureaucrat could have seen him, he would have
recognized a look of such pure murderous sociopathy that it might
have killed him on the spot.

The safe clicked open. Bartleby reached inside, fishing out
a bundle of cash. "Well, anyway. Truly, it's been an honor to have
the legendary Von Grimskull working for m—"

One moment later, people on the street looked up in
surprise as a window on the top floor exploded. A screaming fat
man soon emerged, flailing his arms for a good second before
slamming into the ground with a sound best described as
'incredibly moist'.

~*~

Bristling with weapons, the guards kicked down the door
and stepped into the room.

The assassin makes it clear he will have no more of this 'Von Grimskull' guff.

Present were three details of note:

Bartleby, their employer, was missing.

The very large window behind Bartleby's desk was currently broken.

In Bartleby's place was a very angry man. An angry man currently holding a pair of fully loaded pistols and wearing a sinister bronze nose.

"Cancer," the assassin croaked.

"Holy mother of pearl," one of the guards yelped. "Do you know who that is?!"

"Eh?"

"That's Von Grimskull!"

The assassin sighed, drawing the hammers back with a swipe of his thumbs.

~*~

Several minutes later, the assassin emerged from the building and stepped out into the busy street. He made his way to the post office, heading straight away to the mail box he had rented. As he pulled out the key to unlock it, he found one of the men who worked there sliding an envelope into the slot.

"Good morning, sir," the courier cheerfully sang.

"Mm." The assassin edged his way past the mail-man, opening the box and drawing out the envelope. He tore it open with a finger. Inside was information on his next target—a small-time crook and current escapee by the name of Arcadia Snips.

"Hope you're having a pleasant day," the courier said. "By the way, has anyone ever mentioned you have the same nose as that fellow from those books? I think his name was Von Gri—"

Never lifting his eyes from the document, the assassin drew his pistol from the holster under his coat. The hammer slipped back with a sharp and punctuated *click*.

Suddenly overcome with a wave of wisdom, the courier snapped his mouth shut and went along his way.

~*~

CHAPTER 7: IN WHICH WE MEET MISS PRIMROSE, MR. WATTS, AND THE ARCHITECTURALLY FELONIOUS STEAMWORK

~*~

Snips observed that the front hood of the train was curved into a quarter of a rusty snail's shell, segmented with plates of bolted and tarnished brass. A telescopic periscope popped out its armored side, swiveling with a hiss of pneumatics; the aperture of its scuffed lens blinked and narrowed its gaze on her.

Dusty, scraggly, and looking like something the cat would not drag in for fear of being labeled a sadist, Snips stepped forward and presented her ticket to the large and intimidating contraption that hovered over the train's doorway. It swallowed the slip of paper, nibbled on it, then spat it back out. Snips stepped inside and followed the ticket's directions to her seat.

She was surprised to find that, rather then walking back to the third class compartment, she was expected to head straightaway to the front of the train. She arched an eyebrow and made her way to first-class.

The lobby that Snips stepped into was comfortably wide and lavished with opulence; a coffered ceiling swept over her head, with a midnight indigo divan framed with burled rosewood and trimmed with gold laid out besides a mahogany long table. The table had an extensive needlepoint of gears and cogs contained beneath a glass frame—a silver platter was placed on it, with complementary tea and crumpets provided. Somewhere, Snips could hear a phonograph playing a scratchy arrangement of stately violins.

Sitting on the divan was a graying pear-shaped gentleman who was enjoying a cup of tea with a short heavy-set lady. The man wore a deerstalker cap so absurd that Snips had to fight the urge to swat it from his head. At once, he turned to Snips, inspecting her through a set of rimless spectacles sitting on his nose.

"Oh, hullo. Are you the fellow they sent to bring more lumps of sugar?"

Snips looked down at herself—dressed in the tattered hand-me-downs of a vagrant. She then looked back up to the old man.

"One lump or two?"

"Two, please," he responded with blissful ease.

"Mr. Watts, if I may." The lady stood. She was a brute of a woman built with all the functional craftsmanship of a stone outhouse. Her jaw was herculean, and her face full of stern scowls and disapproving stares—with a tangled mop of wheat gold curls and corkscrews bound up atop her head. Her evening dress was so conservative that it could have made a pastor's daughter look questionable in comparison. At her feet lay a large coal black medical bag. "I am Miss Maria Primrose, and this is Detective Jacob Watts. I assume you are our consultant, Mr. Snips?"

"I most certainly am," Snips agreed. "Although I'm actually more miss than mister."

Miss Primrose's expression slipped from stern authority to shock and embarrassment. "I beg your pardon, Miss Snips! Count Orwick's man failed to inform me that you are a woman."

"I've forgotten a few times myself," Snips said, rolling her hat off and tipping it. "I assume you two are the detectives?"

"Detectives? Are we detecting something?" Mr. Watts asked. "Oh, excellent! I do love a good mystery. What is it we're detecting, Miss Primrose?"

Miss Primrose shot an angry look at Watts, then sighed in reluctant surrender. "We're solving a crime, Mr. Watts. The recent death of Basil Copper."

"Oh, he sounds like an interesting chap. When do we meet him?"

"We're not meeting him," Miss Primrose said, struggling to maintain her composure. "He is dead."

"Oh. How dreadfully dull," Watts said.

Miss Primrose turned to Snips. "My apologies for the confusion, Miss Snips. As you have no doubt already guessed, we are with the Watts and Sons Detective Agency."

"Pleasure to meet you," Snips said. "Arcadia Snips, professional lock enthusiast."

Miss Primrose frowned sternly, looking down at Snips' attire. "May I ask, Miss Snips, why you are wearing such an odd assortment of clothes?"

"Oh, you know," Snips said, shrugging. "Dangers of the profession, that sort of thing." She walked forward, draping herself down on the far-end of the divan. "So, what do we do now? Trade recipes?" She took one of the crumpets, tossing it into the air and leaning back to catch it in her mouth.

Miss Primrose reached forward and snatched the crumpet before Snips could bite down. "Explain yourself. Why are you dressed in such a crude fashion? And exactly what is your specialty? Why were you assigned to our investigation?"

Snips crossed her eyes. "Oh, come on now. What's wrong with my clothes?"

"Your current manner of dress would cause dark alleyways to avoid you for fear of soiling their good reputations," Miss Primrose said.

"I think she's dressed quite cleverly," Detective Watts piped up. "It's likely a disguise—get into the minds of the insane and homeless—"

"I'm a professor of escapology, with a minor in chicanery," Snips said.

A grim expression swept over Miss Primrose's face. "You are a thief."

"Well, I don't like to brag—"

"Count Orwick assigned us a thief."

"—but I am pretty good with sleight of hand," Snips said, taking another bite out of the crumpet.

"I should have known he would attempt some form of sabotage. I cannot believe that—" Miss Primrose stopped and stared, looking from her now empty hand back up to the crumpet Snips was eating. "Oh, for goodness sake. Give me that!" She snatched the crumpet back, placing it aside.

Snips licked the excess butter off her fingers. "So, what is it that we'll be up to?"

"'We' will be up to nothing. You are to accompany us as we investigate this death as thoroughly as possible."

"And I'll be doing what, precisely?"

"Keeping quiet," Miss Primrose snapped.

~*~

Cobbled together from a pastiche of styles, the Steamwork looked as if it had suffered an assault at the hands of a roving pack of mad Victorian architects. 'Something stylish and elegant,' the first had said. 'With Corinthian columns and a Greco-Roman motif.'

'Buttresses! Flying buttresses!' the second had roared. 'With steeples! More steeples! Steeples on top of steeples!'

'And perhaps a bit of wood leafing around the windows. Nothing too flashy, mind you, but just a few subtle touches here and there—'

'—arches! More flying buttresses! Six fireplaces! A balcony! And—'

'Let's slap on some avocado paint and call it a day,' the third had said.

The final result broke six city ordinances and at least two laws of physics.

When the three investigators arrived, they found someone attending to a statue of a muse located near the front door, polishing up her naughty bits with a dirty hanky. The man was just finishing buffing her to a marbleized shine when he noticed them approaching.

"Good afternoon, sir," Miss Primrose announced. "We are members of the Watts Detective Agency, here to investigate the matter of your recent unfortunate tragedy—"

The man spat into his hanky, gave the statue one last swab, then turned to approach the three of them. He was older than old; he was old back when old was still a fad. When God had said 'Let there be light', this was the fellow who had been sitting on the back porch, shaking his cane and complaining about all the racket those whippersnappers were making with their new dang-fangled invention.

"Pleasure t'meet ya," he said, giving Miss Primrose a crooked grin and offering her a grimy palm. "I'm Dunnigan McGee, the janitor. Is this your first time here?"

"I am afraid so," Miss Primrose admitted, refraining from taking the hand. "You have a very, ah, interesting building here," she observed, glancing past Dunnigan.

"Aye, she's a beaut." He gave the door a sturdy kick and shoved it open with his shoulder. "We'll probably have some papers for you t'sign. Indemnities against electrocution, combustion, subtraction, that sort of thing—"

"Subtraction?" Snips asked. "What do you mean, 'subtraction'?"

"Math can get a little out of hand around these parts, ma'am."

The interior of the Steamwork looked worse than the exterior; it was held together by nothing more than springs, duct-tape, and liberal amounts of whimsy. Lengths of pipes speared overhead, spewing out plumes of scalding steam at irregular intervals; tables groaned beneath the weight of alchemical apparatuses and books explaining the intimate details of flying sloths' mating rituals. On quite a few occasions, the detectives could see past the scorched ceiling to the floor above through holes caused by various explosions. These pits had been patched up with a few bits of metal grating and nets.

"What is it exactly that you do here?" Snips asked.

"A little bit of everything," Dunnigan said. "We're a factory for ideas, missus."

Snips hmphed. "Any good ones?"

"Sometimes," Dunnigan admitted. "Sometimes, well—it's complicated."

A case of indigestion stirred somewhere in the bowels of the building. A dull thump and a series of distant explosions rattled the jars on the shelves and sent several experiments clattering to the floor. Dunnigan sighed.

"Things have been a bit stressed since Basil's accident," he said.

"Are you convinced it was an accidental death, then?" Miss Primrose asked.

Dunnigan shrugged. "Accidents are pretty common around these parts, 'specially with someone like Basil. Man couldn't put together his afternoon tea without blowing something up. Mr. Eddington'll want to know you're here, of course; if you wait in the lobby, I'll be with you in a moment."

"Of course," Miss Primrose gracefully replied.

The Steamwork's lobby had been designed to house their more prominent guests; it was lushly furnished in an Egyptian motif, with expensive blue-black sofas lined in gold tassels and sleek furniture built from varnished maple and glass. A roaring fire snarled in an artificial hearth, glutting itself upon a meal of flammable gas.

"I'll be back in a jiffy," Dunnigan said, turning to the three of them. "Make yourselves comfortable." Once he left, they seated themselves and mulled over the turn of events.

"So," Snips said, turning to Watts. "How do you plan on proceeding with the investigation?"

"Oh, well, if I am going to get to solving this mystery, it's best that I begin at the beginning," he said. "Miss Primrose, you wouldn't happen to know where the beginning is, would you?"

Miss Primrose's eyebrows pinched together in intense thought. For a scant moment, she had the look of a calculating machine steadily clicking its way through a difficult problem. At last, she said: "I think that to begin, you must perform a thorough interrogation of the tea and biscuits, so you may eliminate them as a potential suspect."

"Oh, quite good," Watts said, nodding. "Quite good. I knew that, of course. I just like to make sure others are keeping up on their detecting." He reached for a nearby biscuit, preparing it for a barrage of questions with a small knife and a bit of butter.

"In the meanwhile, Miss Snips and I will attend to the incidental details—so you may have no distractions while you pursue this important route of inquiry," Miss Primrose said.

"Ah! Excellent. You are as helpful as ever, Miss Primrose."

"Thank you."

Dunnigan soon returned. "Well, Mr. Eddington'll to speak with you whenever you're ready. In the meanwhile, you're free to inspect the Steamwork at your leisure."

"Very well. If you'll pardon us, Mr. Watts." Miss Primrose rose to her feet.

"Er," Snips glanced between Miss Primrose and Watts, then dropped her voice into a whisper as she stood up besides her. "Where are we going again?"

"To attend to the 'incidental' parts of the crime," Miss Primrose said. "Specifically, the scene of Mr. Copper's demise."

~*~

Basil Copper was seriously dead.

The entire workshop had been consumed in an explosion that had left the far wall and ceiling exposed to the elements; as the three of them stepped in, they found themselves staring out at the vast and bustling cityscape below. Whatever destructive force had been unleashed here had been quite thorough in its destruction; nary a tool or scrap of paper remained in a semi-recognizable state.

Snips looked around. "So he blew himself up."

"That would be the obvious assumption," Miss Primrose said. She lifted her skirts up to step across the scorched debris, crouching down to more closely inspect the rubble. Immediately, she grew pale.

"Mr. Dunnigan," she said, doing her best to smother the quaver in her voice. "Have you already done a thorough search of this room for—ah, his remains?"

"Oh, aye, I swept up a little before you came in, Miss Primrose. Just thought it would be polite. Basil did always hate a mess."

"I think you might have missed—ahem." Quickly, she stood up, straightening herself and pointing down at the pile. "I think you might have missed Mr. Copper's ear."

Dunnigan scooted over and peered down. "Well wouldn't you know it—so I did! Huh. I'll put it in the bag with the rest of him." He reached down to snatch the scorched scrap of skin.

Snips waited until Dunnigan had left with the offending appendage, then turned to adjust her hat in a mirror shard that had fused with the wall. "So what's the deal with Watts?"

Miss Primrose returned to her bag, opening it with a click. Several shelves brimming with beakers, flasks, and mechanical curiosities folded out. Arming herself with a set of brass-framed magnifying lenses mounted on a leather head-strap, she turned to Snips and fired her an optically-enlarged glare. "I think the better question to ask would be what is the 'deal' with you, Miss Snips. Why on earth has Count Orwick assigned what is clearly a criminal to an otherwise legitimate investigation?"

Snips tapped the lens aside, leaving her exposed to Miss Primrose's scalding glare. She waggled her eyebrows. "Maybe he thought you could do with a little illegitimacy?"

Miss Primrose scowled, snapped the lens back into place, and turned back to the ashes. "As for your previous inquiry, Mr. Watts is a brilliant investigator. Age has merely taken its toll. Thus the responsibility for solving this crime falls upon us—or more accurately, myself."

"Then why are you working for him?"

"He was—is—a great man. He deserves respect. As for my other motives, are they not obvious? Apply some modicum of intellect to your own question and I am sure you will stumble upon an answer."

Snips thought about it for a while, scratching at the back of her head. "Because you've got a thing for him?"

"Please! I would sooner be smitten with a toad. I work for him because it is otherwise impossible for me to solve crimes. And since you seem to remain insistent about distracting me from solving *this* crime, perhaps you should go ahead and make yourself useful."

"How?"

"Interrogate some of the staff here."

"About what?"

"About how many lumps of sugar they take with their tea!" she snapped, then sighed. "About the case, Miss Snips. About the victim. About any data that might be pertinent to our investigation.

Now go! Shoo! I am working."

Snips turned to leave; just as she was stepping out, she caught sight of a curious thing poking out from beneath a rock. Crouching down, she brushed aside a few pieces rubble and found what looked to be a burnt slip of colored paper.

Snips frowned. She looked to the oblivious Miss Primrose, then stuffed the paper into her pocket. Doing her best to remain unnoticed, she stepped out the door.

~*~

CHAPTER 8: IN WHICH OUR TITULAR PROTAGONIST MEETS THE DAFFODIL SCION AND MR. EDDINGTON COMPARES NOTES WITH THE MASKED MENACE

~*~

The Steamwork was beginning to sink into a deep lull; only a few men scurried down the steam-choked corridors. No one seemed interested in the small shabbily dressed girl who slipped through its halls.

Snips hadn't gotten very far before she walked straight into someone else and collapsed with them into a heap of surprised cries and paperwork. When she at last managed to extract herself, she was surprised to find a young light-haired man who resembled a frantic rabbit locked in a desperate search for his hole. In an instant, he was down on his knees, snatching up every document he could find.

"Late, late, late," the man said, muttering to himself. "Terribly late! So sorry sir, didn't see you there, have to go—"

Snips rolled forward and perched herself in front of him, thrusting her face into his. The man squeaked and threw himself backwards, scrambling to flatten his spine to the wall.

"Hey," Snips said. "I'm a girl."

"You are! I am doubly sorry, then," he quickly responded. "Uh—"

"Doubly sorry that I'm a girl?" Snips said.

"No! Doubly sorry that—um, I'm sorry, what was I sorry about again?"

"What's your name?"

"William," he said. "Please pardon me, I'm in a bit of a rush with these last changes, and I—"

"Right, right. I'm doing an investigation, though. Real important stuff," Snips said. As the man struggled to arrive on his feet, she sprang up and slapped her palm on the wall beside his head. He was a foot taller than her, but he cowered at her presence, holding the paperwork out in front of him like a shield. "Mind if I ask you a few questions?"

The boy's face began to burn. "Err—questions? I suppose, um, if it's important. Do you mind if you ask me on the way, though?" He ducked out beneath her arm, darting over to pluck up a sheet that had escaped him. "I'm behind schedule as it is."

"Fine, fine," Snips said, sliding her arms behind her back and moving to walk besides him. "What's all this business?" Snips leaned forward to peek at one of the sheets at the top of the pile. "All these numbers—"

"It's for the Steamwork's new calculation engine," William said, quickening his pace to a loose jog. "Bank data that we must input."

"Calculation engine? The Steamwork has one of those things they use in banks?" Snips asked. "To, like, calculate interest and all that junk?"

"We've completed one, yes," William said. "It's one of the more important projects we've been working on."

"Why? Don't the banks have them already?"

"Yes, but the calculation engines they use possess fundamental flaws," William explained. "They can be damaged or disrupted by creative mathematics, or a mistake on the part of an operator. The recent plague of disasters facing the banks is representative of that."

"Oh," Snips said, wrinkling her nose. "Don't tell me you buy into that whole Professor Hemlock business."

William looked surprised. "What's not to believe, Miss...?"

"Snips," she said. "Just Snips. And Hemlock's a joke; a scam they use to sell news rags. A bedtime story mathematicians use to scare their kids into showing their work when they solve for X."

"That may be, but the fact that a misplaced decimal point can bring Aberwick's financial district to a crashing halt remains a problem in need of a solution," William said. "Our new calculation engine *is* that solution."

Snips noticed that as the discussion turned to his engine, William relaxed more; the nervous agitation flickered out of his eyes as he took on a confident stride.

"So, what? You're going to sell it to the banks?"

"Oh, no. It's too large for the banks to build," William said. "It occupies the entire basement of the Steamwork. No, we're going to rent it to them."

"Rent it?" A gentle hum had gradually been growing as they walked; as they reached the wide stairwell, it grew to a clanking purr. Snips peered down the stairs, inching her way forward.

"Yes, rent it," William said, stepping past her and moving downward. Snips reluctantly followed, listening as William explained. "In addition to the calculation engine, we've fitted all the banks with pneumatic piping that connects them to the Steamwork. We're able to send near-instant messages to any bank in Aberwick, and vice versa."

"Like mail carriages," Snips said.

"No, it's not a large carriage," William corrected her. "It's an array of pipes."

"Sounds like grave dealings."

"Anyway, once the improved engine is complete, we'll rent them space on it, which is impervious to disruption via operator error. The banks will send us all their accounting information, we'll do all the calculations, and then we'll send it back to them."

"Seems risky," Snips said. "Letting you guys run all the banks' books."

"Oh, they'd still run their own engines," William said. "We'd only be on stand-by as a back up, in case their engines failed. They could send a message to us, requesting the lost or unavailable information, and we'd help them fill in their blanks. In addition, when their engines go down, we can do the calculations for them."

"I think I see," Snips said, and by then they had arrived in the Steamwork's basement. It was a dauntingly wide chamber that occupied nearly a block of space beneath the city; it was deep enough to swallow entire sections of the apartments that bustled on the streets above it. Every inch of it below the catwalk they now stood on was occupied by a machine—one single whirring, grinding, spinning, humming machine.

It was a consortium of gears and cogs all spinning in tandem, with platforms cutting over it, across it, and through it— brimming with half-a-dozen engineers and mathematicians, dressed neatly and weaving their way through the metal passages that the machine provided, taking notes and making adjustments.

Snips gawked; William smiled.

"This is the machine," William announced. "My calculation engine."

"You—you *built* this?" Snips asked, unable to hide her incredulity.

"Well, not by myself, no," William said. "Mr. Eddington provided much of the funding, and I've only been making improvements on previous designs. But I was chiefly responsible for designing the mathematical functions it performs," he added, a sliver of pride slipping into his voice. He moved forward to his office, which was located in a niche on the other side of the catwalk; Snips followed, trying not to stare at the twisting labyrinth of gears that churned beneath her.

When she stepped into the office, the first thing she noticed was the umbrella. It was long and heavy, and as black as obsidian; it had a stylized hilt made of ivory with a butterfly forming the knob at its base.

William set the paperwork on his desk. "So, what is it exactly that you're investigating, Miss Snips?"

Snips moved towards the umbrella, reaching out to touch it. "Hm? Oh, Mr. Copper's death," she said blankly. "Where did you get this?"

"I think you might be in the wrong place, then," William said. "Mr. Copper wasn't involved in this project. Not as far as I'm aware, anyway. As for the umbrella, ah, well," he hesitated. "It was my father's."

"Really," Snips said, picking it up. It was far heavier than one would expect an ordinary umbrella to be.

"Yes, yes. Actually, I'd rather not talk about it, if it is all the same," William said. "Unless it's important to your investigation, of course. But I can't imagine how it could be."

"No, not very important," Snips admitted, setting the

umbrella down and turning back to William. "Did you know Copper well?"

"We had met before," William said. "I once visited his apartment, a year ago—when I first began working for the Steamwork."

"What was he working on?"

"To be honest, I do not know," William said. "His work was always very hush-hush. I actually didn't see him very often around the Steamwork. He'd report in and more or less disappear. Of course, we worked on opposite ends of the building. I'm afraid I really didn't know the fellow that well," he confessed. "Is there something else I could help you with, possibly?"

"Sure," Snips said. "What's your favorite color?"

"Green," he replied instantly, then paused. "Er, what?"

"These are important questions," Snips said, trying to sound as gruff as she could. "Are you trying to interfere with my investigation?"

"No! Not at all."

Snips was about to say something else, but at that moment she heard someone clearing their throat behind her.

"Mr. Eddington," William said, managing to mix of relief and disappointment with one look. "Hullo!"

"I believe you still have considerable work to accomplish, William. I will deal with Miss Snips," Mr. Eddington said. Nodding rapidly, William turned back to his paperwork. Snips tipped her hat to William and turned to Mr. Eddington, following him out of the office.

Snips huffed. "Odd fellow."

"I assume that you are Orwick's 'government consultant'?" Mr. Eddington asked as they walked over the calculating engine.

"The one and only," Snips said, tipping her hat. "Arcadia Snips, at your service. May I ask who you are?"

"Mr. Timothy Eddington. Chief administrator of the Steamwork." The man glared at her long and hard. "I assume you'll want to discuss the details of the case with me."

"Sure. You got an office?"

"This way."

As they rounded back up the stairs and around the corner, Snips thought she caught sight of Dunnigan stepping into Mr. Eddington's office, but the administrator said nothing. Once they reached it, he opened the door and allowed Snips to enter first.

Once inside, her eyes nearly sprang from her skull. All other thoughts disappeared in a flash: there was not a single object in the room that was not worth stealing. Even the pens looked like they could feed a family of six for a month. A chain of ivory statues sat on an ebonized desk; books with gold leaf foil bindings littered the shelves. Crystal tumblers lined a fully stocked liquor cabinet, filled to the top with the good stuff.

Snips' fingers started to twitch. She shoved them so deep into her pockets that her pants started to sag.

"Is there a problem, Miss Snips?" Mr. Eddington asked.

"Not at all," Snips blurted out a little too quickly. "Just a little, uh, chilly in here. My, you have a lot of expensive stuff." She felt her fingers spasm in her pockets, fighting for freedom. "Quite a lot of expensive stuff."

"Yes. I enjoy the finer things in life," Mr. Eddington said, walking around his desk to take a seat. "Please, make yourself comfortable. If it is all the same with you, I would like to finish this up as quickly as possible."

Snips moistened her lips. "Right, right," she said, sitting. "Just have to, you know, ask you a few questions."

Mr. Eddington raised an eyebrow. "Miss Snips, why are you stuffing my gold engraved pen in your pocket?"

Snips froze, looking down at her hands. She immediately placed the pen back on the desk and proceeded to flatten her palms to the seat of the chair, sitting on them. "Sorry," she said. "You know how people can be with pens. Thought it was mine for a second."

Mr. Eddington's eyebrow continued to lift, disappearing underneath his graying hairline. "I... see."

"Anyway. I was just asking Daffodil back there about the calculation engine project you're running." Snips allowed her eyes to slide across the room, trying to find something to distract her from all the interesting things on Mr. Eddington's desk. She caught sight of something in particular; a small bulletin board that had various newspaper clippings attached to it. They dealt with new groundbreaking inventions the Steamwork had been responsible for. Snips noticed that most of them were dated back from at least a decade ago.

"Yes. It's quite a lucrative arrangement. Mr. Tweedle and his banks gain added security and invulnerability toward mathematical mischief, and in return we charge a considerable yet wholly appropriate fee," Mr. Eddington said. "However, I fail to see precisely what this has to do with Mr. Copper's demise."

"Just coming at this from every angle possible," Snips said. "What else does the Steamwork do? Besides the bank stuff."

"We invent things, Miss Snips. Our improvements on the calculation engine is merely one such example."

"Such as?"

"The original calculation engines. The gas piping that provides the city with light and power. A system of pneumatic tubing that allows for instant communication between parts of the city. In essence, the Steamwork is a factory for science. We mass produce technological wonders."

"What was Basil working on? Mr. Daffodil wasn't quite sure himself."

"At last, something that has to do with your case," Mr. Eddington said with an exasperated sigh. "He was working on several minor projects. Most of them were rather dull. Nothing of any particular interest."

"Well, like what?"

"He had a rather absurd idea concerning replacing gas lighting with bulbs of glass containing lengths of galvanized filament."

"How would that make light?" Snips asked, frowning in thought.

"That was precisely my question. As for what his current project was, I do not know. Although he was my research assistant, he was up for review; he had defied many of my attempts to put him on a more constructive project ever since he became obsessed with matters of electricity."

"Do you think he was working on anything dangerous enough to cause an explosion?"

"Yes. I hasten to add that, on several occasions, Copper has ignored safety protocols when conducting his experiments—and this is not the first time he has nearly blown us all to kingdom come."

"Is there any place Basil might have kept notes on his latest project? Maybe something he had yet to submit to you, or research notes outside of his workshop?"

"If so, I am unaware of it. Copper rarely submitted his projects for approval, because he knew I would not approve them." Mr. Eddington opened his desk, withdrawing a rather large and intimidating pile of paperwork. "There are several matters I must attend to. Please pardon me if I cut this interview short."

"Sure."

"Perhaps Mr. Copper kept some of his notes at his home? You should check there. In the meanwhile, I have work to do. Good day, Miss Snips."

Snips rose to her feet. "Thanks for the hint. I'll keep it in mind."

~*~

Not long after Snips had left his office, Mr. Eddington stood and locked the door to his office. He then returned to his desk and pressed a switch hidden on the side of a drawer. At once, the bookcase gave a gentle hiss as hydraulic pumps edged it forward and to the side. In a narrow niche behind it, a spiral staircase was tucked away. It led deep into the basement of the Steamwork.

Mr. Eddington stepped through the passage, carefully making his way below. When he reached the lowest chamber, he was greeted by the sight of Dunnigan mopping the stone tiled floor.

"Mr. McGee."

"Oh, good evenin' Mr. Eddington," Dunnigan said, throwing the man a quick smile. "Didn't quite see you coming—"

"I have told you to never use my entrance during the

Steamwork's operating hours. If anyone of importance had seen you disappear into my office, the results could have been catastrophic."

Dunnigan frowned and nodded his head. "Well, I'm sorry about that, Mr. Eddington. I just figured—"

"I don't pay you to figure," Mr. Eddington cut him off. "As it was, we were fortunate it was merely a woman who noticed your entry."

Mr. Eddington stepped past Dunnigan, not noticing the face that the janitor made at his back. He stepped through into the Steamwork's Vault—a chamber that lay far beneath even the deeply buried calculation engine.

The fact that the Steamwork *had* a basement beneath its basement was a fact that not many were privy to. Not even William knew of its existence—and with good reason. It was a laboratory choked in dust and secrets, containing several cases in which marvels were kept under glass—preserved and cleaned, disassembled and analyzed. Mr. Eddington paused at the mouth of the room's entrance, reluctant to enter. Though he knew the idea to be absurd, he could not shake the feeling that the laboratory's previous master had left some trap for the unwary to blunder into.

Mr. Eddington threw off the sensation. He knew every inch of this room—every *centimeter*. There was not a particle of dirt present that he had not categorized and neatly labeled. Which was why the other man's presence here was so disarming.

"Mr. Eddington," a voice laced with menace and metal spoke from the back of the room. "Good afternoon."

Mr. Eddington grimaced. How on earth did the bastard keep getting in here without someone noticing? Certainly, Mr. McGee should have seen him enter. Could there be a secret entrance that Mr. Eddington was unaware of? Or was the man always here, sleeping until he arrived—merely another of the previous owner's miraculous machines?

"Good evening, sir," Mr. Eddington responded as politely as he could. "I received your missive, and told Miss Snips what you suggested."

The man stepped forward. Aside from his suit, he only

Mr. Eddington secretly meets with the Masked Menace.

possessed two articles of note—a black jackal mask rimmed in gold and a delicate paper butterfly lapel. The mask distorted his voice into a metal hum, making it impossible to determine his identity. It was one of many unnecessary theatrics that Mr. Eddington had learned to cope with.

"Excellent," the jackal said. "And Mr. Tweedle?"

"Hardly a concern," Mr. Eddington said. "He is easily cowed into submission. I am far more worried over Count Orwick's interference."

"Count Orwick will be dealt with," the jackal said, and there was an edge to his tone that gave Mr. Eddington the chills. "Concern yourself only with fulfilling your end of our bargain."

"We'll have the rest of Aberwick's bank accounts loaded into the engine by tonight," Mr. Eddington said. "And then—"

"And then I will do as promised. So long as you abide by my instructions, everything shall go according to plan."

Mr. Eddington gave a slight start.

"Is something wrong, Mr. Eddington?"

"Merely a sense of *déjà vu*," Mr. Eddington muttered. "I assume you can show yourself out," he added, turning to leave.

~*~

CHAPTER 9: IN WHICH WE ONCE AGAIN RETURN TO THE PAST TO INVESTIGATE ONGOING MATTERS CONCERNING SECRET SOCIETIES AND THE RECKLESS APPLICATION OF MATHEMATICS

~*~

"My apologies, Nigel. Abigail couldn't make it; there's a bit of trouble back at the Steamwork—"

"You don't need to apologize on her behalf," Nigel told him. "I am well aware that she would prefer not to venture into our little 'clubhouse'."

"It's just a little disorienting for her, is all," Jeremiah said. "I mean, you've plunged so deep into it, and only in two years—"

"Do not worry. I more than understand her discomfort."

The pair ventured past the Society chapter-house's thriving garden grounds where cicadas thrummed among the birches and pines, making their way to the brightly lit conservatory. Its framework was built of light oak with bronzed roof panels that flashed in the light offered from a hanging lamp of glass and tin.

Jeremiah made himself comfortable on a padded wicker cot; Nigel sat in an inlaid armchair with a rich foliage motif and lush cushions dyed an imperial shade of blue. They remained in silence until Jeremiah caught sight of someone stirring among the shadows in a corridor behind Nigel.

He sighed. "Nigel, Abigail and I—we're worried. About you."

"Whatever for?"

"We think you're getting too involved in this whole affair," Jeremiah said. "The secrets, the ritualistic trappings, the deceptions —you've cloaked yourself in a cloud of mystery. We're worried you are taking it far too seriously."

"Trust me," Nigel said. "I find it just as absurd as Abigail no doubt does. It is merely a tool to reach our ends."

"Still, one cannot maintain lies of this sort for so long

without letting them seep into their life," Jeremiah said. "We just want you to be careful, Nigel. Don't let your means *become* your ends."

"Wise counsel, yes, yes," Nigel said. "But we can talk of this later."

"If you wish."

"Did you bring the new numbers?"

"Of course." Jeremiah drew the folded papers out from his coat, handing them over to Nigel. The dark-haired naturalist unfolded them, removing a pair of spectacles from his front coat pocket and perusing the mathematical formulas scrawled over its surface.

"I must admit," Nigel said, perusing over the equations, "Your recent work has been magnificent. Some of the predictions your last set of equations made exceeded even my initiates' superstitious expectations."

"Only a few of the equations are actually mine," Jeremiah said. "Abigail is responsible for the bulk of them."

"She has proven to be a far greater asset than I had originally thought," Nigel said.

"She's brilliant," Jeremiah said, and left it at that. "Shall we input the numbers...?"

"Yes, yes," Nigel said. "Let's." He rose from his chair, gesturing for Jeremiah to follow as he moved deeper into his home. Jeremiah stepped inside the dimly lit interior of the chapter-house.

The chapter-house's drawing room was decorated with resplendent textiles; crimson curtains trimmed with gold lining smothered what little light entered through its windows, casting a filtered glow upon the furniture within. The shadows here had grown so thick that they seemed to possess a substance all of their own; Jeremiah could easily imagine that, given the right prompting, they would leap to the defense of the chapter-house's master.

"Your new home is rather disconcerting," Jeremiah confessed.

Nigel laughed, as if enjoying some delightful joke. "Do you know why we are afraid of the dark?"

"Because our imagination fills it with dreadful, wicked things," Jeremiah said.

"Yes," Nigel replied, "that is correct. But do you know why?"

"No, but I am sure you will tell me, eh?"

"Of course. Because the alternative is far more terrifying, Jeremiah. Because the alternative is this: that there is nothing there. That, in fact, we are merely alone. Alone, in the dark."

"Funny," Jeremiah replied. "Maybe it's just me, but I've never been too frightened of getting my face eaten by an *empty* shadow."

Nigel laughed again. He lead Jeremiah down a set of spiraling stairs, down into the very belly of the chapter-house, beyond the realm of the uninitiated.

The basement where they had stored the latest probability engine was large in size, but nearly all the space was taken up by the engine itself. It dwarfed Jeremiah's previous designs; iron and steel had replaced the cheaper brass fittings, with Jeremiah's latest improvements—vacuum bulbs and batteries—providing a source of cleaner, quieter power.

It had been Abigail's idea to build the controls out of a church organ. Each key was labeled with a number or function, and after a bit of practice, inputting data became child's play. Nigel sat the documents on the nearby music stand, cracked his knuckles, and began typing in the values in a blur of finger strokes. "There is something else I wanted your opinion on, Jeremiah," he said as he worked. "Seize the electric torch to your left; use it to inspect the chalkboard over the corner there. I have scribbled down a few equations."

Jeremiah did as he was told, approaching the chalkboard with some consternation. As he lifted the torch up to inspect the numbers, his eyebrows knitted with confusion. The writing went far beyond the meager boundaries of the chalkboard—Nigel's dense, neat script extended over the chalkboard's frame and coated every inch of the wall. "Nigel, what is this?"

"A thought experiment."

"A thought experiment? This is an equation for the engine,

Nigel. I recognize the functions—but I cannot make out what it is you are trying at, here."

"We have used the engine to avert small calamities with the foreknowledge it grants us," Nigel said, still inputting the numbers with focus and intent. "But what if we attempted to make something happen?"

Jeremiah raised a brow, looking back at Nigel. "We've done that. The rain—"

"A paltry parlor trick," Nigel said. "A clever act of chicanery, nothing more. No, what I was thinking was something far more grand."

"Were you not the one who warned us of frivolously using the engine?"

"Yes, yes, of course," Nigel replied. "But this idea is far from that."

"What is it you are proposing?"

"What if we made a person?"

Silence lingered. Jeremiah frowned.

"A person, Nigel?"

"Yes. Imagine it—a person created through the probability engine. If we could distill the birth of a person to mere mathematics, could we not cause it to happen? Furthermore, what would occur? You and Abigail have theorized that events caused by the probability engine lead to all manner of strange coincidences and conflagrations of chance; would a person created in this way lead such a life as well? Could we, in fact, manufacture a living entity's very destiny?"

"It is... an interesting notion," Jeremiah admitted, "yet one best constrained to matters of theory."

"Of course, of course," Nigel said. He brought the cover down over the keys with a loud snap. "I would never think of actually putting the idea into *action*. Not, at least, without your and Abigail's permission."

"Of course," Jeremiah said, although he sounded unconvinced.

"I apologize, Jeremiah. Pardon my rudeness for keeping you so late; it sometimes grows lonely in this house. I have only fawning fools and ignorant believers to keep me company."

"Of course, of course," Jeremiah agreed. "No pardon is necessary. Think nothing of it."

"We will speak next week, then? After I have sent the latest results to you?" Nigel said, staring up at the monolith of a machine.

"Yes, of course," Jeremiah replied. "And, perhaps I will speak to Abigail of this theory of yours—we would never put it in practice, of course, but it might intrigue her—"

"I would rather you not, Jeremiah. She all ready thinks me a schemer; I would rather her opinion of me not grow darker."

"If... if you insist, Nigel."

"I do. Good night, Jeremiah. One of my men will show you out."

"Thank you. And, good night, Nigel."

~*~

CHAPTER 10: IN WHICH OUR TITULAR PROTAGONIST MAKES AN ILL-CONCEIVED JOKE, THE DAFFODIL SCION PONDERS HIS FAVORITE COLOR, AND AN ASSASSIN LEARNS A DREADFUL SECRET

~*~

Snips nearly walked right into Miss Primrose as she bolted out of Basil's workshop. The detective clutched a metal-rimmed flask filled to the lip with a frothing cyan chemical.

"Blue, Miss Snips!" she cried out. "It turned blue! Do you know what this means?!"

"You're expecting?"

Snips considered the error of her ways from the workshop's floor.

"Quite sorry, Miss Snips," Miss Primrose announced dryly, shifting her weight back to the tips of her toes. "My elbow seems to have slipped into your abdomen. Did you say something?"

Snips coughed and spluttered, dragging herself back to her feet. "Where did you learn to, ah, 'slip' like that?"

"Miss Muffet's Finishing School for Ladies," she said. "Blue indicates the presence of an explosive agent."

"So he blew himself up," Snips said.

"He was 'blown up'. We do not know by whom. Did your interrogations bare any fruit?"

"Mr. Eddington mentioned checking out Basil's house to see if he left any blueprints for his current project. Otherwise, he's not aware precisely what Basil's experiments meant, except they involved electricity."

"Then I agree. As this is a simple task, I will entrust it to you, Miss Snips. See about securing the location of Mr. Copper's home at the front desk. Meanwhile, I will investigate the patent office to see if—"

"This sounds like something important," Watts said, suddenly appearing behind Miss Primrose. "Is this something important? Because if it's important, I should probably do it. I mean, after all, I am a very important person."

Miss Primrose instantly went pale. "Err—important, Mr. Watts? N-no, not at—"

"It is of great importance," Snips interrupted, her voice slipping through the conversation like a greased dagger. "In fact, it is of such immense importance that neither Miss Primrose nor myself can be trusted with it. To say that this matter is critical to the case would be an understatement of incredible proportions."

Miss Primrose glared at Snips; meanwhile, Detective Watts looked supremely interested. "Whatever could it be?"

Snips leaned in towards Detective Watts, glancing from side to side to ensure that no one else would overhear. And then, in the hushed tone often reserved for conspiracies of the utmost secrecy, she whispered: "Books, Detective Watts."

Watts gasped. Miss Primrose spluttered.

"Books?!" He asked, then dropped his voice. "Do you think that—"

Snips pressed a finger to her nose and shook her head. Detective Watts immediately snapped his mouth shut and nodded, glancing around the room to eye any nearby books with nervous suspicion.

"Think about it," Snips murmured. "They're everywhere, aren't they? Always just sitting there. Full of *words*."

"Yes, yes," Watts nodded. "I've always said that books are full of words, haven't I, Miss Primrose?"

Snips cut in before the speechless Miss Primrose could reply. "This requires a more thorough investigation, don't you think?"

"Yes. Yes! I will get to the bottom of this matter immediately!"

"To the library," Snips cried.

"To the library!" Detective Watts replied, then with a swoosh of his long coat, he ran off.

Miss Primrose stared after his retreating form for quite some while before turning to Snips. "How did you—"

"I'm fluent in crazy. Where should we meet once I search

Copper's house?"

Miss Primrose withdrew a small plain card from her medical purse; on it was a neat and legible print. It said 'WATTS AND SONS DETECTIVE AGENCY' at the top, and listed an address in the upper ward beneath it. "We will meet here in approximately four hours' time, Miss Snips."

"Right," Snips said, taking the card and tucking it in her coat. "Four hours."

~*~

Daffodil's workshop was a confused jumble of engine parts, diagrams, equations plastered to the walls, and old books on medieval knights. The young man looked more disheveled than ever, holding an ink-pen and scrawling down numbers at his desk. He did not even look up as Mr. Eddington entered.

"Busy," Daffodil announced, eyes transfixed. Mr. Eddington had long learned that the man was absolutely unbendable when he was working on a sufficiently difficult problem. "Finishing up some final equations."

"I simply wanted to check in on you and insure that this 'Miss Snips' had not gleaned too much information from you, Mr. Daffodil."

"Didn't tell her much," he said, licking the tip of his pen and dipping it in the inkwell. "Favorite color."

For the second time that day, Mr. Eddington raised his eyebrow.

"Your... favorite color?"

"Green," William said, and then—quite to Mr. Eddington's surprise—he sat the pen down and looked up at him. "What do you know about women, sir?"

"Only that they are monstrous and inscrutable creatures, best avoided at every opportunity."

"I see, sir."

"Have a good night, Mr. Daffodil. Remember to lock your office up on your way out."

"Yes sir."

Eddington left. Shortly after the door closed, William glanced back down at the equations he had been furiously solving. At their center lay Snips' name, which—so far—had resisted all attempts at subtraction, multiplication, or division.

Even by cat.

~*~

Smoke rolled up from the tip of the assassin's cigarette. His bronze nose winked and glimmered in the dim light of Dead Beat Alley's spluttering and outdated gas lamps.

People in Dead Beat Alley minded their own business; it was assumed by everyone that everyone else was a puppy-murdering sociopath and the less they had to do with them the better. This philosophy had turned out quite well, and had made it a haven for several depraved puppy-murdering organizations throughout the city.

He arrived at Snips' apartment—a fire-trap shoved in between two larger fire-traps soaked in grease and placed next to burning lamps. He pulled out his pistol and kicked the door down with a solid whump, striding in and taking aim.

Motes of dirt floated in sluggish whorls through the book-lined room. But there was no one present; no one downstairs, no one upstairs. Realizing that his quarry was not home, he decided to do a little research.

The assassin hummed to himself, glossing over the titles of several books. Most of them were concerned with some matter of science that applied to the art of breaking and entering.

Upstairs wasn't much different. He considered ransacking the place, but didn't want to leave any clues of his presence; it would probably be best to do a search, wait to see if she was coming back, then move on. As he was scanning the top of one bookshelf, he heard a tell-tale creak beneath the sole of his boot.

"Hn." The assassin crouched down and peered at the floorboard. It didn't take much to pull it up; among the dust and cobwebs that inhabited the niche below, he discovered a small wooden chest wrapped in linen. Sitting down on Snips's lumpy bed, the assassin brought the chest to his lap and opened it, carefully rifling through its contents.

A folded paper butterfly. A small locket with a picture inside of a woman—he assumed it was Snips's mother. Several old post-cards that contained little of interest. A dusty book about medieval knights. But at the very bottom of the chest was a faded yellow photograph that caught his eye.

On its front was a little six-year-old girl with long dark hair and an extravagant dress—likely Snips—and a tall, handsome gentleman in a coal-colored suit and vest. They stood in front of a large machine that had the appearance of a horse-drawn carriage, except without the horses. It had an assembly of contraptions weighing it down and what looked to be a steam-engine attached to its back.

He flipped the photograph over. It read: 'NIGEL AND DAUGHTER'.

The assassin whistled low. He put the objects back in the box, returned it to its proper place, and then quietly made his way out.

~*~

"I'm afraid we don't have Mr. Copper's address," the secretary explained.

"Listen, Sue—"

"My name is Michelle, ma'am."

"Right, Sally. Like I was saying," Snips explained. "I need to know where the poor bugger lived. I mean, how in the world am I supposed to investigate his house if I can't even find it?"

The long-suffering secretary sighed. "His place of residence changed not too long ago, ma'am. He never submitted his new residence to us. I can give you the address for the previous house where he lived."

"Is there a problem, Miss Snips?"

Snips turned to find herself face-to-face with William. The young mathematician had donned his evening coat and held a folder full of what looked to be important documents.

"I'm just trying to explain to Sabrina, here—"

"Michelle," the secretary corrected.

"Right," Snips said. "I'm just trying to explain to her that I need to find out where Copper lived."

"Well, I could take you to his apartment, if you liked."

"Really?" Snips asked, waggling her eyebrows. The expression clearly made William uncomfortable.

"Er, yes," he said, shifting his weight from foot to foot. "I'm just getting off work now."

"Lead on, good sir." Snips paused, before adding: "Actually, I need to make one little stop on the way, first. If you don't mind."

"Erm, not at all," William said, flustered.

~*~

"It's a bleedin' travesty, s'what it is."

"Unghunh."

"Succession of bleedin' governmental authority through bloodlines? Since when is bleedin' heredity any significant demonstration of legitimacy to rule?"

"Unghungh."

"Naw, we ain't bleedin' got that. I mean, th'boss—the *real* boss, I mean—he ain't possessin' no authority on the bleedin' basis of who hooked up with his ma. We thugs are bleedin' civilized, see."

"Unguh?"

"Aye. He's in charge 'cuz he could kick our bleedin' arses."

Mr. Cheek and Mr. Tongue paused in their conversation, having made their way up to the front counter. The teller stared at the two mismatched collection of body parts and proceeded to do the only sensible thing: she fainted.

A moment later and the bank manager had taken her place, providing the two ruffians with a smile. "Hello, gentlemen," he said with a nervous titter. "I'm Mr. Caddleberry, the bank manager. If you give me just a moment, I'll be happy to open the vaults for you. No need for any violence," he quickly added.

Mr. Cheek narrowed his one eye; Mr. Tongue proceeded to gurgle with indignation.

"Unghungh!"

"Aye," Mr. Cheek agreed. "We ain't here to bleedin' rob you, stupid git. We want to open an account."

"Oh—Oh! Oh, of course!" Mr. Caddleberry exclaimed, throwing his hands atop of his heart with shock. "How absurdly ridiculous of me. An account—yes, yes! We'd be happy to have your business, Mister—"

"Just make an account followin' these specific bleedin' instructions," Mr. Cheek announced, thrusting a card out to the bank manager. "Absolutely no bleedin' deviations, understand? Exactly as the bleedin' card says."

"Of—of course," Mr. Caddleberry said, accepting the card with great reluctance. He read the instructions and assumed a rather confused look. "This is a bit... Erm, well, I mean—opening an account here under these conditions... It's quite unusual. You'd stand to lose more money than you'd gain, and—"

"Did I ask for a bleedin' opinion? I can't recall. Mr. Tongue, did I ask for a bleedin' opinion?"

"Ungunh."

Mr. Cheek turned back to the bank manager, bringing one immense fist down to tap on the counter. "No, I didn't bleedin' think so. So if you don't mind, Mr. Babbleworry—"

"Caddleberry," he corrected, and instantly regretted it. "Er, although Babbleworry is quite fine. My closest friends often call me Babbleworry. Kind of a nickname, really."

"—we'd like it very bleedin' much if you'd just open an account followin' those specific bleedin' instructions."

"I'll input these numbers into the calculating engine right away," Mr. Caddleberry said. "I'll do it myself. This instant!" He nearly tripped over the still-unconscious bank-teller on his way to do just that.

~*~

ACT 2

~*~

"Professor Von Grimskull's monocycle roared beneath him as it thundered through the crimson night-sky, the wheel forged from sheer awesomantium snarling its way across the flaming dirigible's upper frame. The legion of steam-powered zombie air-pirates had all ready taken control, their engine-ladened frames churning out thick choking whorls of vaporized smoke; soon, the zeppelin would crash into the swirling energies of the temporal anomaly, completing the necrocthulthic ritual and fulfilling the eldritch prophecy — bringing an end to the universe.

The bronze-nosed Von Grimskull made a low, deep-throated snarl. "The Doctor is in... *VINCIBLE!*""

—<u>Professor Von Grimskull and the Zombie Sky-Pirates</u>, Page 5

~*~

CHAPTER 11: IN WHICH OUR TITULAR PROTAGONIST MEETS WITH A SINISTER CRYPTOZOOLOGIST AND MISS PRIMROSE FAMILIARIZES HERSELF WITH ABERWICK'S ESTEEMED BANKING SYSTEM

~*~

Snips was unaccustomed to traveling by anything other than foot; she had always preferred the feel of cobblestone beneath one's toes to the well-cushioned luxury of a hansom cab. But William seemed rather tired, and Snips was worried about officers in the upper ward recognizing her face. When he sent for a cab, she didn't complain.

She gave the man directions and turned to William, her eyes drifting to his umbrella. He had drawn it off the coat rack moments before leaving the Steamwork; Snips could not wrest her gaze away from it.

"Is something wrong, Miss Snips?"

"Your umbrella," Snips said. "Before, you mentioned it was your father's—"

William grimaced and sighed. "Yes. Professor Daffodil."

Snips nodded. "So you're—"

"I'm afraid so," William said dejectedly, shifting awkwardly in his seat. "I am William Daffodil; Jeremiah Daffodil and Abigail Daffodil's son."

"I heard of them," Snips said, which was at least half of the truth. "Big scientists, right? Ran the Steamwork?"

"*Mad* scientists," William corrected her. "Responsible for endangering nearly half the city in that awful affair a decade ago."

Snips bit down on her lip, turning to stare out the window. Sensing her sudden distance, William tried to put her at ease.

"I'm well aware my father and mother were villains," William explained. "But I am nothing like them. Mr. Eddington and the others have been especially kind, granting me an opportunity to prove myself at their old business, the Steamwork."

"It's not that," Snips said. "Just, uh. It's complicated."

"I understand. It is not easy to accept the fact that I have no connection to my parents beyond biology," William began. "It's just—"

"Whatever your parents did or didn't do has absolutely nothing to do with you," Snips said, cutting him off.

The horse at the front of the cabby gave a whicker as it stopped at the front gates. "Come on," Snips told William, stepping out of the carriage and toward the black iron gates. "You can wait in the lobby."

"What is this place?" William asked.

"Just a guy I know," Snips answered, her voice hollow.

The Arcanum Estate occupied a small block of land in the upper ward; it was surrounded on all sides by metal fencing and signs that made it clear that trespassers would be shot, mauled by angry dogs, and then shot again. It was probably one of the only places in Aberwick that you couldn't have paid Snips to sneak into.

She and William walked past the front gates and straight to the stout oak doors. Snips gave them a solid knock.

The well-dressed servant that answered the door fit the definition of human only in the strictest sense. It was as if a creature with no conception of what a person looked like had been handed a basic description and then asked to craft one out of stone. The final result had gotten the basic gist of it, but there remained several fundamental flaws.

His face was composed of an assembly of harsh angles and drastic, stark edges; it was several inches longer than it should be and was devoid of facial hair. He was as white as chalk and looked just as brittle. His expression was as stoic as rock and had all the cheer of a child's funeral; Snips had never seen the man smile and at this point didn't think that he was capable. A large black scarf swallowed his throat like a constricting serpent of linen.

"Evening, Starkweather," Snips said. "I'm here to see him."

"This way," he said, stepping into the house's dining room.

The home had very little light; neither Starkweather nor its owner required much. What illumination did flow in through the windows shone down upon every manner of curiosity the mind could conceive—glass jars stuffed full of strange and impossible creatures, varying from the naturally occurring to the wholly artificial. William stared in wonder, while Snips resisted the urge to peek in the bottles. She knew there were things inside them that, once seen, were very hard to put out of your mind without a month of steady drinking.

"You can wait here," Snips told William, leaving the young mathematician to make himself comfortable on a couch. William shifted nervously in the seat and threw Starkweather and Snips a meek smile.

The man she had come to see was inside the study. Neatly arranged diagrams of impossible machines framed under glass and pine lined the walls, with books littering the desk and floor. Several of them were opened, with various passages highlighted or underlined by a careful pen. Scarcely a shred of light penetrated this deeply into the home, making it hard to make out the silhouette that sat at the back of the room.

He was a wretched figure; nothing more than a burnt husk swaddled in antiseptic soaked bandages from head to toe. Despite his horrible affliction, he appeared to be reclining in a comfortable chair, wearing a pair of crimson bathrobes, a cherry-red fez, and holding a book in his lap. The cloth-wrapped claw that used to be his hand would occasionally swing over to brush across a page, dragging it from one side to the other; years of practice had turned this once clumsy gesture into an act of casual grace.

"Master Arcanum," Starkweather said, standing at attention. "Arcadia is here to speak with you."

The man struggled to pluck up one of the bookmarks on the table besides him, working to push it between the pages. When he at last succeeded, he slapped the book shut and awkwardly put it aside. His eye and lipless mouth were the only things that were left of his face; one eye had been burned away, but the other was kept safe inside a lubricant-filled goggle that fitted neatly over the socket.

"My dear," he spoke in a moist rasp. "To what do I owe the visit?"

Snips wore a tight-lipped expression. Rather than explaining herself, she reached into her pocket and drew out the scrap of burnt, colored paper, holding it up.

"Ah," he said. "Business."

"Business," Snips agreed.

"So, then. The scorched remains of a paper butterfly. Where did you find it?"

"At a murder scene. An engineer named Basil Copper. Employed at the Steamwork."

"I was unaware," he said, suppressing a cough, "that you were investigating murders, now."

"Not much of a choice. It's a long story and I'd rather not fill you in on the details. I just want to know one thing: Is the Society involved?"

"I have little relevance in the Society these days, Arcadia," Nigel Arcanum said, reaching down for his rubber gas-mask. He brought it to his face, releasing a nearby valve with a hiss and drinking deep of the nourishing oxygen it released. "Mmn. I'm afraid I could not tell you. As far as I am aware? No."

"Was Copper a member of the Society?"

"Again, not as far as I am aware. But such knowledge is outside of my purview. I find it unlikely, however, as the Steamwork is notoriously worthless," Nigel said.

Snips raised an eyebrow. "Howso?"

"At one time, beneath the guidance of its once esteemed founder and his wife, the Steamwork was a factory of innovation," Nigel explained. "It has long since lost such notoriety."

"All the inventions Mr. Eddington mentioned the Steamwork being responsible for are things we've had for at least a decade," Snips said, agreeing. "I assume, then, he's incompetent?"

"Entirely. He has been steadily losing money since half a decade ago. He clearly commands only a trivial understanding of science."

"How has he stayed in business all this time?" Snips asked.

"I am afraid that I have not researched this particular mystery thoroughly," Nigel said. "I only know that Mr. Eddington's books do not properly add up. As for the past two years, the

Steamwork's profits have taken an even deeper nose-dive."

"If I find out that you have any connection to this—"

"Yes, yes, you'll turn me over to the authorities or some such nonsense," Nigel said. "I assure you, this is not some long-winded gambit on my part. If the Society is involved, it is an affair outside my knowledge."

"If you aren't involved in this, fine. But don't interfere. None of your meddling."

"Of course, Arcadia."

Snips turned and left. As her footsteps took her towards the door, she heard Nigel's voice rise up from behind:

"Arcadia?"

Snips turned. "What?"

"If the Society *is* involved, then—you know well enough to be careful, my dear, do you not?"

"I'm not your dear."

She stepped out, slamming the door behind her.

William was waiting for her in the study, staring at one of the objects on the shelves; Snips silently marched past him, her face as rigid as rock. As William rose to follow, she failed to notice what it was that the young mathematician had been looking at so intently.

An umbrella identical to his sat among Nigel's curiosities.

~*~

Miss Primrose boarded the car to find that all available seats had been taken by other passengers; she was forced to stand, gripping one of the bronze handlebars located high over the seats as the train lurched forward.

The train had not been long in moving when one of the passengers—a burly older gentleman in a top-hat and powder-gray suit who was in clear need of a shave—looked the strong-jawed woman up and down and cleared his throat.

"Yes?" Miss Primrose said.

"Pray, are you an advocate of woman's rights, ma'am?" he asked, doing his best to suppress a devilish smile.

Miss Primrose scowled. "Yes, sir, I most certainly am. Why do you ask?"

"Because ma'am," he replied, his face splitting into a broad, toothsome grin. "I was about to offer you my seat; but of course you claim the right to stand!"

As the train came to a hissing halt at the platform, passengers fought with one another to climb out of the car. They were soon followed by a stern-faced Miss Primrose, who was in turn followed by a very sullen and scruffy old man sporting a fresh black eye.

The marble facade of the East Crown bank fitted over the intersection of 3rd and Maple like a comfortable hat. The two story office had scarcely a single edge to it; this had the effect of making the building seem as if it were giving the corner a warm hug.

Miss Primrose stepped past the threshold of the entrance and into its austere lobby, where tellers and bureaucrats were busily shuffling about in the quiet desperation of Aberwick's various financial disasters. The trail of patents she had busily been following since leaving the Steamwork had lead her inevitably to Mr. Tweedle, who had cosigned several of them; she now tapped her finger on one of the countertops, drawing the attention of the woman behind it.

"Yes?" The teller snapped.

"I need to speak with Mr. Tweedle," Miss Primrose said. "It is a matter of great urgency."

"Yes, I'm sure it is," the teller said. "And, like all the matters of great urgency that Mr. Tweedle is facing, it will have to take a number and get in line."

"Madame, this is—"

"Let me guess!" the teller shouted. "You want to take your money out of the bank, don't you? Got a whiff this whole Hemlock business and now you want to slip out the back before your money's all gone, eh?"

Miss Primrose furrowed her brow with displeasure. "Madame, I—"

"You people make me sick!" The teller threw her arms into the air. "Take it! Take all your blasted, misbegotten money! We don't want it anymore! We don't *need* it anymore! Ooh, you people and your fearful terrors. I've—I've—oh, I think I'm going to faint, I think I'm—"

The woman collapsed with a thud. Instantly, someone across the aisle rang a silver bell; a small group of appropriately dressed physicians stepped behind the counter with a stretcher in tow. They proceeded to load her up and march out of the office.

Shortly after, another bank teller was shoved in front of the blinking Miss Primrose. This one was rather short and had a pair of fancy glasses. "Hullo!"

"Uh, good evening, Madame," Miss Primrose began. "I'd like to—"

"Deposit money? Very good, then. How much will you be depositing?" The girl's eyebrow began to twitch.

Miss Primrose frowned rather sternly. "I am not depositing any money."

"Shall I write you down for a ten-note, then? A hundred-note, perhaps?"

"Madame, I repeat: I am not depositing any value."

"Oo, a thousand-note, is it?" The girl started to giggle. "How very industrious of you. A working woman, are you?"

"Madame!" Miss Primrose slammed her left arm down on the countertop, making a very loud sound. "I do not have an account at this bank! I have never had an account at this bank. And, God willing, I will refrain from creating an account at this bank any time in the near future! I only wish to speak with Mr. Tweedle on a matter concerning a recent criminal affair—"

"Oh," the girl said, drawing back meekly. "I understand."

Miss Primrose sighed with relief.

"You'd like to open a new account, then?"

Now it was Miss Primrose's turn to twitch. "Fetch me your manager."

~*~

CHAPTER 12: IN WHICH MR. COPPER'S APARTMENT IS SEARCHED AND A TRAP IS SPRUNG

~*~

Despite his prestigious career at the Steamwork, Basil Copper had long been burdened by a family debt that had left him destitute. This meant he lived in the only place where a man could manage to get by on a handful of pennies and a quick smile: The Rookery.

For Snips, it remained nothing more than a visit home. She had spent most of her childhood here among the dirty faced street-urchins and fast-witted card sharks—cheating and being cheated, stealing and being stolen from.

Snips sucked in the Rookery's stink as if it were a breeze of fresh country air. Meanwhile, William covered his nose with a handkerchief and did his best not to retch.

"Sweet as treacle, eh? It'll put hair on your chest."

"I'm not exactly looking for a hairy chest, Miss Snips," William mumbled. "Now I remember why I've only visited Mr. Copper once during my time at the Steamwork. This way."

They arrived at Basil's apartment just as the sun was tipping its hat and making its way for the door, ushered on out by the indignant splutter of gas lamps. The beggars and con-artists didn't bother to ply their trade this deep in the Rookery; everyone here knew all their scams backwards and sideways. It was a relief to William, who had grown quite distressed at the sight of dirty-faced swindlers struggling to coax a tarnished coin from his pocket.

Basil's apartment was a three story slum rudely crammed into a niche between a pawn shop and a dilapidated warehouse. Curiously, it was also the only building on the street that remained well lit. Snips stepped up to open the door, but found it locked. She paused, glanced back at William, shrugged, then knocked.

A metal slot slid open, revealing a pair of glaring eyes. A woman's voice (one could only assume it was female; it sounded like what you'd get after smoking thirty cigarettes and swallowing a wad of sulphur followed up with an acid chaser) growled. "What y'want."

"Why, to see the face that eyes as lovely as yours must belong to."

The growl turned into a snarl. "You with the gas company?"

That threw Snips off. "Eh?"

"You have to tell me if yer with the gas company," she said, eyes bobbing away from the slot long enough to spit. "It's the law. I looked it up."

"We are not with the gas company," William said, stepping forward. "Miss Snips is looking into a matter concerning Mr. Copper's recent demise, and—"

"S'all right, but if yer with the gas company, I'll clock y'both," she rumbled. The slot slipped closed. Locks rattled, followed by the sound of a chain clinking to the floor and several deadbolts being released. Snips threw William another shrug.

The door opened. The woman behind it was a solid brick of chocolate-colored muscle and fat; she looked as if she were a jigsaw puzzle made up of iron fused together with a blow torch and slapped with a layer of spackle. She wore a coral pink evening gown that had gutted and devoured the remains of several competitors on its way to her closet.

"Name's Marge," she said. "I'm the landlord here. Gas company's been trying t'hook us back up." She waved a frying pan at them as if she were herding cattle into their pens. Snips and William followed her prompting.

The apartment interior was surprisingly clean. The walls and floors were built of cheap lumber and showed the scars of long use, but several of the doors had been replaced and reinforced by a skilled craftsman. The gas lamps still remained in the hall, left dusty from disuse.

But it was neither the competent carpentry nor the unused lanterns which caused both Snips and William to stop in their tracks. That honor belonged to the newly installed lighting fixtures.

Tear-shaped dollops of pearl-white glass were arranged neatly beneath the metal braces that lined the ceiling. Each was no larger than a fist, and produced a steady near-blinding glow; the illumination they provided left the hallway basked in light to rival the sun.

"That's—what is that?" William asked, voice quivering with sudden excitement. "This isn't a gas lamp." Despite his better judgment, he found himself dragging a chair beneath one of the fixtures and hopping up for a closer look. "Miss Snips! Have a look at this! These are absolutely remarkable. How do they work?"

"Electricity," Snips said. "Galvanized filaments contained in glass bulbs. The entire apartment's probably strung up on them." She threw a look back at Marge, who now traded her harsh expression for one of surprise. "Basil's work, I assume?"

"S'how he paid for his rent," she said, nodding. "Worked as a handyman. Fixed th'doors, got the plumbing working, and got us light too."

"And the gas company—" Snips began.

The woman's grip on the frying pan tightened. "Ever since he cut off them pipes—bloody buggers! They been sendin' boys down here, tryin' to turn it back on. But we told 'em, we don't want any. They keep sayin', 'it's fer your own good, missus'. For our own good!" She spat. "Like we're all babes who can't figure out what's good fer ourselves."

"Could I—might I perhaps have one of these?" William asked, reaching to touch the glass.

"Don't touch it!" The woman barked with enough force to nearly send him tumbling off the chair. "They're hot. And we ain't got many left. They burn out after a long while, 'afta be replaced." She paused here, before adding: "You're lookin' after Basil's things? Gonna find out who scragged him?"

"Yeah," Snips said. "Yeah, something like that."

"Since you're anglin' to find some justice fer Basil—you can 'ave one. But just one," she added. "I'll take you to his room."

Snips and William followed Marge as she strode down the hall towards the stairs. As they walked, William started peppering Snips with questions.

"How did you know about the bulbs, Miss Snips? Are you familiar with the fundamentals of galvanization?"

"Eddington mentioned it as one of Basil's side-projects," Snips said. "Called them a silly idea. Completely useless."

William frowned. "Mr. Eddington seems to have gotten it wrong. They don't appear useless to me."

"No," Snips agreed. "Provide better light. No spluttering, no vapors, no explosions."

"Of course, electricity is still a dangerous element," he confessed.

"Is it explosive?"

"Hm? Oh, no. Electrical currents alone could not cause an explosion. The danger is in contact; electrical currents cause seizures and burns."

Marge drew out a ring of keys from beneath the neckline of her tattered dress and counted down from the first brass one. She jammed it into the stout iron-plated door ('In case he blew 'imself up,' she said) and opened the way to the basement.

A wild jungle of geometrically arranged chaos greeted them. Pipes zigzagged every which way, veering off into perfect right angles at the drop of a hat; strange machines with rolling metal coils sat in dark corners, gathering dust as they patiently awaited their deceased master's return. Suits and pants were hanging from one high pipe, with Basil's mattress spread between two that ran into the wall at hip-level. All about the room were brass fixtures with bright bulbs that extinguished all but the most clever of shadows; at its center was a looming steam-engine that steadily chewed away at a feast of coal and wood. The smell of grease clung to every surface.

Snips pressed forward into the room, hopping across pipes and furniture on her way to Basil's workbench. Meanwhile, William did his best to fight through his amazement and ask Marge questions. "How does the electricity—"

"Through the pipes," Marge cut him off. "He said he dipped 'em in rubber. Turned the gas valves off, fed the wires through. S'got a generator hooked up to the engine on the level above."

Basil had arranged several planks of wood atop of a heated pipe to serve as a makeshift table. Atop it were several of his experiments; while Snips scavenged his work desk for information,

William inspected each device in turn.

"There's a bulb, you can 'ave that one," Marge said, pointing to one of the bulbs on the table. William politely thanked her and placed it inside his coat.

One device in particular caught William's fancy: a small metal lever had been attached by insulated wire to a light bulb that was fitted into an iron frame. He pressed the lever down and watched with rapt fascination as the bulb immediately hummed to life; when his finger left the trigger, the bulb instantly turned off. He repeated this action several times, puzzling over what the device could mean. Then he looked up.

"Miss Snips."

"Where did he put his blueprints? Nothing like that in any of these drawers," Snips said. "Just tools, tools, more tools—what is this? Is this a screwdriver? This doesn't look like a screwdriver."

"Miss Snips."

"It's got a spring on it. What sort of screwdriver has a spring on it? We're dealing with a deranged mind here. I think—"

"Miss Snips!"

Something about his tone drew Snips away from the desk. She turned, looking at William. His head was tossed back, his gaze glued to the ceiling. Snips followed his eyes and noticed just what it was he was staring at.

The insulated wire that ran from the lever to the light bulb did not travel directly to its target. Instead, the wire went from the trigger to the ceiling—where it curled over itself in several dozen bundled loops, cluttering the ceiling in coiled bundles that must have been at least a mile's worth of cord. The wire eventually dropped back down, leading up to the bulb.

Staring up at the extraordinary length of wire, William pressed the trigger again. The light bulb reacted instantly.

"Miss Snips," he said, his voice stark and quiet. "Do you know the stories of Professor Hemlock?"

"Bits and pieces," Snips said, eyeing the bundles stapled to the ceiling. "I've heard them, anyway."

"A brilliant inventor so far removed from the common day that his creations resemble magic more than science," he said, voice hushed with awe. "A man who, driven by the fear that his genius would be misapplied, sought to hide it from the world."

"An absurd bedtime story." Snips stepped forward, detaching the trigger from its battery with a snap of her fingers. "It's hogwash. Besides, I don't see the big deal. So Basil invented a light you can turn on from far away."

William's head slowly dropped back into place. "He proved that electricity travels instantly. He invented a way to communicate across vast distances with impossible speed."

"And so Hemlock flew down in a steam-powered chariot and blew Basil to kingdom come to protect us from the horrors of reliable mail service," Snips shot back. "By Jove, I think you've done it, Mr. Daffodil! Excellent work!"

William's distant look was dispelled by a flash of anger. "Simply because you do not understand the significance of Mr. Copper's invention, Miss Snips—"

Marge cleared her throat. Both Snips and William turned, their faces flushed with frustration.

"Yer lookin' for blueprints, right? Because if you are, they're right over there." She pointed the frying pan to the far wall, where several blueprints and notes for Basil's various inventions had been plastered.

"Yeah," Snips said, glaring at William. "Yeah, that's what I was looking for."

"If there's nothing else you need, Miss Snips," William began, gritting his teeth and stepping up to the wall to snatch the blueprints up. It was only then that he noticed the small niche that had been hidden behind the documents. "What on earth—"

He began, but never finished; at that precise moment, the device that was contained within the hidden space activated. The string that had been carefully hooked to the back of the posters was snapped by the violence of his motion, which caused it to wind back into the contraption. It produced a hiss followed by a distinct and unpleasant odor.

And then it exploded.

They had less than half of a second to react. William did nothing but stare with blank-eyed surprise at the blossom of flame that belched forth from the alcove; it was Snips who darted forward and snatched the umbrella out of his hand, unsnapping it as she thrust herself between him and the device.

A wave of fire splashed across the parasol's iron-reinforced canopy, rushing around its edges to eagerly tickle at their shoulders. William coiled an arm around Snips' waist as the force of the explosion repelled them violently back into the room, tumbling toward the exit; when they at last came to a rest, they were left bruised and dazed.

"Oh dear," William muttered in confusion.

"Fire!" Marge roared. "Fire!"

They looked up. The explosion that had been designed to kill them had ignited several small fires throughout the workshop. Bulbs of glass began to pop; tools were engulfed in the rapidly spreading blaze. As they watched, the grease-soaked room went up in a brilliant flash of heat—and the fire showed no signs of contenting itself merely with the basement.

"The rest of the building," William panted. "We need to evacuate it immediately!"

Marge charged out of the room at once. William carefully disentangled himself from Snips, glancing back at the table full of Basil's work.

"We cannot leave his machines," William said, and Snips caught the quivering reluctance in his voice—as if he were under great spiritual duress. "We must—"

"No time. We've got people upstairs we need to warn."

They ran.

~*~

CHAPTER 13: IN WHICH MR. TWEEDLE BEGS FOR A CELL WITH A VIEW AND OUR TITULAR PROTAGONIST MAKES A LEAP OF FAITH

~*~

Mr. Tweedle threw himself down at Miss Primrose's feet.

"Please, I beg of you," he said with a wet and sloppy sob. "I beg of you! Cease with your tireless interrogations, your endless questions! All I ask is that I be given a dry, warm cell. Perhaps one with a view—maybe where I can see a pretty bird once and a while. Maybe a tree?"

Miss Primrose scowled. "Mr. Tweedle, contain yourself. I haven't asked you anything yet."

"But you will!" Mr. Tweedle said. "And then you'll figure everything out. You detective types, you're all so desperately clever."

"Have some dignity, Mr. Tweedle!" Miss Primrose shoved the weeping bureaucrat back towards his desk with the tip of her foot. "Seat yourself at once."

Still cowering and whimpering, Mr. Tweedle crawled his way back to his chair.

"Now, Mr. Tweedle," she said, taking her seat. "Let us start from the beginning, shall we? And this time, try to have a little backbone, please?"

"I'll try," Mr. Tweedle said.

Miss Primrose gave him a polite smile. "Good evening, Mr. Tweedle. My name is Miss Primrose."

"Good evening, Miss Primrose," Mr. Tweedle said with a sniffle.

"I'm here on an investigation on the Steamwork's behalf. Would you mind if I asked you a few questions—"

"I did it!" Mr. Tweedle cried, throwing his hands to the desk and dropping his head into his arms. "I admit to it! Please, just take me away—"

Miss Primrose scowled once again. "Mr. Tweedle!"

"I'm sorry, I'm sorry, I just can't take it anymore. The terrible guilt, the horrible crushing despair—"

"What precisely is it that you're confessing to, then?" Mr. Tweedle looked up with one glassy wet eye. "What is it you're investigating again?"

"Mr. Copper's recent demise."

"Oh yes, that. I killed him! I admit to it! Take me away!" Mr. Tweedle shoved his wrists out in front of him, offering them to Miss Primrose. "Lock me up and throw away the key! Take me somewhere I'll never have to look at another bank figure again!"

"Stop being ridiculous," Miss Primrose said. "You couldn't have killed Mr. Copper."

"Why not? I'm perfectly capable."

"You're an idiot," Miss Primrose said. "And you don't have enough spine to murder a fly. What has happened, Mr. Tweedle? Why is the bank in such a state of chaos? Why are you so desperate to enter into our prison system?"

"You're—you're not going to arrest me?" Mr. Tweedle asked.

"No, Mr. Tweedle. I am not."

"It's so awful," Mr. Tweedle said, sinking his face into his hands. "So wretchedly, terribly awful! I cannot take working at this bank for a day more."

Miss Primrose's hard glare softened a bit. "Why do you not simply resign, Mr. Tweedle?"

"Because I don't know where the resignation forms are! The investors have hidden them from me, the wretched monsters!"

Miss Primrose pursed her lips. "Why do you wish to leave the bank? Certainly, it cannot be that difficult."

"Ever since this whole Steamwork matter has started, it's constant stress," Mr. Tweedle said. "That and this awful Hemlock business. Before that, it was absolutely lovely." He lifted his head, his eyes getting a far-off look. "Every day, I'd come into the bank office, and the secretary would ask me—'One lump or two, Mr. Tweedle?'—and I'd say—'One lump, of course'—and then I would spend the rest of the day enjoying a cup of tea, reading my paper, and watching the birds in the tree from my window..."

"I don't quite understand, Mr. Tweedle. What has changed?"

"Now they expect me to make decisions!" Mr. Tweedle cried. "Big, important decisions! Every day—I have to decide this or that. And what's worse is that they took my window away!" He pointed to the side of the office, where a window had been recently bricked up. "My investors said it was 'distracting me from the important business of a bank'."

"I, er, see, Mr. Tweedle. Still, I only wanted to ask you about some curious matters that I discovered while investigating several of the Steamwork's patents. It seems you've cosigned several of the patent licenses, and I merely wanted some clarification as to why."

Mr. Tweedle wetted his lips. "Tell me something, Miss Primrose. Do you think—if someone does something illegal, and someone else helps them in a rather roundabout way, fully aware that the act is illegal—is that second person performing a crime?"

"In most cases, yes," Miss Primrose said. "They are an accomplice."

"And could they go to prison?"

"Perhaps, Mr. Tweedle." Catching on, Miss Primrose added: "In fact, I am quite sure of it."

"Hm. Interesting. Very interesting." Mr. Tweedle leaned back, twiddling his thumbs. "Well, if I tell you everything I know, and you discover that Mr. Eddington *is* doing something illegal, would it be too much to ask that you assume I knew about it all along?"

"I, er, that is," Miss Primrose said, trying to follow the man's runaway train of logic. "I suppose I could."

"Then it might be worth mentioning that Mr. Eddington is up to his ears in debt," Mr. Tweedle said, leaning back with a serene smile. "And that he is probably willing to do *anything* to escape."

~*~

Fire seeped up from beneath the floor, unfurling into tongues of flame that painted the walls black with their hungry licks. Snips and William gaped at the sight; Marge emerged from nowhere, carrying snot-nosed bratlings under either arm. She gave Snips and William a glare, then started firing off orders with all the bravado of a general on the front lines.

"Upstairs. More folks. Get 'em downstairs as fast as you can," she snapped. "I'll try to rustle up a bucket brigade."

She turned and crashed through the front door, leaving the two blinking. Slowly, their sense of obligation began to reassert itself.

"Upstairs, Miss Snips," William said.

"Right," Snips replied.

They turned and ran up the stairs. Men, women, and children were already tumbling out of their rooms, coaxed into the hallways by the sound of an explosion below. Several looked up at the scorched pair—William in particular, with his charred umbrella and clean suit—and gawked.

"Fire," Snips shouted, flinging her arms back the way she came. "Everyone out!"

Only later would Snips ponder the wisdom in shouting 'fire' to a crowd of people as she stood between them and the nearest exit.

Both William and Snips fought their way through the retreating throngs, working to stay afloat and not be dragged out by the currents of fleeing families. They struggled to the next set of stairs, making their way step by step through the narrow halls.

The flow soon quieted to a trickle, leaving the task of gathering up what few people remained to Snips and William. They knocked on doors, shoved through living rooms, and hollered into bedrooms; it soon became apparent that no one remained.

"Let's cut out," Snips said, eagerly heading to the exit. William was sure to follow. But as they descended down, they found themselves confronted by a suffocating wall of smoke.

"The fire has already spread to the lower level," William remarked between coughs. "We must ascend."

They ran to the top of the apartment, briefly savoring the sweet aroma of air *not* choked with smoke, but this relief quickly faded with the realization of their situation.

The apartment roof was far above the roof of its neighbors. The smoke that had run up the stairs was now emerging from all sides of the building, engulfing them in a growing shell of ash.

"Problem," Snips said, braving the smoke and scooting near the edge to peer down at the street below. "We may have to jump."

William tapped his umbrella against his palm. "How much do you weigh, Miss Snips?"

"Hundred and ten, maybe. What's it matter? We're likely to break a leg with this. Do you know much about—" Snips cut herself off at the sight of William licking his finger and holding it up to the air. "Uh."

"Miss Snips, could you please remove your belt?"

"Huh? Pardon?"

"Your belt," William asked, struggling to be as polite as a gentleman asking for a lady's article of clothing could be. "Please, remove it and give it to me."

Snips glared, but did as he asked. She handed it over and watched with confusion as William wrapped it around his arm and buckled it into a loose loop.

"Your arm, if you would?"

"You know, I'm not sure what you're doing, but—"

"There isn't much time. Please, Miss Snips. Trust me."

Snips sighed. Something about his tone made her relent; she held out her arm. William fed it through the loop, tightened it until they were linked together snugly, then nodded in satisfaction. He raised his umbrella over his head, stepped up onto the roof's ledge, and turned to Snips.

Snips balked. "You—you can't be serious."

"I am dead serious, Miss Snips."

He drew Snips close to him with a strength that took the thief entirely by surprise and then leapt off the building.

~*~

CHAPTER 14: IN WHICH WE ONCE AGAIN RETURN TO THE PAST, TO LEARN OF MATTERS CONCERNING BUTTERFLIES, GENIUS, AND THE DANGERS OF TRUSTING MAD SCIENTISTS

~*~

With gentle but urgent key-strokes, Nigel coaxed the probability engine to life.

Gears ground their precisely cut teeth against his formula, working their way through the problem. Nigel watched intently as his notes unfolded into a symphony of clicks and clacks, building its way to a crescendo; when it was at last finished, the engine offered him a punch card containing the solution.

"A destined life," he said, standing to take the card. He held it with reverence, as if a single misstep would bring his work to ruin. He made his way to the back of the room where a cleverly designed device had been placed.

It was a column of iron half his height and a foot in diameter. Inside of its hollowed shell was a web of exquisitely crafted mechanisms, designed to turn even the most complex mathematics into simple and elegant action. At its very top— connected to intricate geography of ticking pendulums and coiled springs—was a magnificent clockwork butterfly.

Nigel inserted the punch-card into the slot at the base of the column, giving the machine a single crank. Metal spokes wound their way through the card's holes, translating its data into movement. Slowly, the machine's mascot stretched out its colorful tin-framed paper wings; then, rotating two degrees to the left, it brought them down.

~*~

"With the new data we've gleaned from these sources, we can—"

"Abigail."

"—apply it to the equation thusly, here and here, I believe it may be feasible to accurately predict even smaller, more orderly systems—"

"Abigail!"

"—and perhaps even use the engine to—hm?" Abigail looked up from the chalkboard at Jeremiah, who wore a sullen expression.

"I have absolutely no idea what you're talking about," he said. "You've lost me."

"Oh, I'm sorry. I must be explaining the premise poorly."

"No, you aren't. It's beyond me," Jeremiah admitted spreading his hands out helplessly. "I never thought I would be saying this, but you understand the fundamentals of my own theory better than I do."

"You're just saying that to be kind," Abigail said.

"No." Jeremiah narrowed his eyes. "I am not a kind man, Abigail. And I do not hand out compliments lightly."

Abigail hesitated, setting the chalk aside and staring at the dense knot of tangled equations she had scribbled down. "I cannot explain it. It almost feels as if I am merely learning something I already knew—reminding myself of ideas that I had once been acquainted with, but had long forgotten."

Jeremiah rose from his seat. "My mother says it was the same way for my father."

"You rarely speak of them," she said, hesitating. "Your parents, I mean."

"My father is missing, and my mother is quite mad," Jeremiah stated rather dourly.

"I've heard stories of your mother. Terrible stories," she said, but her voice possessed no trace of fear—rather, it had a dash of excitement. "They say that she was a monster in her youth; that she terrorized cities in the seat of mechanical monstrosities."

Jeremiah chuckled. "Oh, yes, she most certainly did. I wasn't aware that you were interested in 'mad' science, Abigail."

"Not at all!" Abigail quickly replied, a swell of heat breaking across her cheeks. "I mean, I am merely curious, is all."

Jeremiah steadied his hands on the back of a chair, leaning over to look up at Abigail. He dropped his eyelids low, wearing a most unwholesome smile. "Are you, now? Perhaps you would like to terrorize a city with me, Madame?"

Abigail scowled, her face red. "Stop being absurd."

"I'm not hearing a no," Jeremiah said, laughing. "I've got a giant mechanical spider stored in the basement. I could have it up and running in under an hour."

"I am most certainly not interested," she snapped, although she was quick to add: "You have a mechanical spider in your basement?"

"And more. Some inventions are mine, some are my father's, some are my mother's," Jeremiah said. "All are quite dangerous." He waggled his eyebrows. "Would you care to see?"

~*~

The air in Jeremiah's basement was pregnant with forgotten secrets and passions long left for dead; countless projects were contained beneath cases of iron and glass, neatly labeled and organized. Abigail sprang between display after display, her fingers soon smeared with dust.

"These machines," she said, breathless. "Some of them are wondrous."

"Be careful," Jeremiah warned her, and then added: "I've been working on continuing a few of their projects, but I haven't had time what with the work we're doing on the probability engine."

"What is this?" Abigail asked, leaning forward to inspect a rusty silver pocket watch. It had been gutted and refitted with a myriad of glass bulbs, dials, and wires.

"That's my father's project," Jeremiah told her. "It was supposed to have been a time machine."

"Do not tease me, Mr. Daffodil," she said, glaring.

Jeremiah laughed. "I'm not teasing," he said. "It doesn't work, though. Not correctly, anyway. Far too unpredictable to be safely experimented with. Ends up stealing time rather than letting you move through it."

"I'm sure," she said, obviously not believing him. She moved to another device. It was one of the few projects not stored away beneath a frame; it consisted of a segmented lead encased sphere approximately the size of a fist, with various valves and pumps attached to it. "And what function does this serve?" She reached out to touch it.

Jeremiah was upon her in an instant. The force with which he seized her wrist gave Abigail a dreadful fright. "Don't touch that," he shouted, and at once it was clear that he regretted his ferocity. "I apologize." He released her, stepping back. "But that project is particularly dangerous."

Abigail rubbed her still-aching wrist, watching Jeremiah and the sphere warily. "Why?"

"It was an invention of my mother's," he said, clearly reluctant to explain the device's function. "Even she was sane enough to stop working on it once she realized its implications."

"What does it do?"

"She called it the radium generator. Under the right circumstances, she discovered certain very rare particles can exert an immense amount of energy for an untold length of time," Jeremiah explained. "For weeks, or years, or decades—perhaps even forever. My mother found a way to recreate those circumstances and harvest the energy."

Abigail's eyebrows shot up. "She created a way to produce a stable source of unending energy?"

"Yes," Jeremiah began. "A machine that creates a spontaneous explosion—"

"Remarkable!"

"—that might never stop," he finished.

The light in Abigail's eyes quickly dimmed. "I see." She shuffled uncomfortably, turning to look at the assortment of machines and struggling to find some way to change the subject. "Is there anything in here that is yours?" She asked tentatively.

Jeremiah grinned. "A few of these things here are mine, but my favorite invention is upstairs. It's not all that amazing, but I'm actually quite proud of it."

"May I see it?"

"On one condition," he replied.

~*~

The highest peak of Jeremiah's home brought them well over the roofs of the other houses in the neighborhood; Abigail stared down at the sight, shifting nervously.

"I have reservations, Mr. Daffodil," she admitted.

"Do not worry," Jeremiah said, standing on the roof's edge with his stylized umbrella in his hand. "Your arm, if you will."

Abigail shuffled. "You said you wanted to show me your invention," she pointed out. "But all you have in your hand is an umbrella."

"The umbrella **is** my invention. Please, Abigail. You gave me your word that you would trust me."

Abigail hesitated, squirming with displeasure. "You asked me to trust you before you brought me up on the roof," she said, wringing her hands.

He laughed, still holding out his arm. "Yes, well, that's often how it goes, isn't it? Please, Abigail. I won't harm so much as a hair on your head; you have my word."

At long last, Abigail submitted; she held out her hand to Jeremiah, who took it into his own, drawing her close.

"Hold my waist tightly, Madame," he told her, and then he lifted the umbrella high above their heads.

~*~

CHAPTER 15: IN WHICH OUR TITULAR PROTAGONIST FLIES, AND MATTERS CONCERNING PERSONAL PROPERTY ARE POLITELY DISCUSSED

~*~

Being dead, Snips decided, was a lot like flying.

There was a strange sense of weightlessness along with the peculiar feeling that came with having one's heart dive straight into the belly, only to change its mind at the last moment and slingshot back up through the throat. There was also very little to see.

"I think that you may weigh a little more than a hundred and ten pounds, Miss Snips."

Snips realized that she had her eyes shut. Despite her brain warning against it, she opened them.

She was not dead.

She was soaring.

"Funny," Snips said with a dry and breathless rasp. "I don't recall having ever possessed the power of flight."

"We are not flying, Miss Snips."

"I mean, that seems like something you'd remember," she continued, licking her dry lips. "'Oh yes, I can fly, silly me'. Or something like that."

"I must repeat: We are not flying."

"At the very least, it seems like something you'd tell mum about. 'Oh hey mum, by the way, I can fly.' And I know for a fact that I never told my mum any such thing."

"Miss Snips!" William's voice was strained to the point of snapping. "We are *not* flying!

Below Snips' feet was the smoldering carcass of the burning apartment; all around her was the night sky. William, his face filthy with soot, was holding her firmly about the waist, their arms linked together. Above them was his umbrella.

It had opened and unfolded, exposing a heavily reinforced iron frame that served as an anchor for the massive canopy that

William Daffodil reveals his father's invention to Arcadia Snips.

extended above and around them. The sturdy weave was catching the air, dragging across the sky like a cat's claw slowly ripping down a curtain.

"Neat," Snips said, scarcely able to produce any other sound.

"A simple matter of air resistance and velocity," he said. "A draft of heat drew us high into the air—far higher than I intended. But we should remain safe until we touch down."

"I didn't know they could do that."

"Yes, it's a rather curious design feature my father added long after the initial design," William said. "By the way, how did you know that the umbrella is fire retardant?"

Snips squirmed in William's grip. "I, uh. Well, you know. Lucky guess."

"You guessed."

"Heh, yeah. Good guesser, huh?" Snips said, grinning.

They floated over the Rookery in silence. Below them were the maze-like streets, the crooks, the tricks, the anguish, the laughter—but from here it all looked like nothing more than a bawdy theater play. Gas-lanterns glimmered like pin-pricks of light in a vast and dark blanket, shining over the unfolding tapestry of city drama. Shouts and cries rose up, distorted by distance and rock until they became nothing more than a collectively mumbled complaint.

But it was William that Snips was watching from the corner of her eye. For a moment, the mathematician's nervous tension had slipped away beneath the quiet satisfaction of a job well done. He was watching the cityscape unfold beneath them with bright and curious eyes.

"Have we met before?" The question escaped Snips before she had a chance to think about it; she wasn't sure why she asked it, but some distant familiarity nagged at the back of her brain.

"I don't know," William confessed, and then added: "I thought so at first myself, but I do not think so. I doubt I would fail to remember a woman such as yourself, Miss Snips."

"Fair enough," she said. She was about to say something else, but William suddenly interrupted her.

"Miss Snips, look! The fire department has arrived."

At last, the pair was coming close to the ground; they were descending within sight of the burning apartment. As they came closer, they caught sight of a massive wagon pulled by a team of horses rushing toward the scene. A giant iron pump was mounted on the center of the carriage. Men in long orange coats and steepled metal hats held on for dear life as the contraption swerved through the narrow alleyways, accompanied by a screeching siren.

"Bah," Snips said. "They're here already."

"So they'll put out the blaze," William said.

"Not before they get their cut."

"Pardon?"

They landed within a block of the apartment. Unbuckling Snips' arm, William gave the belt back and ran off in a swirl of smoke to view the situation for himself. Snips sighed and followed after. As they rounded the last bend, they could see the engine had reached its destination. One of the firemen—a grizzled one-eyed goat of a man who resembled a brigand more than a firefighter— was involved in a heated exchange with a soot-covered woman they soon recognized as Marge.

"—hell we will!" Marge snarled to him just as Snips and William came within earshot.

"If you act now, we'll throw in a Gold membership for half our usual rate," the fireman said. "A quarter off all your gas bills!"

"We'll put the bloody thing out ourselves!" Marge roared, turning back to the throng of tenants who were struggling with buckets and shovels against the fire. "Back to the front lines, you lazy gits! Someone fetch more buckets!"

People darted off to carry out her orders. The firefighter shook his head and tsked. "Wasting precious collateral," he said.

"What on earth is going on?" William asked.

"Business as usual in the Rookery," Snips replied. "Gas company's trying to buy the apartment off her."

"While it's burning?!"

"Yes," Snips said, addressing William much like a parent might speak to a child. "While it's burning."

"But that's—that's—"

"He'll keep dropping his offering price as the fire gets worse," Snips spoke as she found herself a seat on a nearby wall. The blaze gave off a bright light, giving everything it touched a metallic orange glow. The color sparkled off her silver-toothed smile, adding a demonic mien to the thief's expression. "If they can't put it out themselves, they'll have to sell it to get anything back."

"We can't let them do that!"

Snips shrugged. "It's legal."

"But it's wrong!"

"Wrong, right, up, down, back, forward—doesn't change a thing."

They were interrupted by the sound of another siren. A clockwork nightmare stumbled out of a nearby alleyway, awkwardly clambering over the street by means of long, clumsy pincers; it was the very same mess of plates and skillfully crafted spider legs that Snips had ridden earlier that day in the Rookery. Its pilots crawled over it, stoking the flames of the furnace while attaching hoses to valves located along the pump attached to its backend.

"Bastard," the fire chief swore, turning to face the machine while shaking his fist. "McMulligan!"

A galvanized bullhorn atop of the machine activated with a metallic whine, flooding the burning street with a crackling hiss. "Attention! Sign nothing! The gas company's fire department is running a scam! We're here to help!"

"Finally," William said, sighing with relief.

"Step forward to mortgage your property and qualify for *platinum* membership!"

"Platinum?! You're stealin' our schtick!" The fireman said, drawing his axe. "Get out of here, McMulligan! I saw 'em first!" He charged across the cobbled street, joined by the majority of his men. Soon, they were swarming atop of the machine, beating away at the iron carapace that enclosed it and struggling with the pilots who remained on its exterior. Meanwhile, the tenants continued to engage in a futile struggle against the rapidly growing blaze.

William stared at the scene, awestruck by the absurdity of it all. When he turned to Snips for answers, the thief just smiled and shrugged. "Probably decided they wanted a piece of the action," she told him.

Turning back to the tableau of chaos before him, William put his umbrella aside, rolled up his sleeves, and marched toward the fire carriage. He seized one side of the wagon, dragged himself up to the pump, and began turning valves.

Snips watched with all the curiosity of an alien monitoring the peculiar mating habits of humans. When William moved to heft up a wrench, it was enough to coax the thief off the wall for a closer look. "What do you think you're doing?"

"Something," William replied, seizing a nearby wrench and fitting it to a valve. With a great heave of his shoulders, he turned it; the engine creaked and shuddered. Pressure rumbled in the belly of the pump as he worked to rouse it from its slumber.

"Don't be silly," Snips said, and now she was scowling. "You won't make an ounce of difference."

"I can't sit by and do nothing," William said, struggling to turn another valve. "People are in danger."

The other firefighters remained distracted with their battle. Snips looked their way, sighed, and climbed up on the carriage. "Fine," she said. "What do I do?"

"Press that valve down," William directed her to a brass fitting, wiping at a layer of perspiration that had gathered at his brow. "Hold it while I release this pressure."

A few of the tenants fighting the blaze had noticed what Snips and William were up to, and were now running over to help. Snips glared at them, but William was quick to pick up on the momentum and started politely issuing orders. It wasn't long before Marge herself—covered from head to toe in ash and burns —arrived at the pump only to take direction from William without batting an eye.

"Hold onto the hoses," William said, turning one last crank. The pump shuddered as an immense pressure started to churn.

The streams of chemically treated water gushed out in long threads of foam, lashing out at the fire. The pump sprayed out steam and moisture, soaking everyone nearby; as they struggled to control the device, the fire started to writhe and wither beneath the smothering assault.

Mopping the sweat and foam from her face, Snips watched the scene unfold. Children ran about in oversized fire-proofed coats, carrying sloshing buckets of water in their hands. Stern-faced men and women clutched at the hoses, directing an endless stream towards the struggling flame.

The thief hmphed and turned back to the valves.

Meanwhile, several of the firemen had seen what was happening. Abandoning their reckless assault on the armored competitor, they began to run toward their hijacked carriage. "Private property!" The chief yelled, pointing his finger at them. "Private property! That's private property!"

Marge turned. Flanking the landlord were some of the finest thugs that Dead Beat Alley had to offer. As the firemen began to regroup, they realized that the crowd—which had started to swell as more inhabitants of Dead Beat Alley joined in the effort —had grown considerably large.

"There a problem?" Marge asked over the thunderous sound of the hoses.

The fire chief, only now realizing the precarious nature of his situation, cleared his throat and pointed at the pump. "That's mine."

Marge looked over her shoulder, spat out a wad of tar, then locked gazes with the one-eyed fire-fighter. "You don't say."

Several of Dead Beat Alley's denizens were now stepping forward, enclosing the nervous firemen in a loose circle. "Uh, yeah. It's against the law to use it without my permission, and—"

"Law?" Marge asked. "Whassat?"

"Think it's somethin' rich people have," a thug offered helpfully. "You know, to keep out riffraff."

"Huh. Sounds expensive," Marge said. "Don't think I can afford it."

The fire chief swallowed. Nasty sorts of men with nastier knives now loomed on every side. "Well, yes, but—"

"Tell you what," Marge said. "Seein' how it's a nice, warm night—and it looks like I might only be losin' half my apartment—

I'm gonna do you a big favor."

"You are?"

"Yeah. I'm gonna let you have the pump back when I'm through with it. How does that sound? Pretty fair, huh?"

"That's ridiculous," is what the fire chief would have said, but somewhere between the sight of Marge's dead eye stare and those long and wicked knives, the message became garbled and ended up sounding remarkably like "Yes, quite fair, ma'am, thank you very much!".

~*~

CHAPTER 16: IN WHICH MISTAKES, PIGEONS, AND CALCULATION ENGINES ARE THOROUGHLY DISCUSSED

~*~

Nigel Arcanum relished the whimsies of a long dead author, his bandage sheathed hand scraping beneath the book's words as he read. But as he reached the end of the page, he paused; the sound of something tapping against bare glass drew him away from his pleasant reverie.

He cleared his throat and spoke.

"Ah. I have a guest. Good evening."

Silence.

He continued: "There is no need to hide from me. Please, step into the light."

A figure rose from the shadows. He wore a clean suit and a black jackal mask trimmed in gold.

Nigel suppressed a wet and guttural laugh. "Oh, dear. They still have you wearing those masks, do they?"

The man's voice was smothered in metal; when he spoke, it was with the tone of steel. "You sent for me."

"I sent a missive to the Society. A harmless request," Nigel said, "for clarification."

"The Society needs not clarify itself to the likes of you."

"How quickly do the dogs turn against their former Masters," Nigel said, smothering another moist chuckle. "You seem to forget who wrote your charter."

"And you seem to forget who abandoned it for the sake of their own 'salvation'," the jackal spoke, his metallic voice unable to mask his disdain. "It has been suggested among my fellow initiates, Master Arcanum, that a time is rapidly approaching when your goals may interfere with our own."

"Should such a time come, pup, I will gladly remind you why your elders still speak my name with reverence."

Long and wicked iron gleamed in the jackal's hand.

"You're a crippled fool living in a dead past," he said. "What threat are you to me? What threat are you to anyone, anymore? Just a musty corpse that hasn't had the good sense to rot in its grave."

The room grew still. When Nigel spoke next, his words carried a presence that defied his mummified remains:

"There are two types of mistakes, little pup. Small mistakes," he said, "and large mistakes."

"I did not come here for a lecture."

"Small mistakes are simple things, such as forgetting to send a letter to your mother on her birthday, or perhaps leaving your door unlocked," Nigel explained. "But large mistakes—large mistakes are something else entirely." A chill swept through the room; the flames spluttered and dipped low.

"Large mistakes are the kind of errors you find in the old Greek plays. The sort where the tragic hero burns his eyes out with hot pokers and spends the rest of his days wandering the earth, searching for salvation. It is eating the gingerbread house you stumble across in the woods; it is taking a bite out of that apple when you certainly know better."

Nigel leaned forward, the chair creaking beneath his weight. "But most of all, little pup, it is doing what you are thinking about doing right now."

Every light in the room went out.

The jackal stepped back.

"Whatever you and your ilk are plotting, I could not care less," Nigel said, returning to a more comfortable position. "But leave my daughter out of it."

"I will do so, in exchange for one thing," said the jackal.

"Oh," Nigel said, sounding amused. "You think you are in a position to make requests?"

"Stop Count Orwick's investigation into the Steamwork. In exchange, I will see to it that your half-breed of a daughter remains untouched."

"'Half-breed'?" Nigel said, choking on his own chortle. "How enlightened. Very well; consider it done. And tell your fellow 'initiates' something."

"Yes?"

"Remind them that the Heap is still burning."

The jackal hesitated, as if chewing this over. At long last, he left the way he came, leaving Nigel to ponder.

Several moments stretched out in silence; at long last, Starkweather emerged from behind one of the curtains. He turned the hidden gas valve on, causing the room's lights to surge back to life. "How long do you intend to maintain this charade?"

"For as long as my atonement takes," Nigel said. "Fetch me a pen and paper, Starkweather. I have letters to write, and they must be delivered tonight."

~*~

It was late at night when Snips and William finally arrived. Together, they were bruised, burnt, exhausted, and soaked to the very bone. William's coat had been torn asunder and Snips had nearly lost her hat. Yet as they approached their destination, they found themselves riding upon a cloud of euphoria—both had been seized by an inescapable sensation of elation that came with accomplishment in the face of adversity.

The fire had been extinguished. The apartment had been heavily damaged, but it was recoverable; in addition, no tenants had been slain or lost. And although Basil's work had been destroyed in the process, Snips had managed to keep a hold on the crucial blueprints that described his research in intimate detail. At Snips' suggestion, they had made their way to Detective Watts' home to clean themselves up and turn in for the night.

"I don't wish to intrude," William said.

"Nonsense," Snips said. "I'm sure Miss Primmypants will be more than happy to have you. Besides, you're going to have to make heads or tails of these blueprints for me," she added, waving Basil's plans about.

Detective Watts' manor house was nestled away among the rolling hills of an overgrown field tucked neatly inside the upper ward. Trees lined all sides of the grounds, creating the illusion of a forest in every direction; weeds and brambles that had never known the cruel edge of a gardener's shears flourished in a labyrinth of green. The only path was rough and broken, winding its way to the lonely building that lay at the center of the estate.

Snips and William gawked; neither had ever seen so much greenery in their life. As they picked their way carefully along the trail that threaded through the lush landscape, William began asking questions.

"Are—uh, are you sure this is the right address, Miss Snips?"

"It's the address on the card," Snips said rather defensively.

"But this is a little—erm, *odd*, isn't it?"

When they at last arrived at the manor house, they found it to be in a deplorable condition. The once-splendid ivory columns had faded to an ailing yellow; every window was shattered and the front doors were hanging by a rusty iron nail. Vines greedily seized the walls and balconies, glutting themselves on whatever purchase they could find. Snips stepped up to the rotting doors and, with great hesitation, gave a steady knock.

The doors promptly collapsed inward.

They stepped in. Their footsteps disturbed a nest of pigeons, who promptly gave flight amidst a flutter of feathers and dust. William pressed a handkerchief to his mouth to stave off the scent of bird dung. The two pressed on.

They did not have to go far before the house came to an abrupt end. Though the front remained intact, the back had collapsed into rubble long ago; after walking for only a few feet, they found themselves suddenly outside. It was as if the house had been cleaved in half, leaving its innards exposed—rich lengths of vines and thorns tumbled through the open rooms, drenching the entire backside in a tapestry of foliage. A pipe overhead had burst, forming a waterfall that splashed across a lopsided floor before drizzling down into a once-tiny pool that had swelled into a man-made pond. A makeshift dock swept out of the house's first floor, reaching to the center of the lake; there, sitting at a cast-iron table, Jacob Watts enjoyed a very late tea with Miss Primrose.

Snips stared at the sight for some time. William shambled forward, removing his hat and waiting patiently.

"Miss Snips?" Miss Primrose began. "I do believe you are

somewhat late."

"Right. Well," Snips began. "About that. Uh, complications arose."

"Would you care to introduce your... ahem. Friend?"

"Oh, yes," Snips said, quickly recovering from the sight before her. "This is William Daffodil. William, this is Miss Primrose and Detective Watts."

"A pleasure to meet you both," William said, bowing.

"Oh, hullo," Jacob replied. "Please, have a seat. Make yourselves comfortable. Ah, not that chair," he quickly added as William approached the seat opposite of him. "That chair belongs to Corporal Squawkers."

"Pardon?"

"My trusted second in command," Jacob said, and only then did William glance down. A pigeon—one who had been fitted with a tiny spear-headed Kaiser helm and a set of painstakingly crafted miniature medals—cooed up at him from the seat before returning to picking at his half-eaten biscuit.

For a very long time, William only stared. When he spoke, his voice was quiet and meek, addressing Jacob in much the same manner one might speak to the dangerously insane. "Your second in command, sir?"

"Yes," Detective Watts said, setting his teacup down. "Exemplary service record. I know it's not protocol to make an enlisted man your second-in-command, but damn protocol—he deserves it."

"Quite," Miss Primrose muttered, tight-lipped. She threw a quick look Snips' way, as if daring the thief to contradict her.

Snips cleared her throat. "Are these—huh. Are these messenger pigeons, Mr. Watts?"

"Messenger pigeons? Oh, no. These men are not mere 'messengers'. They are *couriers*."

"I, er, see," she said, despite the fact that she actually did not.

"During the last war, they delivered critical correspondence across smoke-choked battlefields despite an abundance of mortar fire and the ever-constant hawk menace," Jacob explained. "And

after the war, what was their reward to be? Honorifics and medals?
Fame and respect?"

Snips and William both admitted that they did not know.

"They were to have a roast," he said, and now a dark
disdain crept into his voice—disdain of the sort often reserved for
crimes of the most horrific nature. "And they were to be the
'guests', as it were. Disgusting, no?"

Despite their many reservations toward entertaining this
particular type of madness, Snips and William were forced to
agree; the thought was indeed disgusting. Both neglected to add
that this was mostly since neither would have eaten a roast pigeon
except under the most dire circumstances.

"So I did what any honorable man would do for those who
had served his country. I used my considerable family fortune to
purchase them in mass and bring them here, where they could
retire with full honors. Here, in these elysian fields," he gestured to
the fields about him, which Snips could now see were thriving with
pigeons—dozens, hundreds, perhaps even *thousands*. "On
occasion, of course, they have taken up certain causes—minor
messages for the banks or a local business, little more than
skirmishes—to keep the blood moving, you understand." He lifted
his teacup, taking a small sip. "Some of them are still imprinted for
several key locations throughout the city."

"Mr. Watts has cared for them for at least a year," Miss
Primrose quickly added.

"Oh," Detective Watts said, placing the cup back down.
"Has it been a year? I haven't even noticed—"

Something plopped into the steaming tea. All four of them
looked up and realized that the culprit was one of the pigeons
circling above.

Watts' reaction was immediate and furious. "Curse you,
Private Jenkins!" He roared, leaping to his feet and shaking his fist
at the offending pigeon. "Curse you and your rebellious streak!
We'll make a proper soldier out of you yet!"

"Uh—" Snips started.

Watts shook his head and sighed, sinking back into his seat.
"Doesn't know the meaning of authority, that one. Impulsive and

head-strong—but no pigeon flies straighter or more true. That reminds me," he said, sitting up straight. "I have considered the matter we spoke of earlier." He pressed a finger to the side of his nose and winked to Snips. "Shall we discuss it further?"

"It's a bit late," Snips said. "I'd hate to interrupt—"

"No, not an interruption at all. I've already taken the liberty of throwing out all the books in the house," Detective Watts said.

Miss Primrose suddenly grew quite pale. "Erm. All the books, Mr. Watts?"

"Yes, before you returned, Miss Primrose. One cannot be too careful when dealing with conspiracies, my dear. Full of rubbish, books."

"But some of those books—your priceless collection of botanical tomes—" Miss Primrose began, rising to her feet.

"Dastardly things!" Watts shouted with great force. "Sitting upon the shelves, waiting to be read—only to ensnare you with their fiendish deceits! I must thank you, Miss Snips, for revealing this plot to me. Countless evenings have I spent beside the fire, held enthralled by the whimsies of a long-dead liar. But now, at last, I am free!"

William balked. Miss Primrose shot a glare at Snips, who provided a helpless smile. Miss Primrose then turned to Watts. "Where, may I ask, did you throw the books out? Not in the pond, I hope?"

"Oh, no. Nothing like that," Watts said, huffing. "I wouldn't think of getting them wet."

Miss Primrose's face immediately flushed with relief.

"I burnt them all," Watts continued. "Far more efficient."

William made a move to catch Miss Primrose as she showed signs of fainting, but she proved to be robust enough to resist the urge. Instead, she threw another withering glance Snips' way and turned to her employer. "Mr. Watts, obviously, Miss Snips and Mr. Daffodil are clearly in dire need of baths, a fresh set of clothes, and a good night's rest. If you would not mind, shall I see to delivering them to separate quarters?"

"Of course, of course," Watts said. "And if you see any books I might have missed—"

"Rest assured, we'll dispose of them in the safest method possible," Snips cut in.

Watts smiled. "Good lass!"

~*~

Despite the manor house's dejected appearance, there remained a considerable portion of the house that had been untouched by the disaster that had rended it in two—William and Snips were not only able to get separate hot baths, but change into fresh clothes in privacy and peace.

When they were finished, they met with Miss Primrose in a smoking lounge that had been meticulously scrubbed down until all traces of pigeon dung were absent. They made themselves comfortable in cushioned chairs, speaking of what they had discovered.

"I believe it may be wise," Miss Primrose observed, "to either allow William to sleep here or send him home."

"Why's that?" Snips asked.

"Well, if you are to discuss matters concerning the case—I work at the Steamwork myself, and may be a suspect," William observed.

"Quite astute," Miss Primrose agreed.

"Oh, come off it," Snips said. "William couldn't hurt a fly. The boy's perfectly harmless."

William gave Snips a look, but didn't argue. Miss Primrose was about to say something in response, but Snips quickly continued:

"Besides, unless you're intimately familiar with matters of engineering, we need him to tell us what this is about," Snips said, producing Basil's blueprints from her coat pocket. "We found it in Copper's apartment. Along with a bunch of really advanced looking doodads." She threw the blueprints to William's lap.

Miss Primrose sat up with interest. "How curious. My own investigation at the patent office followed by a discussion with the bank administrator, Mr. Tweedle, has led me to several extraordinary conclusions."

"This is all quite complex," William said, investigating the blueprints for the first time. "This is—hm."

"What sort of conclusions?" Snips asked.

"For starters, Mr. Eddington is in debt," Miss Primrose said. "His company has been regularly losing money for the past five years. He has taken loans out of Aberwick's banks, using patent licenses on several improvements for their calculation engines as leverage to secure a low interest rate. However, at the current rate, he will soon be unable to even pay back the interest."

"This is *really* fascinating. Copper was really onto something here," William said.

"So the whole pneumatic tubing thing—the new calculation engine—this whole business model of his. It's a last stand sort of deal," Snips said. "If this doesn't go through, he'll be finished."

"Utterly," Miss Primrose agreed. "As will Mr. Tweedle. The loans that were given to Mr. Eddington far exceeded the boundaries of common sense; should he fail to pay them, several of Mr. Tweedle's banks could go down with him. So the pneumatic pipework's success is a necessity for both Mr. Eddington *and* Mr. Tweedle."

"I mean, this is nothing short of brilliant," William said, completely immersed in the blueprints.

"That explains why the banks are so complicit in letting someone else crunch their numbers," Snips said. "What I don't understand is how Copper's involved. We discovered some sort of machine that allows you to send signals over galvanized wire, but I don't see how that's an issue."

"Even if Copper found a way of communication superior to the pneumatic pipes, it wouldn't threaten the business model," Miss Primrose agreed. "I don't see how this invention threatens Mr. Eddington's idea, either."

"Oh," William said casually, "It completely blows it out of the water."

Both Snips and Miss Primrose stopped talking, their eyes turning to the young mathematician.

William flushed underneath the sudden attention, swallowing. "Well, I mean, uh—"

"Please, Mr. Daffodil," Miss Primrose said. "Enlighten us."

"Copper didn't just invent a way to communicate over long distances more effectively," William said. "He invented a way for *machines* to communicate over long distances more effectively. These plans—the process he's suggesting—it's completely automated. There's no human involvement, just electrical signals being sent between calculating engines."

Both Snips and Miss Primrose exchanged glances. Snips spoke first. "So?"

"So," William said, sitting up straight. "The problem with our model is it requires so much work. You get a message over the pipework that has the account information, then you input it manually. But with Basil's model, the information exchange is *instant*. You could just tell one machine to send all the information on it to another."

"So, it's faster and more convenient," Miss Primrose said. "But—"

"Not just faster, not just more convenient," William said, voice accelerating to an excited pitch. "There's just so much more you can *do* with it. In our model, if the main engine fails, all the other engines are in danger—our engine is the safety net. But with Basil's model, *every* engine is a safety net. If one engine fails, you can send all of its calculations to the others—if all the engines but one fail, you can send all of its calculations to the one that's still operational."

"Repeat that in English?" Snips said.

"It is simple, Miss Snips. Because all the machines can work as a safety net, there is no need for a single safety net," Miss Primrose said. "Mr. Copper's system renders Mr. Eddington's engine redundant. Thank you, Mr. Daffodil. You have been of inestimable aid in this matter. We now know why several people would wish to suppress such an innovation. And we know that at least one of them is low enough to stoop to murder."

~*~

The silver pocket watch was a remarkable thing; as large as

a fist, it possessed three ivory faces. The largest and central face tracked the current time, while its two sisters functioned as a stopwatch and count-down timer. It purred in the assassin's palm like a contented tomcat, measuring seconds in steady ticks. When it at last reached zero, he hauled back the length of rope, spinning a pulley overhead and drawing a spluttering Agrippa out of the water.

He had seen better days; one eye was swollen shut and a trickle of fresh blood was beginning to flow from his recently smashed nose. The assassin twirled the rope around a peg protruding from the wall, keeping the dark-skinned giant's torso hanging over the barrel.

"As a rule," he explained with an air of casual boredom, "I don't engage in torture. Not that I object to it on moral grounds," he quickly added. "I just find it doesn't get you anywhere. You rarely end up getting the truth; just what you want to hear."

Hacking and coughing, Agrippa spat a wad of phlegm at his face. It fell several feet short, prompting the assassin to smile.

"No, getting the truth requires something special. You have to make the person want to tell you the truth," he said. "It's just a matter of motivation." He drew one of his pistols from the holster, setting it down on the table in front of him. It was a heavy and graceless thing, built for function instead of style; its hilt was covered in iron treads for an easy grip and its trigger was nearly impossible for a layman to pull. He preferred it that way; those who were hesitant to kill could rarely manage to fire his guns. It required a determined finger. "So let's talk about your motivation."

"Bastard," Agrippa gasped.

"For starters, you probably want to survive," he said. "But let's be honest—that's just not going to happen. I know it, you know it. Regardless of whether you tell me what I want to know, you're going to be dead when I walk out of this room."

Agrippa grew silent and sullen, allowing his eyes to do much of the talking.

"So if you know you're going to die, what else could possibly motivate you?" he asked. "What could I ever offer you that would convince you to tell me what I want to know? Well, that depends. Do you want a quiet funeral? Or a noisy one?"

Agrippa's eyes narrowed.

"Because if you tell me what I want to know, then I'll just kill you quick and painlessly and walk out of your life. But if you don't tell me what I want to know—or even worse, if I find out you lied to me—then I'm going to be angry. And when I get angry, I go to funerals. You don't think there'll be anyone you care about showing up at your funeral, hm? Do you?"

A low and rumbling growl escaped from his throat. "You sonofa—"

"So what will it be? A quiet funeral? Or," and here he tapped the pommel of his pistol with his index finger, "a noisy one?"

A long and tense moment stretched out in the quiet of the house's basement. At last, Agrippa grunted and closed his eyes. "What d'ya want to know."

"My contacts tell me there was a little barbecue in the Rookery the other night."

"What about it?"

"Apparently, a couple was in attendance. One of them was Arcadia Snips; the other I don't know. Introduce me."

"William," he said, spitting. "William Daffodil."

"What are they doing together?"

"Investigatin' something. About Basil Copper, an engineer who worked at the Steamwork. Got 'imself killed a few days back, Snips is out to find out by who."

"Where can I find Arcadia?"

"Don't know," he said.

"That's a step towards a noisy funeral."

"I don't know!" he snapped, straining his muscle against the ropes—and for a moment the assassin grew agitated at the possibility that Agrippa could snap through them like a train snapping through twine. But he soon relaxed when he saw that the giant could not escape the bindings.

"Give me something."

"She's with that other fella," Agrippa said. "She might be holed up in his place."

137 -- ARCADIA SNIPS AND THE STEAMWORK CONSORTIUM

"I see. Is there anything I should know about her? Any surprises she might have in store for me?"

"Snips?" Agrippa said. "You might manage to kill her..."

"I expect that I will."

"But she'll charge you an eye for the right."

The assassin shrugged. "Whatever." He plucked his pistol off the table and slid it back into its holster. Then, just as he was turning to go, he stopped and looked back at him. "Oh, I almost forgot—remember what I said about a quick death?"

"Eh?"

He tugged the rope free, dropping Agrippa back into the barrel full of water on his way out. "I lied."

~*~

CHAPTER 17: IN WHICH, TO NO ONE'S SURPRISE, OUR TITULAR PROTAGONIST ACTS SCANDALOUS

~*~

The smoking lounge was drenched in the tangerine haze of the morning light. The sun-drizzled stretch of Snips' slumbering figure was draped next to William's in a manner that might have been described as scandalous if it were not for the several mathematical books and blueprints that lay beside them on the cot.

Those readers familiar with fiction of a more racy sort (though we would never accuse you, dear reader, of such indiscretions) might recall that scenarios such as these are often followed by a rapid succession of disasters leading to the most embarrassing situation possible. As the man awakens, the shock of realizing he has spent the night arm-in-arm with a woman incites him to leap to his feet and trip over a strategically placed feline, landing him straight atop the now-awake companion; the ruckus this produces soon rouses the butler to action, who bursts into the room and, seeing the young damsel in the arms of the gentleman, assumes scandal is afoot. This is followed by the stuttering red-faced explanations, the prideful shouts, the accusations, the inevitable attempts at reconciliation, so on, so on, et cetera, et cetera.

These readers may be both surprised and disheartened to learn that no such event occurred. The reason why can be traced to several facts: William Daffodil slept like the dead, Jacob Watts had neither feline nor butler (he considered both to be beastly creatures), and Snips awoke first and was sufficiently well-versed in fiction of this sort to avoid that very scenario.

Snips withdrew herself from William with all the care she gave to barbed wire, slipping free without disturbing so much as a wheatgold lock. She brushed herself off, straightened her clothes, and paused in front of the mirror.

A dirty silver-toothed vagrant stared back.

"Hmph," she said, arching back to admire her profile. There wasn't much *to* admire; she was hard where she should have been soft and sharp where she should have been smooth. She looked back to William, sleeping serenely on the cot. She glanced about to make sure neither Miss Primrose or Detective Watts were up and about; she then skillfully slipped back into William's arms.

She wriggled about until she was comfortable, drawing in a slow breath. Then, with great care, she took William's wrist and slapped his hand down to the side of her bottom.

"Ah! Villainy!" she cried, springing from his grip with enough violence to rouse the mathematician from his slumber. "Scandal!"

William was awake in an instant, flailing about as he fell from the cot. At once, he leapt to his feet, red-faced and surprised. "Wh—what? What's happened? What's going on?"

Snips pointed her finger at him, her eyes flashing with accusation. "You, sir, are a beast. Taking advantage of a hapless damsel. The shame!"

William stuttered for a reply. "I—I beg your pardon, Madame?"

"No pardon will be given, not today," Snips said. "You have stained my reputation as an upstanding Lady—"

"I beg your pardon?!"

"—and now you must make restitution," she said, and then she darted forward, pinning him. She shoved her palms against the wall, keeping his waist between her arms; she threw her head up, her face looming just beneath his chin. "My honor demands it!"

Rather than try to escape, William grew still. The mathematician watched her with a thoughtful expression that quickly made Snips uncomfortable; she imagined it was the sort of look he gave mathematical equations right before completing them. It made her feel as if he was about to solve her for X.

Snips narrowed her eyes. "What?"

William squinted back. "You are a very peculiar person."

"Yes, yes, I know." Snips dropped her arms and stepped away. "No need to rub it in."

"Oh, no," William said. "I don't mean it like that. I like

peculiar people."

Snips peered at him; William did his best not to blush.

"Don't get any funny ideas," she told him. "You're a pleasant sort of fellow, but I don't do relationships. Too complicated. Not worth the trouble."

"You are making a rather large assumption there," William pointed out.

She stiffened. "Well, what I mean is—"

William smiled. "But truth be told, I think that under different circumstances, I'd be quite smitten with you. You're very lovely when you aren't acting like a brigand."

"Um—" Snips shuffled where she stood, taken aback. "—uh, that is—"

William took her hand; he brought the back of her knuckles up to his mouth and gave them a gentle kiss. It was the sort of silly gesture that was supposed to inspire fancy ladies to swoon; it was the kind of romantic flop-trop best reserved for third-rate plays and guileless Romeos.

"Your pardon, Madame." William straightened back up and headed down the stairs.

For the first time that she could remember, Snips' cheeks burned.

~*~

Miss Primrose was enjoying breakfast out on the makeshift dock. Snips adjusted her hat as she made her way towards her hostess, humming a soft tune.

"Did you sleep well?" Miss Primrose asked, voice buzzing with disapproval.

"Oh, come off it," Snips said, still working off the previous blush. "I didn't do anything. We just fell asleep while trying to iron out the details of Basil's model."

"As you like, Miss Snips," she said, although it was clear that Miss Primrose remained unsatisfied.

"What's our next move?"

"Mr. Eddington is our chief suspect," Miss Primrose said.

"It seems certain he is up to no good."

"Yeah, that's what I was thinking. We're going to need more evidence, though. Right?"

"Correct."

"So I'll head on down to the Steamwork," Snips said. "See if I can't dig anything up that I shouldn't dig up."

"Mr. Eddington is unlikely to cooperate. Besides, the Steamwork is closed today."

"I won't be going there during working hours," Snips pointed out.

Miss Primrose blanched. "You intend to break in?"

"What? Did I say break in?" Snips feigned outrage. "Me? Break the law? Madame, I am *offended* by your insinuation!"

"Miss Snips, I cannot condone—"

"Relax. You don't need to 'condone' anything. Just go and tell Susan what we've found so far."

"Susan?"

"Count Orwick," Snips said.

"Very well, then," Miss Primrose said, scowling. "You will go about your own particular 'investigation', and I shall inform our employer as to our recent discoveries. Shall we return here by, say, eight o'clock?"

"Eight o'clock it is," Snips said.

"Very well. Try to get it right this time, Miss Snips."

As Snips turned away from the deck, she caught sight of William picking his way around the manorhouse. Ignoring Miss Primrose's disapproving glare, Snips ran off to catch him on his way out the gate.

"Hey," Snips said. "Wait a moment, eh?"

"Erm, oh, I beg your pardon," William said. "I've only now just realized I'm late for my grandmother's little party—"

"Oh, visiting your grandmum, eh? Mind if I tag along?" Snips asked.

"I—um. I'm not sure if that's entirely wise," William said.

"Really, now? Afraid I'll scare her off?" Snips grinned.

"Oh, I doubt that," William said. "I doubt that very much."

"Well, I want to talk with you a little bit, before you run off to wherever," Snips said. "So I'll come along, if that's alright."

"I suppose," William said, resisting the urge to squirm about in his clothes. "But, you must understand. My grandmother's very, ah, *strange*..."

"I'm sure I'll manage."

~*~

CHAPTER 18: IN WHICH WE RETURN TO THE PAST ONCE AGAIN TO DISCUSS GRAVE MATTERS CONCERNING WAR AND MATHEMATICS

~*~

"Good evening, Nigel," Abigail said, greeting him at the laboratory doorway. Mrs. Daffodil was dressed in a sky-blue high-collar blouse with a frilled lace front and cinch belt above a pair of dark mahogany bloomers. Her cheeks were stained with grease and her favorite pair of goggles were pulled high upon her temples. She had bound her hair up into a tightly curled bun, so as to avoid getting it caught in the churning network of machines that ran behind her. "Here for Jeremiah, I take it?"

Nigel removed his hat. "Indeed," he said. "Well, for the both of you, actually."

"Hn. I assumed this was a social call of some sort."

"No, not at all. It is a matter of grave business. Where is Jeremiah?"

"Playing with his toys," she said, her voice containing no small amount of disapproval. She stepped deep into the laboratory, picking her way past tables brimming with all manner of alchemical reagents and strange contraptions. Among them was placed a cradle of pine containing a bundled up babe. Nigel paused a moment to admire the Daffodils' child; he slept despite the laboratory's noise, the constant snarl of gearworks serving as a mechanical lullaby.

"We're a bit worried about him," Abigail said, noticing Nigel's interest in the child. "I moved him down to the laboratory, where I can keep an eye on him. While keeping an eye on Jeremiah, I mean."

"Worried?" Nigel asked.

"He has bouts of weakness," she said. "I fear he may have inherited my father's weak heart."

"Hm."

An explosion flared up in the back of the laboratory, rattling Nigel's molars. Abigail spat a series of unlady-like curses and stomped her way toward the smoldering corridor.

"Jeremiah!" she cried. "Stop it! We have a guest!"

"Guests?" Jeremiah said, thrusting his head out from the door. His own goggles were pulled over his eyes; his entire face was covered in a thick layer of ash and soot. When he saw Nigel, he immediately grinned. "Oh, hello Nigel! I was just thinking about you—"

"Jeremiah, Abigail," Nigel continued. "It is a pleasure to see you both, and a meeting between us is long over-due—but I am not here to exchange pleasantries, I fear. There is a matter we must discuss. Immediately."

Jeremiah frowned; Abigail nodded. "We'll talk in the lobby," she said.

~*~

"The numbers do not lie," Nigel said from the comfort of a lush chair. "War is coming."

Abigail leaned against the crackling hearth. Jeremiah sat beside her, trying to soothe their babe in his arms. Neither seemed particularly dumbstruck by Nigel's announcement.

"Perhaps you do not understand," he said. "After analyzing the last packet of data you sent, the result is clear. Our country will soon be at war—"

"We know," Jeremiah said, sounding particularly sullen.

"I beg your *pardon*?"

"We've known for some time," Abigail agreed.

Nigel blanched. "How?"

"We have our own probability engine, now," Jeremiah explained.

"You—you what? But we agreed—"

"We agreed to not misuse the probability engine for our own ends," Abigail replied. "And we have not. Our only purpose for building the engine was prediction and experimentation; we have not used it to create results. We have, however, used it to monitor *your* use," she said, her voice thick with ire.

Nigel sank back into the chair, turning his attention to the fire.

Jeremiah nodded. "I told her about our discussion concerning the thought experiment you presented to me a year ago. Despite your desire for secrecy, I had to tell her. I was terrified at the notion that you would actually try it."

"I suggested that we build our own engine, solely for the purpose of monitoring whether or not you were making changes without our knowledge," Abigail continued. "And lo and behold— not quite to my surprise—we discovered you were. Extensively."

"You've been changing things without our permission," Jeremiah said.

"Yes," Nigel said. "I confess. But the changes I have wrought—they have all been for the greater good. I have prevented famines; averted calamities. Saved lives—"

"And created at least one," Abigail said, her voice as penetrating as a syringe. "Do not act as if you have done this in the better interest of the world at large, Nigel. Your motivation has always been curiosity. Moreso than even my husband," she added, throwing Jeremiah a look as he gently bounced young William on his lap. "You did these things because you wanted to see if you could."

"Perhaps," Nigel said with reluctance. "Yes, perhaps you are correct. But now—now, we are faced with a true calamity. A catastrophe of immense enormity. If these numbers are correct, this will be a war that will swallow up hundreds of thousands—"

"Millions," Abigail corrected him. "It will be a war to end all others. It will be fought with horrible weapons beyond comprehension, placed in the hands of kings and queens leading armies of nationalists and patriots. It will be accompanied by plague, disease, and famine. Entire generations will cease to exist."

"We must stop it," Nigel said. "Surely, if the engine has ever had a purpose, this must be it!"

"No," Abigail replied. "No, we musn't."

"I beg your pardon?"

"Think of all the world's civilizations as an immense boiler;

famine, drought, conflict—these are the valves through which pressure is released. Over the past few years, you have been shutting each of those valves off, gradually increasing the pressure," Abigail said.

"Are you saying I am responsible for the very war these numbers predict?"

"No," Abigail said. "Of course not. It would have come, one way or another, as a natural consequence of technological progress. But each disaster you have stopped has only added to the strength that this disaster shall inflict."

"How long do we have?" Nigel asked.

"Two decades at most," she said. "We could delay it, but that would only make the event more horrific than it already is."

"Is there no way to stop it?" Nigel asked. "No way we can stifle it?"

"It is too soon and too vast," she said. "No flapping of a butterfly's wings can deflect it. Only an enormous event could hope to counter it, and even then, I am not sure if it would be stopped—only postponed."

"How can you be so calm about this?!" Nigel fumed.

"Because there is nothing that can be done," Abigail told him. "No remedy, no cure, no panacea. There will be war, Nigel. The world will suffer. We cannot save it. All we can do is care for those around us and pray for the best."

"You spoke of an enormous event being able to counter this," Nigel said. "How enormous?"

Abigail shook her head. "It's an absurd premise to begin with, Nigel. There is no way to fight this."

"Tell me. How enormous?"

"We meddled in matters best left to chance. Leave it be."

"Tell me," Nigel said, and there was a force and fury behind him that gave both Abigail and her husband reason for pause. "Tell me what would be necessary. If only to convince me that it is impossible."

Abigail sighed. "A nation collapsing. A world-wide depression. Tens of thousands dying. A city disappearing overnight. Any of these events could accomplish the task, in theory

—and do you notice what they all have in common, Nigel?"

Once again, Nigel turned back to the fire.

"They all involve murder," Abigail said, pressing on. "They all involve inflicting harm now, to deflect harm later. They all involve taking the matter into our own hands, and doing violence to our fellow man."

"Abigail," Jeremiah said, speaking softly. "None of us would do something like that."

"No," Nigel agreed, staring unceasingly into the heart of the fire. "None of us would."

~*~

CHAPTER 19: IN WHICH OUR TITULAR PROTAGONIST LEARNS OF THE DAFFODIL SCION'S GRANDMOTHER, COUNT ORWICK DISCUSSES KINGSMEN, AND MRS. DAFFODIL MAKES HER INTENTIONS CLEAR

~*~

"It was difficult, growing up with everyone around you knowing your parents were villains," William said.

"Huh," Snips replied, her hands shoved down deep into her pockets. "Kids gave you lip over it?"

"Sometimes. Most of them were convinced that I was plotting to build some sort of devastating steam-powered automaton to wreck the school with," William said.

"Heh."

"Which is fair, since I actually was."

Snips froze in mid-step, the sole of her shoe hovering over the cobblestone. "I beg your pardon?"

William cleared his throat as heat surged into his cheeks. "Well, I mean—I wouldn't have. But mad science, well... You must understand, Miss Snips. It's in our blood. My father was a mad scientist, my mother was a mad scientist, my grandmother a mad scientist, my grandfather a mad scientist..."

"Right. So." Snips squinted one eye and popped the other open wide, leaning forward to inspect William closely. "You're telling me every so often you feel the urge to terrorize the city from the seat of some mechanical monstrosity?"

William drew back defensively. "No!"

"Oh. Well, okay, then."

"I mean, I'd much prefer a dirigible, anyway."

"*I beg your pardon*?!"

"Not that I would!" William threw his hands up in front of him. "Never, ever! I stick with mathematics—with theory. I mean, I don't want to have an episode, like my grandmother did."

"Wait. Episode? Like your grandmother did? Exactly where

are we going, again?"

"Erm, well—that's a bit of a funny story," William said, smiling apprehensively.

~*~

Napsbury Asylum, Snips decided, was precisely where she wanted to be put once she went off the deep-end.

It was a pleasant looking brick building that, under different circumstances, could easily have been mistaken for a very rich man's house. Snips walked behind William, who seemed to be growing more and more depressed with every step towards the front door.

"You don't have to actually meet her," William said. "I mean—"

"After the stories you just told me about her? You bloody well better *believe* I have to meet her," Snips said.

"I just don't want to frighten you with my family history," William said.

"Trust me, you won't."

William sighed, slumping as he stepped through the door. Snips quickly followed, grinning all the way.

Various people throughout the asylum wing were dressed down for the birthday, wearing brightly colored hats and sitting in their seats. There were several trays of food set out, and an extraordinary number of cats meandering around the scene.

The centerpiece of the event was a slim middle-aged man with a bushy moustache and a look so full of serene cheer that Snips had a hard time imagining he was a patient. He looked more like a man who had finally discovered his place in the world—plus, his cake was carved in the shape of a brown tabby.

"Hello, Mr. Wanewright," William said, removing a small wrapped package from his coat. He sat it besides the growing pile of presents that were placed at the man's left. "A pleasure to see you once again."

Mr. Wanewright smiled; the expression was pure sunshine. "Oh, hullo, Mr. Daffodil. A pleasure to meet you again! Have you met Professor Snugglewuggums?" He reached forward, picking up a nearby black cat and holding him up for William to greet. It was only now that Snips realized that every cat in the room had some sort of accoutrement to it—an article of clothing or fashion that had somehow been cleverly attached to them. Professor Snugglewuggums had a top hat and monocle.

"No, I'm afraid I haven't," William said, suppressing a sigh. He reached forward to take Professor Snugglewuggums' paw, giving it a shake. "A pleasure to meet you, Professor."

The cat meowed.

"Oh, dear, he's quite taken with you." Mr. Wanewright exclaimed, setting the cat down. "Very good, Mr. Daffodil. Very good!"

Growing very uncomfortable, William quickly smiled and slipped back into the crowd of partygoers. Snips followed, glancing back over her shoulder.

"So, is that guy—"

"Criminally insane? Yes," William said. "I'd rather not explain the details. Suffice it to say there was an incident involving a very loud tax-collector and several dozen very hungry cats."

Snips grimaced.

Mrs. Daffodil emerged from the crowd to greet William; the old woman instantly looked between him and Snips and produced a dazzling smile. "Oh, William, is this lady a friend of yours?"

"This is, ah, yes. A friend of mine. She works for a detective agency," William said, gesturing to her. "Miss Snips, this is my grandmother, Mrs. Daffodil."

"A pleasure to meet you, Miss Snips," she said, taking the thief's hand. "You have extraordinary taste in clothing."

"Uh, thanks," Snips said.

"I can't help but notice you're not wearing my sweater, William," Mrs. Daffodil said. "Don't you like it?"

"Oh, you know, I'm terribly sorry," William said, smiling nervously. "I completely forgot about it."

"That's a shame," Mrs. Daffodil said. "Anyway, I'm very glad you could come to the party. Would you mind being a dear

Arcadia Snips and William Daffodil are formally introduced to Professor Snugglewuggums.

and getting me a slice of cake?"

"Sure," William said, stepping back toward the table. For a moment, Snips and Mrs. Daffodil were alone.

Snips noticed she hadn't let go of Snips' hand. Her grip was, in fact, uncomfortably strong.

"Uh, anyway, I'm just, you know, happy to meet you," Snips began. "William's told me a little bit about you."

"Has he?" Mrs. Daffodil said. "He hasn't mentioned anything about you."

"Oh, well," Snips said. "I mean, I guess I'd expect that. We only met yesterday, you know. He's a very nice fellow," she quickly added.

"Oh, yes. He's quite good-natured," Mrs. Daffodil quickly agreed. "You know, I'm very good at measuring a person's character at a glance, Miss Snips."

"Are you?" Snips shuffled, suddenly nervous.

"Yes," she said, and her grip tightened to steel. "Miss Snips, I may be old and senile, but I can still smell a fink from a mile off. I don't know what your angle is, and I don't care. But before you play my grandson like a third-rate fiddle, I want you to know something." Her voice dropped to a dreadful whisper:

"I'm not in here because I shoplifted, or forgot to feed my cats, or otherwise acted like a naughty little minx. I'm here because I built things. Terrible things. Horrible things, Miss Snips. And so help me God, if you so much as put a dent in my dear little boy's heart, I will unleash a mechanized Armageddon upon you that would cow the Devil himself."

Snips blinked, stared, and swallowed. "Uh..."

William returned, a plate of cake in hand. "Here you go, grandmother."

Instantly, the icy aura vanished beneath a mask of warm affability. Mrs. Daffodil took the slice with a broad, motherly smile, releasing Snips' hand. "Thank you, William. You're such a dear."

"Are you two getting along, then?" William asked.

"Smashingly," Mrs. Daffodil said.

"Oh, uh, yeah," Snips responded, scratching at the back of

her head. "Yeah, she's, uh, quite something, your grandmum."

"Well, I have to be off, anyway," William said. "I hope you don't mind, grandmother. I have an appointment to keep." He threw a nervous look at Snips, but she appeared too distracted to notice.

"Of course not, dear," Mrs. Daffodil said. "Just try to remember to come by a little more often, hm?"

William nodded.

"Oh, and feel free to bring your friend, too," she added, throwing a meaningful look Snips' way. "I'd love to hear more about her."

~*~

"Are you familiar with the Kingsmen, Miss Primrose?" Orwick asked, staring out of his office window and toward his trains.

"No, sir, I do not believe I am," Miss Primrose said, shifting in her seat. "However, I am not here to discuss historical trivia. I have a matter of great urgency—"

"They're a fascinating organization," Count Orwick said, cutting her off. "Dissolved by royal mandate over four decades ago. Founded a century prior by one of our less esteemed monarchs, they performed all manner of horrible crimes and obscenities in the name of maintaining the power and prestige of the Crown."

"Ah," Miss Primrose said, not without disdain. "Government-sanctioned assassins."

"No, no," Orwick replied. "Nothing so base. Indeed, if that was all they were, I would find them far less fascinating. No, the Kingsmen were knights, but they were knights of a peculiar breed. They were given no extraordinary rights, no powers of law, no official capacity. They were simply informed of the situation and told to do what they felt they must."

Miss Primrose frowned. Count Orwick always struck her as an awful sort of person; she dealt with him only out of the necessity of dealing with one's client. This entire conversation of his was absolutely confounding, and merely serving to reinforce her impression of the man. "Count Orwick, I've come here to tell you about Mr. Eddington. We believe he may be involved in serious matters of—"

"They broke the law, Miss Primrose. Killed, assassinated, stole, so on. But they were not *above* it," Orwick explained. "They were given no official orders to do so, and if they were caught in the act, they were brought to justice just as readily as any real criminal. They were, in short, the vigilantes of the Crown."

Miss Primrose stiffened in her chair.

"How is Miss Snips performing? I hope she is not causing you too much trouble."

Miss Primrose's lips thinned into a line. "None at all, sir," she said, trying to contain her agitation.

"Well enough," Orwick said, turning back around to face Miss Primrose. "As for your case, I'm afraid we have encountered a problem. I am not sure how, but overnight, we have received several very angry letters from very important people demanding we close this matter immediately."

"I was unaware Her Majesty is subject to the approval of her peers," Miss Primrose said.

"I'm afraid that she sometimes is, yes. Especially when those peers are as important as these," Orwick noted. "She has commanded me to cease with my little investigation into Copper's demise. And without royal mandate, I am outside of my jurisdiction. Of course, you will still be paid in full for your services..."

"Of course," Miss Primrose agreed, clearing her throat.

"And tell Miss Snips that I will see to the abolishment of her little problem as well," Orwick added. "All in all, it seems that this matter is officially closed."

"I see," Miss Primrose said.

"It is quite a shame there aren't any Kingsmen around these days," Count Orwick said rather wistfully. "You know, I've been thinking about advising Her Majesty to reinstitute the organization."

"If there's nothing else, Count Orwick—"

"No, nothing else," Orwick said. "Do be careful, Miss

Primrose."

~*~

It took an hour for William to arrive at the Arcanum estate; he had nervously retraced his steps to make sure that Snips was not following him.

Once there, he found it difficult to resist the urge to take a peek at the oddities that lined the manorhouse's halls. But rather than satisfy his curiousity, he cradled the cup of tea Starkweather had brought him while he waited to see Master Arcanum, pausing to blow away the rising steam.

As he lifted his head, he noticed that everything had gotten abruptly quiet.

The crickets outside were no more. William could not even hear the tick of his own heart. He frowned, searching the room; his eyes fell upon the large and stately clock that occupied the far wall.

Its second-hand was trembling, struggling to get past the five.

"Not again!" William cried, and before he could stop himself, he had dropped the cup. The mathematician flinched with expectation, then stopped when he realized that the scalding tea had never reached his trousers.

He peered down at the teacup, which was now hovering in mid-tumble directly above his lap. Its contents were paused in mid-spill, resembling a dark ice sculpture. Staring with rapt fascination, William reached out to touch the side of the tea—and immediately drew his finger back with a yelp. Although solid, the substance was still quite hot.

He looked back to the clock. The second-hand continued to wrestle with the future, skipping back to the five with every attempt. And as William stood up to get a closer look, the hand suddenly snapped back—lurching to the four.

"Master Arcanum will see you now," Starkweather announced.

William spun around, facing the towering monolith; he saw now that the teacup was sitting neatly on the table, undisturbed and still steaming. He turned back to the clock, only to find that the second-hand was happily marching forward, well beyond the seven.

"Um," William said. "Did you—did you just notice anything, uh, odd?"

Starkweather raised his eyebrow.

William shook his head. "Nevermind," he said, and then he walked on.

The study contained all manner of oddities that drew William's interest; the designs for strange machines that cluttered the walls caught his eye in particular. The owner of the estate even apparently had a mummy still in its sarcophagus, the withered corpse still bedecked in the ancient jewelry of its long-dead empire.

As William was inspecting the mummy, it suddenly spoke. "Good evening."

William nearly screamed, springing back and hoisting his hat up to protect him from what he assumed was the freshly arisen corpse. It took him a moment to realize that it wasn't the mummy who had spoken, but someone else—a figure who he had missed in his initial appraisal of the room, sitting on a chair in a nightgown and cap.

The figure was, apparently, yet another mummy.

"Uh," William began.

"You wished to speak with me," the second mummy said.

"Hullo," William said, shifting uncomfortably. "I'm sorry, I don't actually know who you are, but—"

The mummy made a gesture. As if conjured from thin air, Starkweather appeared behind William and dropped a heavy hand to his shoulder.

"I was here earlier with Miss Snips and I just wanted to ask you a few questions," William squeaked out just as that grip turned to iron.

"Wait," the mummy-man said, shifting to sit up. At once, the servant's hand fell away. "You know… Miss Snips?"

Well, yes, somewhat," William said. "I mean, we've fallen off a building together, and fought a fire. I'm not sure if that

William Daffodil is startled while inside Professor Arcanum's study.

qualifies me as 'knowing' her, but I've certainly met her."

"Pardon my earlier rudeness. I've had some trouble with unwelcome guests in the past," William's host said. "My name is Nigel Arcanum. May I inquire as to whom you are?"

"William," he said, wetting his lips. "William Daffodil."

There was a long pause.

"Oh, er, I suppose I should explain," William said, having long grown used to such moments. "Yes, I am related to *those* Daffodils, but I assure you that I am in no way like the villains."

"How disappointing," Nigel said.

William blanched. No one had ever reacted that way before.

"I knew your parents, William," Nigel continued. "And though they were many things, they were certainly not villains."

~*~

CHAPTER 20: IN WHICH OUR TITULAR PROTAGONIST DISCOVERS THE TRUE PURPOSE OF THE STEAMWORK, THE DAFFODIL SCION DISCOVERS MORE OF HIS PAST, AND MR. EDDINGTON IS THREATENED WITH PI

~*~

Snips jammed the business end of her crowbar between the planks of wood that now guarded the hole in Basil's workshop wall, twisting them off with a loud pop. She glanced below to make sure no one had heard the sound (nor noticed the thief who had clambored up the side of the building), then tossed the timber up to the roof. Without further delay, she slipped inside.

Basil's workshop was as dark as Snips expected. The thief withdrew a hollow glass stick, gave it a steady shake to rouse up the lightning beetles inside, then held it up as the azure glow seeped into the room. After a quick glance to make sure nothing was waiting for her in the corners, she tossed the empty burlap sack over her shoulder and moved to enter the halls of the Steamwork.

Snips muttered thanks to whatever God was listening that the Steamwork didn't have some sort of clockwork automaton patrolling it after hours. The hallway was completely empty, with the only light provided by Snips. She skulked up to Timothy Eddington's office, found the door locked, then set the light stick down and got on her knees.

Locks were one of Snips' specialties; while others had spent long years learning how to put things together, Snips had been studying how to take them apart. Her long and clever fingers traced the width of the keyhole, gave the knob a jangle, and figured it to be a fairly simple warded lock. She unfolded the leather flap of tools she had brought with her, plucked out an appropriate pick, and began her work.

"Really, Mr. Eddington," Snips said aloud as she twisted the pick about, attempting to fit it into the grooves. "You'd think you'd put a little more thought into your security. It's almost like you want me to steal everything you own."

The lock soon snapped open with a satisfying ka-chunk. Replacing her tools, Snips rose to her feet and stepped inside, holding the light stick high above her head. Its glow permeated throughout the room, shining down across the many baubles and trinkets Snips had admired on her previous visit.

"Hello, gents," Snips said. "Don't suppose you'd fancy a night out with a pretty lady?" She swept her burlap bag up into her hand and went to work.

She had snatched an ivory Buddha, three expensive looking pens, a lovely amethyst paperweight, and was considering the matching set of ebony bookends when she noticed the filing cabinet behind Mr. Eddington's desk. This one had been triple-padlocked.

"Oh dear, oh dear," Snips said, tsking. "This will not do! Three padlocks? Really, Mr. Eddington. How over-zealous." She squatted down and went to work on them; one by one, they rattled off beneath her quick fingertips and razor-sharp tools. Once the last one clattered to the floor, she opened the cabinet up with a serene smile and held the light stick low to see what she had found.

"Hm." She let her fingers dance across the files, searching for something with a provocative name. Her hand froze over a file with the title of 'HEMLOCK INITIATIVE'.

She bit down on one end of the light stick as she leaned against the far wall and glanced through the documents. She couldn't make out two thirds of it—as far as Snips was concerned, mathematics might as well be Swahili—but there were several things that popped out immediately.

She shoved the documents in the burlap sack along with the other goods. That's when she noticed the button.

It was small and delicate, stashed away beneath the desk in a spot few would know to look; designed to blend in with the wood grain, she only noticed it thanks to the shadows cast by her light-stick. She gave the beetles another violent shake to brighten the glow, then leaned forward to give it a closer look. Tilting her head to the side, she reached forward and pushed the button in with a click.

The bookcase on the other side of the room slid away with a low hiss, revealing a narrow passageway.

Snips' eyes were as wide as saucers by this point. She stifled her urge to whistle low and crept back out from behind the desk, counting slowly back from ten. Once she was satisfied no one was charging up the passageway to see what was going on, she crept up to it and stepped in.

The bookcase clicked back into place.

Dunnigan's disappearance into the office earlier had made her suspect a secret passage was stashed away somewhere in Mr. Eddington's office; this confirmed it. The hidden niche was filled with a set of cramped stairs that spiraled down into the heart of the Steamwork. Snips moved carefully, keeping her eye out for the telltale glow of a far off lamp. But by the time she reached the bottom of the stairs, all thoughts of being discovered had disappeared.

The base of the stairway opened up into a stone lobby, which in turn lead to a large hall; as Snips stopped and stared at the sight before her, an unknown hand turned on the lights. They came on slowly, flickering near the back as machines roused from their slumber with a splutter of dust and a distinct electric hum. And then, like a curtain being drawn from the stage, row after row of bulbs shined down upon marvels and miracles.

Each well-oiled contraption cheerfully hummed as it set about its predetermined task with no more fanfare than ants going about their daily toil. Iron rods crackled as arcs of electricity leapt between them; relentless engines rumbled behind sets of spinning wheels and levers.

In a glass case was a wheel of iron as tall as Snips. Inside it was a seat attached to a plump looking steam-engine, suspended on a series of pipes and valves that attached to the wheel's inside curve by two metal sleeves at the bottom and the top.

In another case was a series of glass bulbs of every fashion, shape, and design; some flickered, some flashed, and others remained steady. The light they gave off was brilliant, and Snips had to keep her eyes averted lest she be blinded.

And yet in another case lay two machines which seemed to resemble the innards of several dozen clocks that had been regurgitated into a pair of boxes made from mahogany and glass. A small crank attached itself to each box's left side, with several dials each bearing a series of symbols from 0 to 9 on the top. Snips realized that they were miniature models of calculation engines; furthermore, the two engines had a wire connecting both of them, and seemed to be interacting with one another.

Next to each display was a framed and mounted set of blueprints, and beneath each set of blueprints was a patent signed and purchased by the Steamwork.

"What are you doing here?"

Snips whirled around. Behind her was Dunnigan, squinting and holding a mop up to her as if it were a gun. Snips sighed with relief and shook her head.

"Continuing my investigation," Snips said. "What is this place?"

"You shouldn't be here," Dunnigan said. "It ain't right."

"This place—these inventions. They're amazing," Snips said, walking between the tables. "But they look so old. Some of the cases are rusty, and..." Snips drew a finger across one table, lifting it up and peering at it. "There's dust everywhere."

"Aye, I'd like to clean the place out, but Mr. Eddington refuses to let anyone touch anything in here without himself being present," Dunnigan said. "'Cept for Mr. Copper, of course." Dunnigan instantly threw his hand over his mouth.

Snips turned. "Copper. This was Copper's laboratory? No," she said, frowning. "It couldn't have been."

"Not, uh, exactly," Dunnigan said, squirming. "But Mr. Copper did most of his work here. Cataloguin' and figurin' out how it all works, and that sort of thing."

"Who's laboratory is this?"

"Well," Dunnigan said, stepping back. "That's a little complicated, see—"

"My God," she said, realization hitting her in a bolt. "I

understand, now. How Mr. Eddington is trying to make money. These devices—what do they have in common?"

"All of them could make history," a voice said. "Revolutionize the industry." A low and threatening chuckle followed. "Annihilate the competition."

Snips turned; Mr. Eddington was approaching from the back of the room, dressed sharply in a suit and bow-tie. He held a pistol in his hand and wore a grin on his face; by the way his eyes gleamed, Snips could tell this was not a social call.

"Er, Mr. Eddington," Dunnigan began, stepping back. "Sorry, sir, she popped in without me knowin' about it. I was just showin' her out—"

"Silence, Mr. McGee."

Dunnigan stiffened.

"I'm here on official business," Snips began.

"None of that, now," Mr. Eddington said, gesturing with the pistol. "Hands over your head. Nothing clever, Miss Snips. I've done a little research on you since our last meeting—I know all about the duck incident."

Snips grimaced. "I am never going to live that one down, am I?"

"Mr. Eddington, the gun ain't necessary," Dunnigan said. "Come on, now."

"Mr. McGee, I told you to to be silent. If you value your occupation, you will take my advice." Mr. Eddington responded. "Miss Snips is an intruder, and must be dealt with properly."

"In case you weren't paying attention, Dunnigan, that means murder," Snips said. She stepped back and lifted her arms.

"Let's all just calm down," Dunnigan said. "We can have a spot of tea, I've got a kettle brewing over there in the back. I'm sure if we all sit down and 'ave ourselves a bit of a talk, it'll all be a lot more clear."

"I have to admit," Snips said. "You've got quite the clever operation here. I never figured you for an extortionist, though."

"It pains me to be associated with a lowly crime. Extortion is such a common word." Mr. Eddington said, pistol aimed steadily at Snips' heart. "After all, I am no common thief."

Snips took yet another step back. "You inherit the Steamwork from Daffodil over a decade ago. Great, but just one problem—you can't keep the business floating on your own because no one's brilliant enough to continue his work. But then you come across this little treasure trove. An entire laboratory stuffed full of his brilliance."

"I admit, my first idea was to sell it all," Mr. Eddington said. "I could have made a small but tidy profit, then tossed the Steamwork aside like the empty shell it is."

"But you thought bigger," Snips said. "You realized that inventions aren't where the money is—it's in the patents."

"Precisely, Miss Snips," Mr. Eddington said, grinning. "My. You are clever for your sex. I patented all the technology around his inventions, then proceeded to call a meeting between several heads of business. I showed them my little discovery, and made the new arrangement clear: They would either pay me a considerable yearly stipend, or I would sell the technology to their competitors."

"And Copper's role? I assume he was the one who figured out how all the inventions worked," Snips said.

"Exactly."

"How do you stop other people from just inventing this stuff on their own, though?"

"Oh, they're free to invent it on their own," Mr. Eddington agreed. "And quite a few have. But in each case, I have used my patents to sue them into destitution."

"You've been trying to create a monopoly on ideas. You're suppressing scientific progress in the name of your profit margins," Snips said, eyes narrowing. She had nearly reached one of the display cases.

"But sadly, the well has started to go dry," Mr. Eddington said. "Many of the businesses I've been extorting have either diversified or found ways to deal with the competition on their own. For the past half decade, my profits have been going to the proverbial outhouse—which means I've been forced to find another source for my profits."

"The calculation engine. Let me guess: You're responsible for the attacks on the banks. You're Professor Hemlock," Snips said.

"Not quite," Mr. Eddington laughed. "Although I suppose that's close enough. How fortunate it was that I came across the scion of the Daffodil legacy—and he proved to be as ingenius as his father!"

"And when Copper managed to figure out how to make calculation engines communicate with one another via electrical wiring—and proposed a bank model that threatened yours—"

"Eh?" A moment of confusion flickered over Mr. Eddington's face. "Copper had a new bank model?"

Snips seized the moment. She brought her elbow down hard against the glass of the display case, grimacing at the pain that bolted up through her arm as the pane shattered. In a moment, she had plucked up the weapon inside; it was an odd affair, being slender and elegant and yet bulging out at peculiar places; entirely encased in iron, it was far heavier than it had any right to be. The barrel looked as if it had been built from an elegant candlestick, with all manner of electric coils, wires, and glass bulbs protruding from the back half.

Snips ducked behind the case, hefted the gun up, and pulled the trigger. At once, it growled to life—and a gear-driven butter knife popped out, desperately trying to slather butter into the air.

Snips blinked and turned the gun about in her hand, staring at it in confusion. Mr. Eddington chuckled.

"What a ridiculous note to die on," he said, then lifted his gun to fire.

Dunnigan brought the kettle of scalding tea down like a hammer across the top of Mr. Eddington's head, throwing him forward. Mr. Eddington had precisely the amount of time it takes to say 'ungh' before he slammed face-first on the floor.

Dunnigan threw the kettle aside, disgusted. Snips peeked out from behind the case, shuffled to her feet, and walked over.

"Dunnigan—"

"Consider this my letter of resignation, you rat-faced scum-sucker," Dunnigan said, spitting down at Mr. Eddington.

"Dunnigan," Snips repeated. "Could you go fetch me a length of rope?"

~*~

"The umbrella in your lobby," William said, settling in the chair. "I have one just like it. I—" He suddenly realized that he had left it at Detective Watts' house. "I don't have it on me now, but I recognized it when I visited here prior."

"Yes," Nigel said. "It was your father's, wasn't it?"

William accepted the second cup of tea that Starkweather offered. "Yes. It's all I have of him, really."

"A shame. Your father was a brilliant man."

"A terrible man," William added, then blushed. "I mean, that's what I've been told."

"Of course. That is what most people have been led to believe."

"You would claim otherwise?"

"I would," Nigel said, as Starkweather laid out a cup of tea on the nightstand besides him. "A grievous one. Your parents' story is not a tale of villainy, but one of tragedy."

"They nearly destroyed the city," William said. "I mean—didn't they?"

"In a roundabout way, I suppose they did," Nigel admitted. "But they were victims of circumstances beyond their control."

"Could you—could you possibly tell me more?" William asked.

"Yes, of course, of course. But first, answer me this: How have you come to know my daughter?"

"Your daughter? You mean—Miss Snips?" William blinked. "She's *your* daughter?"

"Yes, although she would likely be loath to admit it," Nigel said. "We have not always gotten along, her and I."

"Well, she seems quite sociable to me," William said.

Nigel's lipless mouth twisted into a smile. "Oh, yes," he said, stifling his chuckle. "Very sociable."

~*~

Timothy Eddington awoke to the feel of cold iron and the glint of a silver tooth.

"Comfy, Timmy?" Snips asked, grinning. "Nothing chafing?"

Eddington jerked with a start; he was wrapped in great lengths of chain linked together by a sturdy padlock. The entire ensemble had been latched atop a pulley that kept him suspended upside down above the massive calculation engine he had helped design. The workers had all gone home for the night; there was only him and Snips.

The engine roared to life; gears ground and cogs growled. Snips had a dreadful sort of look on her face—the sort of hungry stare that Eddington had seen on William when he was deeply immersed in some difficult equation. At that moment, Mr. Eddington knew precisely how a math problem felt when it was about to be completed

Mr. Eddington swallowed. "My nose itches."

Snips leaned forward, scratching the tip of his nose. "I bet you're wondering why you're hanging over the calculation engine," she said.

"The question might have occurred to me," he admitted.

"Are you familiar with the concept of Pi, Mr. Eddington?"

"Yes," Mr. Eddington said, speaking over the engine's constant hum. "I believe I am."

"Well, just for fun, I've set the engine to figuring out Pi to it's final digit."

"That's, er, impossible."

"Is it? I must confess, I've never been very good with maths," Snips said. "But I'm curious to see whether or not adding you to the equation might help us find out if that's true."

Snips tugged the chain that held him aloft in the air. Mr. Eddington inched towards the grinding gears. Swallowing, he stiffened. "I don't suppose there's any way I could dissuade your, ah, mathematical curiosity?"

"Maybe if you satisfy some other curiosities in exchange," Snips said. "Answer my other questions, and I won't indulge. Clear?"

"Crystal," he said.

"Copper. Why did you kill him?"

"I didn't."

Snips twisted the chain and let some of it spool between her fingers. The pulley rattled as he dropped an inch or two. "Oh, come on now, Mr. Eddington. Let's be friends here, hm? Go ahead and spill the beans. You can trust me. I'm great at keeping secrets."

"I didn't kill him!" Mr. Eddington shouted, his face growing red with fear and frustration.

"Then who? One of your minions? A business partner?"

"I don't know!"

Snips let the chain slip further. Mr. Eddington could feel the vibrations of the engine's calculations traveling up through the catwalk, down through the chain—all the way down to his teeth. They chattered with stark terror.

"Please! Oh, God! I've killed men before, but not him! Not him!"

Snips gave the chain a harsh pull, reeling Mr. Eddington up. "Wait, what?"

Gasping and wriggling, Eddington fought for words. "I'm telling you the truth! I've killed men in the past, but not Mr. Copper. I had no reason to! He analyzed the technology, figured it out, but even if he wanted to, he couldn't do anything with it! He could never find the funding for the inventions. Every business man in the city would refuse to provide funding for his work, and even if he did find one, we'd drive him out of business."

"Then who killed him?"

"I told you, I don't know! It must have been the fellow in the jackal mask!"

Snips released the chain.

Eddington screamed as he descended down a good six feet; the chain jerked hard as his head dangled only inches away from a furiously churning cog. He could smell the grease, even *feel* the heat of friction rising up in great swelling waves. "Oh, oh God—"

Snips' voice had changed now; gone was the jovial charm and playfulness. Replacing it was nothing but frost and murder.

"Jackal," she said. "With a butterfly."

"Y-yes!" He stammered. "A butterfly pin made of paper!" She hauled Mr. Eddington back up until the red-faced administrator was eye-level with her. "Tell me everything," she said. "Starting with the Hemlock Initiative."

Mr. Eddington gulped. "You—you must know that this is illegal! You are committing a crime!"

"Oh sweet mercies, am I?" Snips asked. "Do you think they'll lock me up in prison?"

Realizing the futility of his tactics, Mr. Eddington started to speak rapidly. "The fellow in the mask gave me equations to use against the banks—a list of formulae that, when inputted into a calculating engine, causes a chain reaction leading to a break down."

"So you've been posing as Professor Hemlock, attacking banks and generating a need for your new and improved calculating engines," Snips said. "But how do you get the banks to input your equations in their engines? It's not like you can just walk up and jam the numbers in. Banks guard those things like their private vaults."

Mr. Eddington panted. "The jackal-masked fellow devised a way to open accounts at different banks using very specific instructions that will, when those accounts are inputted into the engines, reproduce the circumstances that lead to an illegal operation."

"So you've been making a bunch of dummy accounts in these banks, creating ticking mathematical time bombs," Snips said. "You then throw out some bogus message about Hemlock doing it for whatever reason, throwing the police off your trail."

"Y-yes. Now, if you'd please—as you can see, I'm merely a pawn in this whole affair—"

"I have more questions," Snips said, eyes narrowing.

"If I answer, will you l-let me live?"

"I'll take your request under consideration," Snips said.

~*~

ACT 3

~*~

"Nothing in the history of Aberwick has captured the city's fear and imagination as intently as that of the Lost Hour. Ten years ago, our fundamental understanding of the universe violently changed.

In that moment, a quarter of the city disappeared beneath a wave of fire and brimstone; thousands outside of the blast radius disappeared, while thousands more found themselves in a place they did not remember traveling to. And perhaps most inexplicably, men and women across the world realized that approximately an hour's worth of time had been forever lost.

What transpired on that day remains an enigma; all we know for certain is that at the event's center lay the mysterious experiment conducted by Jeremiah and Abigail Daffodil, and—for better or worse—they are the cause and reason behind 'The Lost Hour'."

—Page 136 of A History of the Isle, by Count Vladimere von Orwick

~*~

CHAPTER 21: IN WHICH MR. ARCANUM DISCUSSES THE DAFFODIL SCION, AND THE ASSASSIN MAKES HIS MOVE

~*~

"William Daffodil," Nigel said, thinking out loud long after his guest had left. "How absolutely fascinating."

Starkweather gathered up the remaining teacups, piling them on a tray. "Did you not tell me you were responsible for saving the boy's life a little over a decade ago?"

"More or less," Nigel agreed. "I am surprised I did not recognize him immediately. He's grown to resemble his father, although he is far more meek."

"He struck me as quite scared," Starkweather observed. "You would do well to treat him gently."

"Yes," Nigel agreed. "Terror describes him aptly, I think. Most men are valiant out of ignorance; they have blinded themselves to reality, believing that the universe shall reward their virtue."

"And he is different?" Starkweather asked.

"Quite," Nigel said. "He clearly understands that the world is best compared to an indifferent storm; one which dooms the virtuous man even as it delivers his villainous brother to a safe and familiar shore."

"And as for his concern over your daughter—"

"Oh, yes," Nigel said. "He is quite obviously smitten with her. Very inconvenient, all things considered."

"For you, Master Arcanum?"

"No. For him," Nigel said. "My daughter loves only two things—the city of Aberwick and herself. And I daresay there is precious little room in her heart for the latter. She is more likely to treat him like a pet than a suitor."

"What shall you do? You told him so little of the truth."

"I will watch him, of course. I owe his father and mother a debt that cannot be repaid," Nigel said. "Perhaps, through him, I can acquire some small means of atonement."

"And you wonder why your daughter loathes you."

"I beg your pardon, Mr. Starkweather?"

"You use those around you as tokens in your ongoing battle against the universe," said Starkweather. "You see the world as a challenge, and all of its inhabitants as your instruments."

"And what is wrong with that?" Nigel asked. "So long as you are good at what you do, and do not sacrifice your pieces fruitlessly?"

Starkweather shook his head. "Life is more consequential than moving pieces on a game, Master Arcanum."

~*~

William's home was the saddest shade of blue he had ever known; it sat in a lonely niche among the upper ward, with white trim lacing that run across the edges of the roofs and domed windows. Although it looked like it hadn't seen a repairman's hammer for years, it still managed to look quite stately among its cohorts, resembling an unmarried duchess dressed in splendid but fading attire, maintaining her dignity despite the scorn of her peers.

The house had been in his family for over a century. He had considered selling it, but had never found the heart to do it; his grandmother loved it, and he still nursed a secret hope that one day she would be able to return.

William stepped inside, stomping his feet down on the welcome mat. The interior of the house resembled a museum more than a place where someone lived; furniture that had not seen use for decades gathered thick layers of dust, with expensive-looking relics and pieces of china preserved under glass like fossils on display. Every so often, there was a hint that someone actually lived here—a teacup out of place, a folded newspaper here, some spare crumbs lining the edge of one table—but for the most part, the entire home seemed to be frozen in another time.

William pondered and sorted over all the information that Mr. Arcanum had revealed to him. There was a great deal to think over, but he was slowly discovering a much different story concerning his parents then he had originally believed—a story that William was intensely interested in learning.

He was thinking over what he should do next when he noticed that his grandmother's grand piano was missing.

"Huh?" William peered down at the spot on the floor where it had once been; he could make out the silhouette of the piano where dust had failed to gather. A note had been pinned there. He reached down for it, plucking it off the floor and reading it.

DON'T LOOK UP.

He sprang backward just as the grand piano crashed through the ceiling, sending a swell of broken splinters up in front of him. It hit with a discordant WHANG, exploding in a snap of wires and timber as it hit.

"Agh," William gurgled, falling to the ground and sliding away on his hands and bottom. "Agh!"

"You're not Arcadia," a voice called out from above.

William looked up. Staring down at him from the hole the grand piano had left was a sinister looking gentleman in all black. His head was shaved, and he had a false nose of bronze; his eyes burned with discontent. In his hand was a pistol.

"Um, no, I am not," William said. "You know, that piano was quite expensive—"

"You don't say. You have no idea how long it took me to lug it upstairs," the metal-nosed man said, and then he jumped down.

The man moved like liquid from one container to the next; there was a terrible grace about him, much like a spider descending upon its prey. He seemed to float atop the wreckage of the piano, crouched over it and staring down at William. The pistol was aimed at the floor, but the young mathematician had the sense that the assassin didn't need it to do away with him if he so wished to.

"Arcadia," the man in black said. "Where is she?"

"I, ah, I don't know," William began, swallowing.

"See, that's not a very cooperative answer," the man in black said. "I'm sensing that you just aren't a very cooperative person." The pistol slid up, aiming at William's head. "And I hate uncooperative people."

"I'm very cooperative!" William squeaked. "I'm the most

cooperative person you'll ever meet!"

"Good to know. Arcadia. Where is she?"

"I don't know!"

There was a terrible bang.

The pistol flew from the assassin's grip, knocked aside by a bullet. Miss Primrose stood at William's doorway, a smoldering pistol held in one hand; hooked over the crook of her arm was William's umbrella.

The assassin looked from his empty hand to Miss Primrose. "Nice shot."

"I came to return your umbrella, Mr. Daffodil," Miss Primrose said. "You seem to have forgotten it. I assume that this gentleman is not a friend of yours."

"No," William said, scrambling to his feet and making his way towards her. "He most certainly isn't, Miss Primrose. He seems to be after Miss Snips."

"Is that so. I wonder why?"

The assassin smiled. "Old friend. Met her back in boarding school. Just want to share a cup of tea with her, talk about old times. That sort of thing."

"Really, now," Miss Primrose said.

The assassin was fast. *Bloody* fast, William realized; in an instant, he was moving. Miss Primrose squeezed off a second shot, but by then the assassin was halfway across the room and drawing another pistol. William snagged the umbrella out from under Miss Primrose's arm and threw it open, hurling it in front of them both.

Both of the assassin's shots glanced off the umbrella's reinforced iron canopy; William edged back with Miss Primrose towards the doorway.

"Not bad," the assassin lazily remarked. He slipped to their side like a grease-slathered peel, flanking them both; at once, he produced a wickedly hooked knife and brought it down to for a blow meant to hook straight into William's heart.

The blade made a 'clang'.

"Clang?" The assassin said, confused. "Meat doesn't cl—"

William snapped the umbrella shut and swung it around like a sledge-hammer, meeting the assassin's chest. There was a loud snapping sound as the man in black was catapulted to the far wall, tumbling over the shattered remnants of the piano. William quickly opened his umbrella back up and held it in front of a perplexed Miss Primrose, urging her out the exit.

As they reached it, a small glass sphere rolled toward them. The device had several chemical mixtures inside of it, all separated by a thin wafer of metal with an attached pin; the assassin had already withdrawn the pin several moments ago, allowing the chemicals to mix in a volatile rainbow of colors.

"Oh, fiddlesticks," Miss Primrose said. She seized William's arm and jerked the umbrella down to aim at the sphere. It shattered with great violence, spraying hot glass in every direction —William felt a bit of it catch his ankle as the fire-retardant umbrella did its best to hold back the ferocity of the blast. They were both thrown back several feet, sending them sprawling on their backs.

The umbrella clattered to the floor. William struggled to get to his feet.

And found himself staring down the barrel of the assassin's pistol.

~*~

CHAPTER 22: IN WHICH MR. EDDINGTON RECEIVES HIS JUST REWARD, OUR TITULAR PROTAGONIST DISCOVERS THE DAFFODIL SCION'S ABDUCTION, AND A GRAND RESCUE IS PROPOSED

~*~

Mr. Eddington awoke to the sound of a gentle sigh, followed by the clink and clatter of chains. He was jerked back into the air, left dangling over the now-inert calculation engine; he struggled to make out the shape of the approaching silhouette that now stood on the catwalk before him.

"Oh, thank goodness," he said.

"Hello, Mr. Eddington," said the jackal.

"What a terrible affair this has been," Mr. Eddington began. "I'm afraid that Miss Snips has managed to figure out quite a bit of our little plot on her own."

"Not all of it, I pray?"

"No, no, not all of it," Mr. Eddington readily agreed. "I left out the crucial bits, or at least as much of it as I could. She thinks *I'm* Professor Hemlock—ha! But she knows that I'm responsible for inputting your bank exploits, at least," he said, shivering. "And she threatened to kill me!"

"Is she aware of our plot to bring the banks crashing down?"

"No, no, not at all," he said. "She thinks that they're just harmless pranks—she's yet to realize our plan to make my engine the *only* engine in all of Aberwick. Now, if you wouldn't mind, my ankles are aching quite a bit and—oh. Oh, dear," Mr. Eddington said, growing quite pale. "Oh my."

"Is something amiss?"

"This is the part where you murder me, isn't it? Tying up loose ends and that sort of nonsense. That's how these things work, isn't it?"

"As perceptive as always, Mr. Eddington," said the jackal.

"My mother was right," Mr. Eddington replied with a sigh. "I should have been a professional hit man."

A gunshot rang out in the basement of the Steamwork.

~*~

It was growing rather late before Snips returned back to Detective Watts' home; she steeled herself for the sound verbal thrashing she'd get at the hands of Miss Primrose. But when she arrived, all thoughts of reluctance evaporated.

"What happened?" Snips asked.

Miss Primrose sat on one of the many chairs in the smoking lounge, grimacing as Mr. Watts finished bandaging her forehead. Soot stains marred her dress, and her left arm looked as if it had suffered some manner of injury.

"Miss Snips," she said, glaring beneath the wrap. "You are tardy."

"Yeah, I had to suspend a guy over a calculating engine. What's going on?"

"An assassin," Detective Watts said, frowning as he snipped the last of the bandages with a pair of scissors.

"One who was apparently sent for you," Miss Primrose added.

Snips blinked. "Well, you're all right, obviously. I assume —"

"Mr. Daffodil is missing," Miss Primrose added.

Snips went as silent as stone.

At that very moment, there was a loud knocking at the (currently collapsed) front door.

Everyone turned their attention to the corridor that lead to the lobby; crouching down over the collapsed doorway was a man in a ridiculous red suit with gold trimming and a leather satchel attached to his side. He looked like he ought to be at the head of a parade, spinning a baton while it was lit on fire.

"Ahem," he said. "Are you—let's see here." He fished a card out of his satchel, reading it carefully. "Are you Miss Arcadia Snips?"

Snips frowned. "Yes."

The man reached deeper into his satchel. Snips, Miss Primrose, and Jacob watched with amazement as he drew out a fez with a gold tassle. As the three of them looked on in silent shock, he put it atop of his head, unfolded a bit of paper, and started to dance and sing:

"Dear Arcadia Snips, the gentleman is in my grips. I'll kill him quite soon, unless you prove to be a loon—and meet at the steepest greet in the Heap."

"Singing telegram," Snips said, grimacing. "We're dealing with a real sociopath here."

"Sounds like a trap," Detective Watts said.

"Oh, it's not a trap, he just wants me to come over for crumpets. Of course it's a trap, you silly git! He's not even bothering to disguise it. I'd have to be a loon to show up, he even said it!"

"So, are you going to?"

Snips sighed. "Of course."

"Very good," Watts said. "I'll get my coat, and we'll—"

"The Heap is dangerous. I'll move faster there if I'm by myself," Snips said.

Detective Watts looked crestfallen. "I see. Well, at the very least," he continued, picking up William's charred umbrella. "Could you return this to the poor lad?"

"Of course." Snips took the umbrella, looked at it cross-eyed, then shoved it through her belt hoop as if it were a sword. "Don't worry. I'll get him back in a jiffy." Snips turned toward the path, but was suddenly blocked by a stern-faced Miss Primrose.

"Right, then," she said. "How shall we arrive?"

"Oh, no," Snips responded, scowling. "You're *definitely* not going."

"I'm afraid I am, Miss Snips. Not only is this my investigation, but seeing William safely home was my responsibility. He was abducted beneath my very nose, as I watched, helpless to do anything—"

"Oh, hush up," Snips said. "This isn't some visit to the local Lord and Lady's dance hall for a fancy cup of tea. We're heading to the Heap, lady. It's the most dangerous place in the entire city."

"I am aware, Miss Snips," she said. "And I am going. William was my responsibility," she added, her voice tense. "I lost him."

Snips and Miss Primrose gave each other hard, long stares. For a moment, the women seemed ready to lock horns; it was Snips who finally relented.

"Fine. But you do as I say, all right? This is your investigation, but the Heap is out of your league," Snips told her. "It's a nasty sort of place, full of nasty sort of people. *My* sort of people."

Grimly, Miss Primrose nodded.

They turned to go; the courier intercepted them, holding out his hand. "Ahem," he said.

"Oh, right," Snips said. "Your tip. Here's one: Get a new job." She darted around the courier and ran down the road with Miss Primrose by her side, heading back toward the Rookery.

"Right then! Ha! I've never heard that one!" The courier shouted after Snips' retreating form. "Completely original, that!"

~*~

Nearly a decade ago, a mysterious explosion had raged through one of the poorest sections of the city, tearing through the cheaply built slums as if they had been little more than oil-soaked kindling. Rather than deal with the rapidly growing inferno, the king at the time had ordered the entire area to be quarantined to prevent the crisis from reaching the upper ward. Walls were erected, bridges were cut off, and leaflets apologizing for the inconvenience were dropped by hot-air balloons.

After a few years, most of the smoke and screaming had come to a stop. The current queen ordered the walls to be torn down and the bridges restored. A celebration was organized. There was to be cake.

But rather than being greeted with flowers and cheers, the soldiers discovered that many of the prior inhabitants were quite miffed about the whole affair, and still held a bit of a grudge. After a decade of fire and isolation, several of them had gone just a little bit mad.

Following an unfortunate incident involving several soldiers, a sausage grinder, and a new-and-improved cake recipe, the queen and her advisers determined that the people inside the district were not yet ready to rejoin society. The walls were re-erected, the bridges re-cut, and new leaflets promising they'd make another go at it in a decade or so (also, this time, there would be proper cake, and not that cheap stuff they tried to foist on the survivors last time) were dropped.

And that was how the smoldering slag known as the Heap came to be.

Nowadays, the Heap was for people who found the occasional presence of a lost policeman in the Rookery to be overbearing. It was a place where the law was whatever you happened to be hollering while holding a very large stick—and it was a place where those skilled in violence could go far. The fact that the assassin lived on its tallest peak did not speak in Snips' and Miss Primrose's favor.

They slipped in through a crack in the wall guarded by men not paid enough to care. At once, the stench seized their noses in a clenched fist and twisted; Miss Primrose retched and even Snips grimaced.

The streets were mostly intact, although the buildings that flanked them were burnt out husks. Even stone buildings had crumbled under the heat of the fire. There was little left but broken glass and the charred skeletons of once-prosperous businesses.

Miss Primrose instinctively drew closer to Snips, who seemed to project a sense of fearlessness into the grim desolation. "My God," she said, not daring to speak over a whisper. "People still live here?"

"Not all of them are people anymore," Snips said. "Stay close."

"To think," she said, looking off towards the distant pillars of smoke that rose from the heart of the Heap. "In some places, the fire still burns."

"More or less," Snips said. "Lots of stories about what

happened that day. Some say it was a gas fire; most people blame Professor Daffodil," she added, sounding rather distant.

"I remember the story, but only vaguely," Miss Primrose confessed. "Something about an experiment gone horribly wrong —"

"A weapon," Snips said. "Meant to end all others."

"And this is the ultimate result."

"If you believe in that sort of thing," she added. "Watch your step. Sometimes, they set traps."

"Hm? Who? And to what end?"

"The survivors here," Snips said. "And for food."

"But what manner of animal would they hope to—oh. Oh, goodness," Miss Primrose said, growing pale with the realization.

"Like I said," Snips explained. "Not people. Not anymore."

Something scurried in the shadows of a nearby building; Miss Primrose gave a jump. "I have a pistol in my medical bag. Perhaps I should fetch it?"

"Relax," Snips said, and then there was a distant howl. "Um. Then again, maybe you should."

Miss Primrose began to reply, but then there was a cacophony of whoops and hollers. A creature sprang from the scorched shingles of a hollowed out tavern and landed in front of them.

The thing was human, or humanoid at least; its dark skin was bare save for a pair of tattered leather chaps, suspenders, and a mud-encrusted shirt. Around its waist and through its hair were tied strings of feather and bones; over the upper half of its face was the stitched together mask of a hound, its eyes flashing behind it like coins catching a fire's glow. On top of the scraggly mane of its hair was a top hat. It landed in a crouch, keeping hunched over as it lifted its head to look at them both. And then it grinned.

Its teeth resembled a platter of steak-knives.

"BOOGEDY BOOGEDY BOO!"

Miss Primrose cried out and leapt back, drawing her pistol from her bag. Snips caught her wrist and pulled it up just as the gun went off, firing a bullet high into the night air.

"Don't scare the tourists, Jack," Snips growled.

Arcadia Snips confronts Jack of the Heap.

Jack laughed; it was a deep and guttural sound, half-choked on razor-sharp teeth. He thrust his head towards the wide-eyed Miss Primrose, sniffing. "Why is my dinner wearing perfume?"

"That's soap, you mutt," Snips fired back. "And she's not your dinner. She's with me. We're here to find a gentleman."

"Oh. Has the fair Lady Snips finally found the dashing knight who can tame her savage heart?" Jack cackled.

Snips glared at him. "As I remember, the last man to try and 'tame' me ended up with six inches of iron in his gut."

Jack smiled. "I still have the scar."

Snips leaned forward, dropping her lashes low and smiling back. "Would you like a matching set?"

"There's more of them!" Miss Primrose cried, pointing her gun frantically around them. Indeed, Snips and Miss Primrose were surrounded; a legion of men and women adorned in tattered clothes and war-paint were rising around them, emerging from behind rubble and rock.

Snips never batted an eye. Jack met her, stare for stare, tooth for tooth. "Why have you intruded on my lands, Lady Snips? This is not your territory."

"A man has kidnapped someone I know," she said. "He's taken him to the highest peak in the Heap. I want him back."

Several of the people drew back. Jack gnashed his teeth. "Him," he snarled, then threw his head back and howled. A few joined him, although none could match his savagery and volume.

"Friend of yours?" Snips asked.

"He came a month ago, claiming the peak for himself. He killed any who came near," Jack growled.

"Sounds charming."

"As always, you have chosen difficult prey, Lady Snips," Jack said. "He will give you trouble."

Miss Primrose had started to calm down, lowering her gun to her side. She directed her attention to Snips. "Who is this man?"

Before Snips could answer, Jack replied. "City-dweller," Jack said, addressing Miss Primrose. "What is your name?"

Miss Primrose narrowed her eyes, holding the pistol at her side. "Miss Maria Primrose," she said.

"Lady Primrose," Jack said, bowing with mocking reverence. "Pray tell, such a dashing, handsome damsel! Might you consider allowing me to court such a ravishing beauty?"

Miss Primrose hmphed. "I have absolutely no interest in matrimony," she said. "Besides, I am fairly certain that you have fleas."

"Ease off on her, mutt," Snips replied. "As for our problem, I just need a half-decent air balloon. Doesn't need to fly far, just straight. Know where a girl could pick one up this time of night?"

Jack laughed. "The Committee has one."

"The Committee," Snips said, sighing. "It'd have to be them, wouldn't it?"

"I will help you secure your chariot, Lady Snips, but beyond that you must fend for yourself."

"What's your price?"

"Remove the man from my lands," Jack said. "Permanently."

"Done."

Jack threw his head back yet again, laughing and whooping in a display of wolfish jubilation. His followers did much the same, until the street was filled with a furious clamor; when he looked back at Snips, his eyes were gleaming. "A pleasure to hunt with you again, Lady Snips."

"Let's just get this over with," she said.

~*~

CHAPTER 23: IN WHICH WE BRIEFLY RETURN TO THE PAST TO LEARN OF THE DAFFODIL SCION'S CLOCKWORK HEART, THEN DISCOVER THE ASSASSIN'S DREADFUL AMBITION AS WELL AS MEET THE COMMITTEE FOR THE FAIR DISTRIBUTION OF CAKE

~*~

The sound of thunder was nearly enough to blot out the frantic knocking at Nigel's door; bleary-eyed, the doctor threw it open only to find himself confronted by a soaked Jeremiah.

"It's William," he gasped, and then he seized Nigel by the sleeve and drew him out and into the cold rain.

They took the waiting cab to Jeremiah's home, where Abigail sat besides the bedridden boy. William's skin was as pale as the underbelly of a fish, a cold sweat leaving him drenched.

Though otherwise young and healthy, the eleven year old had always had a particularly weak constitution; a quick inspection confirmed Nigel's suspicions. The boy's heart was failing.

Nigel straightened, turning to the husband and wife. "Abigail. Go down the street to Doctor Morganton's house. Tell him it is an emergency, and that Nigel Arcanum requires his surgical instruments immediately."

Abigail nodded. Though flushed with color and worry, the woman still kept her head about her; she darted off at once to carry out Nigel's orders. He turned to Jeremiah, staring at his old friend evenly.

"Nigel," Jeremiah began, swallowing. "Can he be—"

"You were right to come to me," Nigel told him. "Most doctors in this city are little more than butchers. I think that, with your help, I may be able to save him."

"My help?" Jeremiah asked. "But I'm no biologist—"

"You've heard of my experiments in flesh grafting, have

you not?"

"Oh, God," Jeremiah said, shuddering. "You don't propose to—"

"No. I've yet to master the technique; the animals I've experimented on invariably reject the organs and die. Replacing his heart with another heart is not feasible," Nigel said, turning back to the boy. "However, I have something else in mind."

"How can I help?"

"Help me take the boy down to your basement," Nigel said. "We will need the instruments of your mother's trade, as well as my own."

~*~

They worked deep into the night and long into the morning; the work was not complete until the afternoon of the next day.

When it was finished, William's color returned. The boy remained asleep, but it was clear from the warmth of his skin and the regularity of his breath that he was on the road to recovery.

But when Abigail finally beheld the fruits of their labor, it was not a sigh of relief that escaped her lips; rather, it was a scream of horror.

"What have you done!?" she cried, beating at Jeremiah with her fists. "What have you done to your son?!"

"There was no other way to save him," Nigel said. "Abigail, please—"

"You've butchered him! My God, you've—"

Jeremiah was as white as a ghost, his eyes dark from lack of sleep. He seized Abigail by the shoulders, holding her still. "Had there been another way to save him, I would have taken it. Were it possible, I would have happily torn out my own heart and given it to him."

Abigail's fury finally began to abate, clutching at Jeremiah's clothes with her fists. Her snarls melted into sobs, her head pressed to his shoulder as he held her close.

William's chest was bare; over his heart was now a circular plate of bolted iron fused to his flesh. Somewhere beneath it, a mechanical heart regularly ticked—pumping blood with the ceaseless precision of a clock.

~*~

William awoke slowly, drawn from the pleasant oblivion of sleep by the sound of steady clicking. He pulled his lids back, gasping at the sharpness of the light; when his eyes had last adjusted, he began to inspect his surroundings.

The room was built of straight timber, its grain exposed; no clever woodwork or design obscured the planks that enclosed it. A snuffed gas lamp hung from the ceiling, with a plain table beneath it; swirls of languid smoke gathered into choking clouds around it, brushing at the ceiling and walls. The clicking came from a nefarious looking gentleman with a false bronze nose and a shaved head patiently cleaning his pistol. The smoke came from his ebony pipe, cradled between his lips and freshly lit.

Understanding struck William with the force of a lightning bolt. Despite his better judgment, he cried out; his coat had been shorn open, revealing the iron bolted plug that sat over where his heart should have been. He had been bound to a chair, his arms tied behind its frame.

Without so much as looking up, the assassin addressed him. "As a rule, I don't engage in torture. Not that I object to it," he quickly added. "I've simply found that it rarely accomplishes anything. People tell you what you want to hear, not what they actually know."

William swallowed.

"Getting the truth requires a little something special. You have to make someone want to tell you the truth," he explained. "So let's talk about motivation."

The assassin rose, circling him slowly—like a wolf who had scented a wounded animal. "My motivation is simple. I want to know about this," he said, reaching forward to tap the metal socket at William's chest. "I want to know where you got it. I want to understand how it works. I want," he whispered, leaning close, "one of my own."

"You're mad," he said, cowering back.

"You don't quite understand what you have here, do you?" His voice was sheathed in a haze of opium, but beneath it lurked murderous intent. There was not a shred of mercy to be found in his glazed eyes. "If a heart can be replaced with mere gears and cogs, what is to stop us from replacing legs? Or arms, or eyes? Indeed, what is to stop a man from becoming a living automation?"

William shuddered; the man in black laughed.

"Let's discuss your motivation, shall we?"

"I won't help you," he said, forcing himself to act more bravely than he felt. "Under any circumstances," he added. "Threaten my life if you will, but—"

"Threaten your life? Don't be absurd," the assassin replied. "You *are* going to die."

"But—"

"There are two types of funerals, boy. Those with open caskets..." The assassin smiled devilishly. "And those with closed caskets."

~*~

"Who are these people?" Miss Primrose asked in a hushed voice. "How do you know them?"

"Blundered in here when I was just a kid," Snips said, picking her way through the rubble with Miss Primrose trailing behind. "After I ran away from my father. Jack found me. Tried to cook and eat me."

"What?!" Miss Primrose had to strangle her voice, lest she draw the attention of the tribesmen around her. "I mean—I beg your pardon?"

"He always got hung up on me," Snips said. "I don't know why."

"Wait, he did this when you were a child?" Miss Primrose asked. "How old is he?"

"Don't know. Don't think anyone knows," Snips replied. "He's been here ever since the Heap started—and I remember reading something about him being around even before that."

"Who are these people who are following him?"

"I don't know," Snips said. "There's all sorts of people here —beggars, bankers, merchants. I guess some people need to embrace something mad to express themselves."

"If I may interject," a man wearing a strap of hide around his shoulder and waist said, jogging to catch up with the two of them. "I myself joined up because of the exceptional realism in their portrayal of pre-historic man. I'm a huge fan of the era of pre-history—"

"Oh, yes," a woman in war-paint carrying a nasty sort of club agreed. "And, you know, what Jack is doing is absolutely wonderful—rejecting the tyranny of mainstream culture and capitalism—"

"Rejecting mainstream culture? That's not what this is about! It's about authenticity and reverence concerning tribal life —"

"Yes, and his rejection of the evils of an industrial society!" the woman excitedly exclaimed. "To think, we're emulating the very first anarchists—"

"What the blazes are you talking about, woman?" the man shouted. "There wasn't any industry to rebel against! Just rocks! You can't rebel against rocks! This movement is about wearing the right set of clothes—"

"Well," a third member of the group said, "being an archeologist myself, I feel it necessary to point out that prehistoric man never wore a shoulder strap like yours—"

"I think we've started something horrible," Miss Primrose whispered.

"Quiet," Jack hissed, clenching his fist and lifting it high. Everyone present went as silent as the dead. The dog-faced leader of the pack crouched low, grinning back at Snips.

Snips crept forward with Miss Primrose, eyeing the cathedral that lay in a scorched valley beneath them.

"You think these guys are crazy?" Snips asked, throwing a thumb back at the tribesmen. "Wait till you get a load of the Committee."

~*~

The old man was as ancient as the rock that surrounded him, and twice as haggard; his beard was so long it nearly dusted the floor, while his eyes gleamed with all the calculated brilliance of razorblades in an alleyway. When he spoke, the church congregation listened; when he shouted, the congregation whimpered.

"And lo," he said, speaking in a voice that crackled like lightning. "In the beginning, there was only a great and pleasant darkness. And then the skies rumbled, and a voice came. And the voice spake: Let there be light."

The men and women in the congregation cried out in fear. They knew about light, all right; they knew that they wanted nothing to do with it.

The old man gripped the podium, leaning forward with a glare that could wilt dandelions at thirty paces. "And so did the Wicked One seek to lead us astray from the blessed darkness, with low premiums, and special interest rates, and a free toaster for every gas bill paid a month ahead of time—"

The congregation wailed, bemoaning their foolish greed for gas-powered toasters. Arms were thrown into the air as dirty-faced children looked on in absolute confusion.

"—and so did we fall for the Wicked One's honeyed words, and his insidious Platinium Payment Plan, and his free toasters; and so did we allow him to build his wicked gas pipes in our houses, and so did the righteous and mighty Lord smite us for his wickedness—"

The cries reached a wild fury as the congregation rose to their feet. Men wept openly for their sins while women cried and clutched their husbands' shirts, burying their faces into their chests.

"—but so did the Lord promise atonement and salvation for those who remained true to the lack of light. And so did he promise that for the faithful and meek, there would be cake!" the old man roared, pointing at the tattered leaflet that was stapled to the wall.

"Cake!" The cry rose up, pushed on into absolute hysterics;

women fainted while men fell to their knees, tears streaming down their cheeks. "Cake!"

It was at this precise moment that the front doors of the cathedral burst open.

Every member of the crowd turned around to face the girl in the funny hat. And as they donned their expressions of befuddlement, Arcadia Snips cleared her throat.

"Hi," she said, tilting her body to the side and assuming the most innocent expression she could manage. "Did anyone in here order cake? Because I'm here to deliver a truckload of it to someone called 'The Committee for the Fair Distribution of Cake'."

Eyes were widened. Whimpers were suppressed. Men and women rose to their feet.

Snips grinned—and ran like hell.

~*~

As the mob of eager Cake-ites ran after the fleeing Snips, two figures slipped into the cathedral's back room through a shattered window.

"Near here," Jack said, clicking his tongue as he darted on all fours across boxes and crates. Cobwebs grew thick as thieves here; Miss Primrose pressed a hankerchief to her mouth, trying her best to muffle the choking cloud of dust that every step coaxed into the air. The roof of the room was long gone; the stars and moon shone down upon them as they searched for their prize.

"My God," she whispered. "Is this—is this it?"

"Your chariot awaits, Lady Primrose," Jack said, cackling.

~*~

CHAPTER 24: IN WHICH THE CAKE ARRIVES, THE ASSASSIN ATTACKS, AND THE DUCK INCIDENT IS MENTIONED

~*~

Snips stood at the edge of the cliff, wind swirling at her back. The Committee for the Fair Distribution of Cake had cornered her, all of them bristling with an array of savage-looking weapons.

"I'm failing to see any cake," the old man said, standing at the front of the mob. Every so often, his left eyebrow would give a frightful twitch.

"Right. About that. The cake thing, I mean," Snips said, grinning. "Funny story, actually. There isn't any."

"I beg your pardon?"

"There is no cake," she repeated.

"Oh, wait," one of the Cake-ites behind the old man said. "I think I've heard of this before. It's like, you know, one of those zen koans."

"Zen what?" the old man asked, looking over his shoulder.

"It's like a riddle," the Cake-ite said. "You have to try and solve it. Like, if a tree falls in the woods and nobody's around to hear it, does it make a sound?"

"Of course it makes a bloody sound. Why wouldn't it?" the old man shouted, frustrated. "That's a stupid riddle!"

"Well, I think the point is that zen Buddhists are horrible with riddles," the Cake-ite said.

"So if we solve her stupid riddle," the old man said, "we get cake?"

"Or maybe the cake is a metaphor," the Cake-ite said. "Like, you have to reject the cake and all its worldly temptations —"

"And then you get a better cake?" the old man asked, getting impatient.

"That'd be the gist of it, aye."

The reverend turned to face Snips. "Right, then. So, about your stupid riddle."

Snips crept back another step, glancing over her shoulder at the yawning chasm that lay behind her. She caught sight of something, blinked with surprise, and looked back to the mob with a smile stocked full of cheer.

And then she stepped backwards, dropping off the cliff.

The reverend blinked. He looked back at his followers, then back to the cliff. "Well, erm—that was... That was unexpected."

"Huh. Usually, they at least have the courtesy to let us lynch them first," a Cake-ite sniffed disdainfully. "I mean—that's just unprofessional."

"You'd think people would have more courtesy these days," another follower agreed.

And that's when the cake arrived.

The gondola was no more than a puzzle of junk fitted together with wedges of wood and rusty iron; its balloon had been woven from an assortment of fabrics, giving it a lumpy shape. The fact that it flew at all was basis enough for a theory proving the existence of divine intervention.

The balloon itself had once been painted into the likeness of a pig, its paint faded and peeling. On either of its sides were smeared drawings of wings; its front bared the worn-but-still-cheered face of a porcine grin, complete with stubby nose. And on its side was a torn and tattered placard, which read: FREE CAKE!

At once, the Cake-ites fell to their knees. Snips slid down from the top of the balloon where she had landed, dropping in next to Miss Primrose—who was covered in soot and busily feeding fire to the brazier at the airship's center. They exchanged glances, looked back to the Cake-ites below, and then turned their gazes towards their destination—the tallest steep in the Heap.

~*~

The assassin searched the patterns of smoke with his eyes, raking through them like a fortune teller in search of his destiny.

He had picked the highest hill in the Heap for several

reasons, not least of which was the ability to see anyone
approaching it from a good hundred yards away. He had set an
array of traps on all sides in preparation for Snips' ascent; it was
very likely that the poor girl would get herself killed without ever
even reaching the top. And if that didn't work, well...

That's what the rifle was for.

The assassin tore his gaze away from the smoke that
unfolded from his pipe, returning his mind to his perch. He swept
across all sides of the crumbling ruins with the gun's lens,
searching for some sign of the thief in the night. Nothing.

Maybe she was smart enough not to come, he thought.

Despite his dedication to the task at hand, he found his
mind drifting up with the streams of smoke that emerged from his
pipe. More than once, he caught his eyes drifting away from the
telescope and up to the moonlit sky. On one such occasion, he
began to ponder the moon itself, and wonder what kept it afloat.

It was on this occasion that he noticed the distant cloud.

"Bastard," the assassin swore, realizing his mistake. Of
course! Why hadn't he thought of it? His advantage was height and
time; it only made sense that the thief would seek to outdo him.

The assassin stood up and took careful aim at the airship
that was rapidly approaching from beneath the moon.

~*~

The gunshot took them both by surprise. Snips had
assumed the assassin wouldn't bother to look up, preoccupied with
his assumed cleverness in setting the encounter somewhere high;
the fact that she had put the moon directly behind them only
occurred as an afterthought, prompting Snips to curse her own lack
of foresight.

The bullet tore a gaping wound through the balloon's body.
Miss Primrose grasped the rudder and did her best to steer, but the
ship only groaned out a complaint and kept going the way it was
going. They were sinking, and sinking fast—at this rate, they'd be
hitting the spire of rubble somewhere above its center.

Another gunshot rang out. Snips ducked for cover as

another hole appeared; that bullet had come far too close for comfort. The smart move would be to stay low until they landed, then try to scramble for cover.

"When we hit," Snips yelled, "stay low and out of sight. Just look for cover, all right? I'll get William."

Miss Primrose shouted something, but by then it was too late; the airship crashed against the spire with all the grace of an anvil dropping on a pile of manure. Snips had avoided getting herself shot, but now she had to worry about falling—and whatever traps the assassin had no doubt set. Already, Snips could see what looked like a figure descending down the labyrinth of junk, rifle in hand.

Leaving Primrose behind to the cover of the airship, Snips dove behind a half-sunken sofa and pressed her back against it. She closed her eyes and tried to steady herself, pondering over her options.

"Arcadia Snips?" The assassin shouted down. "We haven't formally met. Anyway, in case you're curious, here are my terms: Come out by the count of three and let me shoot you or I'll shoot the boy."

Snips sighed. The direct approach; she had to admire that in a killer. She drew out the length of twine from her pocket, swinging it over the top of her hat.

"Three."

Like water, Snips thought, clenching her teeth. Be like water. She slid the string over her hat, pulling it down and knotting it under her chin.

"Two."

She adjusted the parasol looped through her belt, making sure it wasn't in the way.

"One."

"Soar," she whispered, rushing out in a sprint; before her was the most complicated obstacle course she had ever beheld. It made her days of leaping among the vendors and carts of the Rookery look like child's play. Everywhere she looked, there was a sharp edge to catch her—a rusty hook to snag her. She steeled herself and dove forward, hands reaching out for hard surfaces to latch onto.

She heard the thunder-crack of a rifle; something popped behind her. But she was no longer paying attention to *him*, only the world around her. Like a mad acrobat, she leapt and cavorted among buried ovens and the rusty husks of long-broken bathtubs. She kicked off a shattered cabinet, rolled up and sprang from a bed frame, and ducked between two slabs of concrete arranged in pillars.

Another rifle-shot sounded out somewhere behind her; she vaulted up to one pillar, kicked off it with her foot, then kicked off the next. By then, she was high enough to catch the top of the column with the edge of her fingers. She dragged herself up and leapt into the air, descending down for the next pile.

Directly below and in front of her was the top of the assassin's little house. And sitting on its roof was William, eyes wide, mouth gagged—tied down to a chair.

Snips leapt and landed in front of him, pulling the umbrella out with one hand. Opening it with a snap in hopes that it would ward off the next shot, she darted up to snatch the gag out of William's mouth.

"It's a trap!" he screamed.

It was only then that Snips noticed the abundance of small glass spheres placed in a weighted net beneath the chair. Each one contained two chemicals, separated by a thin wafer of metal; each had an odd looking pin. And tied to each pin was a length of string, which bundled together into a single metal wire that extended from beneath the chair to the distant perch from which the rifle shots were coming...

The metal wire drew back with a snap. At once, every pin was drawn free. The chemicals mixed and fermented into an array of brilliant colors.

"Bloody hell," Snips said.

~*~

The assassin smiled.

He set the rifle aside and rose up from his perch, moving to circle around and make his way towards the smoldering slag where his house had once stood. There remained only one final task; to collect whatever remained of Snips' body and turn it in for his reward.

But as he approached the smoking ruin, he could not help but notice that there was a distinct lack of gruesome body-parts decorating the ground. He glanced high and low, frowning. Had he used too many explosives? He had wanted to make sure, of course; could her remains have been disintegrated?

Something clunked behind him. He turned around, instinctively drawing his pistol—but what he saw left him too startled to pull the trigger.

Snips was floating down from above, clutching the umbrella in both arms, its S-shaped hook jammed underneath the back of William's chair. The boy was currently unconscious, but Snips was very much awake, and staring straight at the assassin. Her hat was missing.

Regaining his composure, he lifted his gun to fire just as she touched ground. She managed to bring the parasol down to deflect the shot, then disappeared with William and the chair beneath a mound of rusty metal. The assassin cursed, stepping back to take measure of the situation.

"Lucky little bugger," he said aloud, addressing Snips. "By the way, do you mind if I call you Miss Arcadia Arcanum?"

Silence greeted him. The assassin smiled.

"Oh, yes, did I forget to mention that I know all about your little secret? The missing scion of the Arcanum estate. Daughter of the great genius, Nigel Arcanum." He crept forward, gun in hand. "So why did you run away from home, hm? Didn't daddy give you enough love?"

Almost there. He leveled the gun towards one side of the mound expectantly, bending his knees and tensing his legs.

Something leapt out the left side of the mound; the assassin had already swiveled and fired before he realized it was just the umbrella. The girl darted out from the opposite side with a speed that took him by surprise, swinging her crowbar around like a jackhammer. It cracked hard against the assassin's forearm, forcing him to drop the pistol.

He spat out a series of curses and darted back, nursing the injured limb. He quickly reached for his second pistol, but before he could even slip it out of his holster, Snips was wearing a smile.

"Oh, *you*," she said, eyes gleaming with recognition. "I remember you."

"Huh?"

Snips lifted her clenched fist to her mouth, rolled open several fingers, and proceeded to produce a single sound:

"*Quack.*"

Jake 'The Beak' Montgomery shrieked like a little girl and started to fire.

~*~

William's recollection of the previous few minutes was groggy at best. Despite this, he was gradually becoming aware of his surroundings. He realized that he was propped up against a wall of rusty bedpans and broken cabinets, listening to the sound of wild gunshots and screaming.

"You!" The assassin shouted somewhere behind him. "It was you! Do you have any idea how long I had to go to *therapy* —"

The chair he had been sitting in had snapped nearly in half; it was a simple matter to slip free of his bindings. He crept around the mound, trying to piece together what was going on. Snips was currently struggling arm-in-arm with the assassin who had captured her previously, a gun held between them; shot after shot flew off into the air.

"Oh, shove it," Snips said, violently head-butting the man in the temple. The second gun tumbled from his grip and into the burning slag nearby.

"I'm going to mount your skull on my wall, you snarky little twit," he hissed.

William caught sight of the pistol that the assassin had previously dropped. He plucked it up, testing its weight in his hand and raising it up to take aim. Still dazed from the concussive force of the explosion, he walked towards the struggling pair.

"William!" Snips cried at the sight of the mathematician. "Get back—"

The assassin used the moment of distraction to slam his elbow into Snips' stomach and send the thief reeling to the ground. At once, he turned and sprang towards William, murder shining in his eyes.

William pulled the trigger.

It refused to budge.

"Typical," the assassin said. He chopped his hand across William's throat; the boy gasped for air as he crumpled to the ground. The gun was plucked from his limp hands and brought to bear on Snips.

Except she was already flying like an arrow, slamming headfirst into the assassin's chest. The gun fell from his hand as he stumbled back, teetering at the side of the mountain. He waved his arms for balance, looking at Snips with wide-eyed shock.

Snips plucked the large revolver from the ground and pulled the trigger in a single, fluid motion.

The bullet darted past the assassin's face, skipping across his left eye; he cried out in anguish as he slapped his hand over the wounded socket. His balance lost, the assassin fell—tumbling tumbling along the side of the mountain. Trap after trap went off, leading to an avalanche of rock and metal.

~*~

CHAPTER 25: IN WHICH WE ONCE AGAIN RETURN TO THE PAST AND DISCOVER THE DAFFODILS' FATE AS WELL AS THE EVENTS THAT LEAD TO THE 'LOST HOUR'

~*~

"You started a war," Jeremiah said.

"Extraordinary problems require extraordinary answers."

"You started a war," Jeremiah repeated, stepping forward. "You used your contacts throughout the Society—throughout the whole damn city—and you started a goddamn war."

"Only a small one, Jeremiah."

"Was that supposed to be a joke? Am I supposed to be laughing?" Jeremiah asked. "Blood will be spilled, Nigel. Over nothing more than a boundary on someone else's map. People will die because of this."

"I fail to see the significance. People die every day," Nigel said. "And it's certainly not as if our country could lose this little conflict."

"That's not the bloody point, and you know it!"

"Really, Jeremiah, you need to consider the broader picture," Nigel told him. "This war will help release some of the pressure—help reduce the severity of the war to come. It may even delay it," he added, "buying us precious time to reconsider our method of attack."

"We can't stop it," Jeremiah said. "Any attempt to do so will only make it worse."

"Obviously, this minor scuffle will not do so. But I refuse to believe that stopping the Great War is impossible," Nigel said. "A decade ago, if I had told you that it was feasible to replace a heart with a machine, you would have called me mad. Do not tell me what can and cannot be done. With determination and genius, anything is possible."

Jeremiah stiffened. "If it weren't for what you did for my boy, Nigel, I swear I'd—"

"What? Turn me into the authorities?" Nigel asked. "On what grounds? I've done nothing but send letters to a few public officials. Or perhaps you'd release information concerning my little social club? Tell the world how it's all a sham? No one of importance would believe you, and the only way to convince them would be to reveal the existence of our probability engine. Which would leave it in the hands of men far more capable of evil."

"Neither Abigail nor I will allow you to use the engine anymore," Jeremiah pointed out. "We won't submit any more data for it. We're both through with it."

"Yes, yes; it doesn't matter. I no longer need your help," Nigel said. "I've learned how to program the original engine myself."

"We'll stop you."

"How? And more importantly, why? You and Abigail made it clear that you are unwilling to do what is necessary to prevent the Great War. I am. I shall take the burden, Jeremiah, and I will bare the consequences. Alone."

"You're insane," Jeremiah said.

"I'm a moral pragmatist, Jeremiah. A few thousand lives are of less value than a few million lives. Can you not see the simplicity of it? One man's life now is not worth a hundred tomorrow."

"Morality is not a matter of simple arithmetic, Nigel!"

"And why not?"

"Because it's murder!" Jeremiah replied. "It's villainy!"

"In an era such as ours," Nigel said, "one must sometimes play the villain to remain a gentleman."

~*~

The probability engine growled angrily beneath the Steamwork as Abigail fed the last equations into it. As it reached the end of the problem's thread, the dials began to spin wildly out of control; a valve hissed inside the machine as it began to choke on the results.

Something gave. A belt snapped; a gear popped. Abigail

shut the engine off, leaving it to splutter with impotence.

"He's sabotaged the engine," Abigail said, voice grim. "It's nothing more than an overglorified adding machine, now. Bloody brilliant, really."

"How?" Jeremiah asked. "No one works with it but us. The vault is locked—no one else can get in. I don't understand how he could—"

"By using his engine," she said. "He set a chain of events in motion that lead to our engine failing to function. But for an effect that specific, he must have been planning this for some time. For a very long time," she added. "Perhaps ever since we realized that the war was coming."

"If he's willing to use the engine to sabotage us," Jeremiah began, shuddering. "The things that one could accomplish with a machine like this—"

"Once we stop him, we should destroy our own," Abigail said. "Back then, we thought it was too much power for one man. We were wrong; it's too much power for any number of men."

"If only we knew what he intended."

"He intends to create a disaster powerful enough to stop the coming war," Abigail stated flatly.

"But how?"

"That I do not know. But it would be best for us to keep William away. He is safe with his grandmother, for now."

"Wait—back then, when Nigel asked you how to stop the war. What were the possibilities you told him?"

"A nation collapsing," she said. "Or perhaps a city disappearing overnight—Jeremiah? Is something wrong?"

Jeremiah's face had gone stark white. "I hadn't even considered it at the time. Such forethought! Such horrible, murderous forethought!"

"What? What is it, Jeremiah?"

"When we replaced William's heart," Jeremiah said. "The only way to power the machine was with my mother's invention—the radium generator. We disassembled it, and I explained its operation to Nigel—some time afterward, I noticed that the blueprints and several key parts that had been left over were

missing. I thought nothing of it at the time, but—my God!"
Abigail's jaw dropped. "He wouldn't—he couldn't—"
"An entire city," Jeremiah said. "Gone, overnight."
"Tens of thousands dead—"
"To save hundreds of thousands more," Jeremiah finished.
"We must find him. We must stop him before it is too late."

~*~

The device resembled a boiler more than a bomb; pipes and
valves protruded from every inch of it, keeping tabs on the reaction
that struggled to escape from deep within its belly. Nigel checked
the readings a third time, nodding in approval.
"Nigel."
He turned; several of the society's initiates stood around
Abigail, watching her warily. One of them opened his mouth to
explain her presence here in the center of the chapter house—
despite Nigel's very specific instructions that he was not to be
disturbed—but Nigel dismissed him with a wave of his hand.
"Madame," Nigel spoke, bowing. "I wish I could say I was
surprised. Is Jeremiah with you?"
"I only have one question," she said, her eyes like steel.
"What you did to William—was it part of your plan? Was it
unnecessary?"
"No," Nigel told her. "It was merely fortunate coincidence."
"Of that I remain unconvinced." Her eyes strayed to the
device as it trembled and shuddered. "I assume, then, that this is
the bomb?"
"A brilliant machine," Nigel said, "both fascinating and
terrifying in design."
"You intend to destroy the city, then."
"Only half," Nigel said. "Only half should be sufficient, if
my calculations are correct. And they always are," he added.
"I have come here to convince you to give up this task,
Nigel. I hoped to appeal to your sense of decency—"
"The stakes are too high for a sense of decency, my dear.
The stakes are too high for anything at all," Nigel said. "If it brings

you some peace of mind, denounce me as a villain, but the actions I take now are wholly necessary. As for you..."

The initiates shifted, stepping forward to surround her. Abigail's eyes narrowed.

"Do not fear, Abigail. You will be spared, as will Jeremiah, if he has the good sense to show up," Nigel said. "I have a dirigible ready to flee the city; the device will detonate shortly, but we will be well out of range."

"Always so bloody analytical," she said. "Always so bloody well thought out. Well, Nigel, there's something you haven't considered—an element you missed."

Nigel gestured to the initiates as they moved to seize her by the shoulders; at once, they stepped back. "Tell me," he said. "Tell me what I have missed. For I would certainly quite like to hear of it."

Abigail smiled grimly. "You forgot who you're dealing with."

Somewhere above them, there was a gentle thrumming; a buzzing that built to a maddening hum. Nigel frowned, looking up.

"We are not scientists, Nigel," she added, and now the hum grew to a steady, throbbing roar.

"What on earth—" Nigel began.

"We are *mad* scientists."

The ceiling of the Society's chapterhouse collapsed inwards as a massive mechanical spider slammed down feet-first directly behind Abigail.

Smoke and dust swirled up in a thick and stifling cloud as the initiates stumbled backward, climbing over one another to get away. Nigel narrowed his eyes and stepped back, trying to pierce the fogging shroud; a figure stood atop the machine, equipped with a dreadful looking device.

"You know," Jeremiah said, hunched over with the weight of the battery strapped to his back, "I've always wanted to do that." Long coils of insulated wires ran up along his arms and to a set of electrified gauntlets. His goggles gleamed brightly in the room's fluttering gas lights.

Abigail leapt to his side, arming herself with a modified

blunderbuss. Rather than having to be manually loaded, the rifle was equipped with a device that used the energy of the gun's shot to snap the next round into place. She swept the weapon's barrel about, squinting one eye to peer down its barrel as she aimed at Nigel.

"Now," she said, "if you would, please kindly disarm your bomb."

"This is absurd," Nigel said. "I've already activated the device. There's nothing left to be done."

"I mean, ever since I was a little kid, I've secretly wanted to crash into someone's secret lair like that. It's a shame I didn't have some clever line at the ready," Jeremiah said.

"Deactivate it," Abigail said. "Now."

"Or what?" Nigel suppressed a laugh. "You will kill me? If a man is willing to kill for something, he damn well better be ready to die for it. And I am."

"Maybe something like, 'so sorry to interrupt, just thought I'd drop in'," Jeremiah continued. "Oh! That's a good one. I must remember that one."

"Darling," Abigail said, sighing. "Focus, please."

"Oh, right." Jeremiah turned his attention to Nigel. "Come on, then. Turn the bloody thing off, eh? You've gone far enough with this nonsense."

"I am afraid I cannot do that," Nigel said.

Jeremiah frowned. "Nigel, please—"

A screeching howl emerged from the bomb; pressure escaped from the vents, spewing out great clouds of steam throughout the room. Nigel dashed to the side, reaching for an antique flintlock mounted on the wall; Abigail cursed and fired in a blaze of flame and pitch, riddling the room with buckshot.

Jeremiah darted forward. An initiate who had yet to flee tried to intercept him, but the engineer backhanded him with a galvanized fist, sending him crashing to the floor; he reached the bomb just as the dials began their wild and frantic spin.

Nigel reached the flintlock, spinning about and taking aim for Jeremiah; Abigail descended upon him in a wild fury, swinging the blunderbuss down as if it were a hatchet. It cracked across the side of his skull, sending him reeling to the floor.

"Jeremiah!" Abigail cried, running to join her husband. "Can you turn it off?"

Jeremiah had thrown the iron gauntlets down and was now studying the valves intently. As he looked up from them, Abigail saw the dark look that passed over his face.

"The only thing that could stop the reaction at this point is another opposite reaction," he said. "And we don't have the tools or the time. It's progressed too far. In only a few minutes—"

"Then we have no choice," Abigail said. She drew his father's invention from her pocket.

"I'll do it," Jeremiah said, reaching for the modified watch; Abigail glared at him and kept the device out of his reach.

"I will do it," she announced.

"But William needs you."

"You can look after him," she said. "Barring that, your mother can help," she said. "And besides, I may be able to return."

"I told you, my father never got the blasted time machine to work right," Jeremiah said. "We have absolutely no idea if either of us can come back. Or if we'll even survive. Or if it'll even work like we think it will," he added.

"We have to do something," she said. "And I refuse to let you do it alone."

"And I refuse to let you do the same."

"Then what shall we do?"

Jeremiah paused. Behind them, the bomb groaned and creaked as the pressure mounted.

"We must do it together," he told her.

At long last, Abigail submitted; she held out the watch to Jeremiah, who took it into his own, drawing her close.

"Hold my waist tightly, Madame," he told her, and then they lifted the pocket watch high above their heads.

And then, all around them, time began to slow to a crawl...

~*~

CHAPTER 26: IN WHICH BREAKFAST IS HAD AND EMOTIONS RUN HIGH

~*~

When Snips finally awoke, she was surprised to find herself in a rather comfortable bed, stashed away in Mr. Watts' manor house. She could tell it was Mr. Watts' manor house because the far wall was missing—instead, she had a lovely view of the distant trees and a sweeping waterfall that flowed down and splashed across the edge where the floor ended.

She blinked groggily and moved to sit up; at once, a blossoming flare of pain erupted in her left side. Deciding to take her body's advice, she dropped back into bed and tried to piece together all that had happened.

Before she got very far, she discovered she was not alone.

"Good morning, Miss Snips," Miss Primrose announced, stepping into the room. She was dressed in a fresh gown, as conservative as ever. However, a new bandage was attached to her forehead and her right arm was in a sling. "I trust you are doing well?"

"Hat," Snips croaked.

"Oh, yes. I forgot," Miss Primrose said, reaching to the front of the bed. Snips' favored hat sat on top of a bedpost; she quickly nudged it over. Snips snatched it up greedily and shoved it on her head.

"What happened?" Snips asked, finding her voice was rough from lack of practice. "How long was I out?"

"Only for the rest of the night," Miss Primrose explained. "You've suffered a few mild injuries, nothing too grievous. Apparently, you had a mild concussion."

"William—" She began. "There was something on his chest. I can't recall the details, but—is he all right?"

"He is," Miss Primrose said, nodding. "It's actually quite an amazing phenomenon, Miss Snips. His heart is a machine."

"Figures," Snips said, and then she laughed, looking down

at herself. Her previous attire was long gone; in its place was one of Miss Primrose's ivory nightgowns. Snips glared furiously as she drew the covers up over it. "Uh, do you have my old clothes?"

"Yes, but they are in a wretched state at the moment," Miss Primrose said. "At the very least, I insist that you allow them to be properly cleaned before wearing them once more."

"Where is William?"

"Downstairs. But please, Miss Snips. Rest. You've been under considerable strain," she said.

Snips closed her eyes, laying back against the pillow. "I didn't get a chance to tell you what I found out last night—"

"Neither did I," Miss Primrose said, looking down at the floor.

"Mr. Eddington didn't kill Copper—"

"Count Orwick has closed the case—"

Both spoke simultaneously; both gave the other a start. When they had calmed down a bit, they explained each other's discoveries in turn; Miss Primrose's realization that Orwick wanted them to continue the case in an unofficial capacity, and Snips' discovery that Eddington was not responsible, but another party was—controlling Mr. Eddington for unknown reasons.

"This man in the jackal mask you mentioned," Miss Primrose said. "Do you know him?"

"No," Snips replied begrudgingly. "But I know the fellows he works for."

"Who?"

"The same ones who probably gave William his mechanical heart," Snips said. "The Society of Distinguished Gentlemen."

"It sounds like some sort of polite book club," Miss Primrose said.

"In a way, that's what it is," Snips said. "But I can assure you, their intentions are anything but polite. Look, I need to speak to William. There are some very important things he needs to know."

"Very well," Miss Primrose said.

~*~

William was enjoying breakfast with Jacob near the docks; although they were immersed in conversation, they both quieted down when Snips limped her way out and towards William. Jacob suddenly excused himself ("A certain matter concerning a certain private who will remain unnamed," he explained), leaving the two alone.

Snips sat down across from William. William cleared his throat and studied his half-eaten plate of eggs.

"Hey," Snips said, flustered.

William looked up. Arcadia was wearing her patchwork hat and a nightgown; somehow, the ensemble managed to make even her look vulnerable. Some long forgotten memory tugged at the corner of his mind, but he dismissed it. "Good morning."

"Morning," Snips said, looking down.

"Thank you for saving my life."

"Uh, no problem," she said, still peering down at her feet. "William?"

"Hm?"

"Can I tell you something—something personal?"

"Certainly."

Snips looked up, meeting William's eyes with her own. "When I was a little girl, I ran away from home. Stupid reasons. I wanted to find my father. I wanted to make it on my own. Kid stuff like that," she said. "After I found him, I ended up on the streets."

"I understand," William said.

"No, you don't," Snips replied. "You think you do, but you don't. A guy like you? The hardest decision you've ever had to make was probably whether to have your eggs fried or poached. Me, I've spent most of my adult life making decisions like whether it's worth bashing a fellow's skull in to avoid getting locked up. You get what I'm saying?"

"No," William said. "I don't."

"I'm not a nice person, William. Oh, I can act the part," she said, "but that's just when the situation lets me. When the decisions are easy. Like, right now, if I wanted to have one of those strips of bacon there—"

"Would you like one?" William asked, holding the plate up.

Snips sighed. "That's what I'm talking about. All I've got to do is ask, and hey, food. But put me in a situation where eating means breaking somebody's nose? And I'll do that too. I just don't want you to get the wrong impression about me, alright? Because you've seen me when I don't have to get nasty, and you might start to think I'm a nice, pleasant sort of person—"

"I don't think you're a nice, pleasant sort of person," William said.

Snips eyed him critically. William smiled meekly.

"I mean, I like you, but I don't like you because you seem to be pleasant," William continued. "I don't know what you've done in your past, but I also know that I do not care. Perhaps that makes me irresponsible and selfish? I do not know. But, for some reason, I feel as if I can trust you. You've given me no reason to believe otherwise."

"That's stupid," Snips said. "You realize how easy I could scam you? Maybe this is all a con."

"Pretend to be good long enough and you may one day succeed in fooling even yourself."

Snips shook her head. "That's silly," she said, but she didn't push the point. Instead, she dropped her eyes down to his chest. "I see you're doing well enough. Not broken, anyway?"

· "No, not at all," William said. "It's functioning quite well."

"Good," she said. "I mean, good that it's still working. Um, so. Do you know where you got it?"

"The heart?" William asked. "My father, I believe, although I never was told the full story; only that my original heart was too weak to carry me."

"William, there are so many things I need to tell you," Snips said. "I know things about him—Professor Daffodil. I didn't say anything before, because I was so thrown off when you mentioned he was your father, and I wasn't sure about you or what you wanted, but—"

William smiled, reaching out to touch the back of Snips' hand. "It's all right. I already know a little bit, at least."

Snips stiffened with surprise. "You—you do?"

"Yes. I know that he worked with your father."

"Wait, what? How do you know that?"

"Your father told me."

Snips drew her arm away with a snap. "He *what*?"

William slid back defensively. "I went to him, yesterday morning. I had seen a copy of my umbrella there, among his trinkets on the shelf, and I wanted to know—"

Snips' voice dropped to a low and forceful hiss. "You spoke to my father? You spoke to him *alone*?"

"Well, yes, you were gone, and I wanted to know more about—"

Snips' arm flew forward with a strength that William didn't even realize she had. At once, she had seized him by the collar and dragged him halfway across the table; fine china tumbled to the dock and clattered along the planks. "Do you have any idea what you did? How much danger you put yourself in? Do you have any concept of who my father is, or what he's capable of? The things he's done?"

William was momentarily cowed by the fierce show of violence; but a fiery indignation flourished in his eyes. "How on earth am I supposed to know anything about him? You didn't even tell me who he was. Besides, he hardly seems like a monster—"

"Don't you dare think of defending him. Not even for an instant," Snips snarled, hurling him back to his chair. William nearly toppled. Snips rose over the table, slamming both hands down atop it. For a moment, she resembled the dragons he had admired in tapestries of old as a boy; William had a notion that streams of smoke would swirl out of her nostrils and she would incinerate him in a blast of flame. "If you knew a fraction of what I did about him—"

William scurried up to his feet. "What? Does he secretly devour babies by moonlight? I imagine someone has to bring them to him and mash them up for his dinner, seeing how he's essentially a mummy now," William snapped back. "If this bothers you so much, then why don't you just tell me the truth instead of shouting at me and treating me like a child?"

"Because you *are* a child," Snips growled. "You run around

and thrust your head into danger at every opportunity. If you're not trying to put out fires, you're getting yourself kidnapped or trying to play hero. What the hell were you even thinking back there, grabbing that gun like that? That assassin could have torn you in two by looking at you funny."

Rather than back down, William roused himself up and slapped his palms on the table right in front of Snips'. "The same thing you were thinking, Miss Snips. I wanted to help."

"And all you managed to do was nearly get me shot," Snips fired back.

William stiffened at that; something about the mathematician seemed to change. Rather than reply, he reached for his hat and umbrella, donning both as he walked off the deck.

Rather than feeling triumphant, Snips deflated to her chair. She watched as William left, then stewed over the remains of his breakfast.

"Bloody hell's bells," she said, sinking her head into her hands.

It was not long before Miss Primrose emerged from the house to join Snips, looking about for William.

"Where did Mr. Daffodil go?" she said.

"Away," Snips said, huffing out a sigh. "Miss Primrose, can I ask you something?"

"Hm?"

"What do you know about men?"

"Only that they are monstrous and inscrutable creatures, best avoided at every opportunity," Miss Primrose said.

"I see," Snips said.

Miss Primrose paused, glancing back over her shoulder towards the distant figure of Jacob Watts. He had extended both of his hands, and was sporting a legion of pigeons on either arm; he seemed to be lecturing them all on the proper conduct of an officer. "Actually," she said, "I am being somewhat unfair."

"Eh?"

"Mr. Watts has always been especially kind, if not necessarily sane," Miss Primrose said. "He took me in and sheltered me when there was absolutely no need to do so, and has always sought to do right for me. In fact, beyond his penchant for madness, I have yet to see a negative quality manifested in the man," she added, before looking back to Snips. "Kind-hearted people are difficult to find. But they do exist."

Snips sat up. "Hm," she said, thinking.

"So," Miss Primrose said, changing the subject. "What do we do now? The case is closed, our primary suspect is no longer one, and our only lead is an odd sort of gentleman's club."

"Now? Now, we solve the case," Snips said, and then she stood. "But first, I've got to go try something different."

"Something different, Miss Snips?"

"Telling the truth," Snips said, walking on after William.

She hadn't gotten three steps before Miss Primrose cleared her throat. "You might consider attempting to tell the truth in something other than a night gown."

"Oh," Snips said, suddenly looking down at herself. "Right."

~*~

CHAPTER 27: IN WHICH OUR TITULAR PROTAGONIST IS ACCUSED OF A CRIME, A BOMB IS DETONATED, AND THE MATTER OF MR. COPPER'S MURDER IS AT LAST ADDRESSED

~*~

Shortly after stepping into the belly of the Steamwork, Snips was seized by several officers dressed in crisp, black uniforms.

"This is nonsense," Snips said. "I wasn't—"

William poked his head out of his workshop, peering across the catwalk. Snips was there, struggling between two of the uniformed men; Mr. McGee and several other police officers were present. Dunnigan didn't look very happy, and Snips was furious.

"I have absolutely no idea what you're talking about!" Snips said.

"She was here, last night," Dunnigan said. "Snuck in—I didn't think she'd actually *hurt* him, officers," the janitor said, shaking his head and looking to the ground. "I thought she was, y'know, just carryin' out a right and proper investigation-"

"There is no official investigation into the Steamwork," one of the officers said.

William climbed up out of the calculation engine, making his way to the platform. As soon as he landed, Snips recognized him; her face brightened. "William!" She said. "Tell these buffoons to unhand me—"

"What on earth is going on?" William asked, trying to look as stern and authoritative as he could manage. It was a rough fit, but the officers seemed to be convinced.

"Mr. Eddington," Dunnigan said, turning around to face William. "They found him, last night. Sorry t'be the bearer of bad news, Mr. Daffodil, but he was murdered."

"Murdered?" William said. "By whom? For what reason?"

"Miss Snips was the last t'see him," Dunnigan said. "Broke

in here last night."

"Miss Snips was with me last night," William said, but then he paused. He hadn't known where Snips was before then; could she have broken into the Steamwork? "Besides, why would she kill Mr. Eddington?"

"We intend to find out," one officer said. "Now, if you'll pardon us, we need to take her back to Count Orwick's train—"

"Susan? You're taking me to Susan?" Snips asked. "Why didn't you say so? He'll clear this up in a jiffy."

"I doubt it," another officer said. "Seeing how his assistant's the one who issued the arrest warrant."

Snips blanched, turning to William. "William, listen—"

William frowned. "Did you break in the Steamwork, Miss Snips?"

"Yes, yes," Snips said, as if that detail was trivial. "Listen, I came here to tell you—"

"Did you kill Mr. Eddington?"

No sooner had the words left William's lips than did he regret them. Though he asked the question softly, its force was sufficient to flatten Snips' will. At first, she stiffened with shock. Then her expression faded to one of muted surrender. She sagged between the two officers, becoming no more than dead weight in their hands.

"No," she said at last. "I didn't."

"I'll fetch Miss Primrose," William said, but Snips shook her head.

"Don't bother," she said, something hard slipping into her voice. "I can handle this myself."

William watched helplessly as they took her away, unsure of what to do.

~*~

Mr. Peabody brought over a flask of sherry and two glasses on a silver tray. The Count gestured for the tray to be put on the lacquered table beside him; he absently poured himself and Mr. Peabody a pair of glasses.

"The matter of this investigation has been troubling me," Orwick said.

"How so, sir?"

"The suddenness of pressure from Parliament and several others to close the case—I am still unaware from what quarter these pressures originated. There must be another player, one who I am not yet aware of," Orwick said. "Someone with considerable clout who could convince several officials in power to oppose me."

"Perhaps they merely opposed the Steamwork's investigation on ideological grounds, sir."

Orwick snorted, sipping from his glass. "Only the young oppose something on ideological grounds, Mr. Peabody. The experienced know better. No, this is the result of some connection I had not foreseen—some link that I am blind to."

"Perhaps Miss Snips, sir?"

"Perhaps," Orwick agreed, taking another sip of sherry. "I had thought I had investigated her thoroughly, but perhaps I have yet to discover the whole picture. I—hn."

"Is something wrong, sir?"

"Quite curious," Orwick said, glancing down at the empty glass. "I am not usually this talkative. And I often have no difficulty feeling my legs," he added, glancing down at his own feet. Suddenly, he found himself slipping to the floor, clambering for a grip on his way down. "I—hn. I think I require a bit of assistance, Mr. Peabody," Orwick said, voice wavering. He looked up and was quite surprised to see his assistant stepping forward, donning what seemed to be the mask of a jackal.

"Having a bit of trouble, sir?" Mr. Peabody said, his voice smothered into a metallic hum. "Need a bit of help, sir? Is there something I can get you? Hm? Perhaps a clue?" He crouched besides Orwick.

"You," Orwick said, his voice dropping off into a whisper. "Poison."

"Oh, quite clever. Did you just figure that out? Very good, sir," Mr. Peabody said.

"Why," Orwick groaned.

"Because the system you have maintained for so long with

your clever bag of tricks is a system doomed to failure, Count Orwick. Because, rather than evolve, it is sometimes better for creatures such as yourself to go extinct. And because in an era such as ours, one must occasionally play the villain to remain a gentleman."

Orwick licked his lips. "Who?" he croaked.

"Who do you think? I have served you faithfully for years —and yet all this time I have been in the service of another. Who can inspire that sort of dedication, that level of loyalty? Who possesses that much foresight? Who else but the Society's true master, Orwick?" Mr. Peabody lowered his face down to the Count's ear.

"Who else but Hemlock?"

Orwick groaned. Mr. Peabody straightened his coat, stood up, and left the Count to die.

~*~

Left confused and perplexed, William returned to the only thing that ever made sense—his work. He was buried elbow deep in purring machinery; a labyrinth of gears and cogs surrounded him on all sides. He sat in a well-cushioned chair that swiveled with his every move, a brass periscope neatly fitted over his eyes. Every so often, he violently heaved his body to the left or right— twisting the entirety of the wheelhouse's clockwork innards with him, swiveling around with the grace of a suspended gyroscope. His fists were clenched around a set of levers, squeezing and tugging them intermittently.

The entire contraption was suspended within the heart of the calculation engine, and served as a way to directly manipulate and observe the furious mathematics that rumbled within it. William had been running the machine and observing its various results by hand; when he at last completed the final calculations, there was a terrible sound.

The engine snarled as gears grinded backwards. Sparks flew; belts snapped. A cog broke free with a metal *twang*, flying over another engineer's head and smashing into a wall. Daffodil seized the panic switch and threw it, bringing the entire machine to a growling halt.

William blinked owlishly, tugging his goggles down around his neck. He searched the dozen or more dials that lay in front of him—moments ago, they had been purring with calculations, displaying an array of values; now all of them had reset back to zero.

"My God," he whispered.

"Mr. Daffodil!" A female's voice called for him over the din of noise. Briefly, he thought it was Snips; he found himself popping out of the wheelhouse with a speed that surprised even himself. When he saw it was Miss Primrose, he was somewhat crestfallen.

"Oh, hullo," he said. "Ah, oh, yes—I was going to go fetch you." William added. "Miss Snips has been arrested. Mr. Eddington was killed last night."

"He—he was?" Miss Primrose grew pale. "You don't think —"

"No," William said, and he felt a pang of regret spear through him. Though Snips was certainly stubborn, she was far from a cold-blooded killer. "No, I think that something else is afoot. But we have another concern. I have made a terrible discovery."

"More terrible than the recent discovery of your employer's demise?"

"The engine," William said. "My calculation engine. It just divided by zero."

Miss Primrose gave him a blank stare. William sighed.

"We've completed entering all the data from all the banks in Aberwick into the engine from a few days prior," William explained. "We don't have all the information in it yet, but we have enough for a dry run, so I ran all of the calculations through it—to the end of today's business hours. And it divided by zero. Every account," he added. "At every bank."

"I do not understand. What is the significance?"

"If these calculations are correct, every bank engine in Aberwick except for this one is due to fail today at the close of business," William said. "All of them are going to divide by zero. All of them are carrying mathematical time-bombs, set to go off today."

"How is that even possible?"

"I do not know," William said.

"Well," Miss Primrose said, moving to give William a hand as he stepped off the deck of the engine. "The banks still have hard copies of all their data, do they not? Certainly, they can merely restore all the information they'll lose."

"The hard copies were kept here, for security reasons," William said. "At Mr. Eddington's insistence. They were confiscated only a minutes ago by Orwick's men, shortly after they had taken Miss Snips away. As evidence," William added, frowning in thought.

"Evidence? Why would bank documents be considered evidence?"

"I do not know," William said. "However—when all of the banks of Aberwick collapse at the end of today's business, the Steamwork's engine will remain the only available source of bank data."

"How fortunate that you have a pipe network connecting you to every bank in the city," Miss Primrose pointed out.

"Quite fortunate," William agreed, and then he paused. "Miss Primrose? Is something wrong?"

The woman had grown quite pale. When she spoke, her voice was trembling: "A thought has just occurred to me, Mr. Daffodil."

"Yes?"

"All of the banks in Aberwick are set to fail today at the end of business hours, yes?"

"Yes, Miss Primrose."

"And all of the hard copies of their data have been secreted away by a dubious government bureaucrat," she added, the quaver growing more pronounced.

"Er, yes," William said. "I don't quite see what you're getting at—"

"And this engine—the engine we are now standing before

—remains the only source of reliable financial information in all of Aberwick," Miss Primrose added.

"Yes, I suppose you are correct—"

She seized William by the arm, pulling him towards the exit. "RUN!"

~*~

The silver pocket watch steadily ticked, slicing time into equal increments. The assassin flipped it closed with a snap and leaned back in his chair, admiring the sight of the city through the curved glass that capped the entire front-end of the luxury train.

He glanced over to Snips. The girl was giving him a rather sullen look, hanging upside down from the ceiling—having heard a great deal concerning her abilities to escape constraints, Mr. Peabody had seen to binding her in a straitjacket and rope, as well as a gag. She resembled a cocoon with only her head poking out from the bottom. On top of this, she had been placed directly above a trap door set to trigger should so much as a mosquito's whisker touch it.

"I want you to know," he told her, "that this isn't about the duck. Or the eye."

"Mmph."

The assassin drew one of his throwing knives out of his coat, tapping the blade's tip against eyepatch that now covered the permanently damaged organ. "Really, all things being equal, I actually like you, Arcadia. I think that, if we had met under different circumstances, we'd get along smashingly."

Snips glared.

The assassin rose to his feet. "When you kill people for a living, you get to be pretty good at getting into a fellow's head. Not that I've got you figured, oh no," he quickly added. "But I can sniff out a thing or two about you."

"Most people," he continued, "think that peace and civility are the standard operating procedure. To them, barbarism is an aberration. People like me—people like you—there's something 'wrong' with us." The knife fluttered from one hand to the other as he approached.

"But we know better, don't we? Civilization is the aberration; peace is the odd man out. We both know the distance between a kind word and a knife in your gut," he said, standing close to her now. "We do what we've got to do so we can eat." The assassin suddenly grinned. "And you know what, Arcadia? I eat *very* well."

"Mr. Montgomery," Mr. Peabody interrupted. "Your services are no longer needed here."

The assassin straightened as Peabody entered the room. He stepped back in deference, wearing a quick scowl. "I'm busy," he said.

"Your business is not my concern," Mr. Peabody said. "Let us not forget that you've failed on your mission. You remain under my payroll by the grace of my employer alone."

"Oh, come off it. It's not like she turned out to be an issue anyway. And besides, you decided you didn't want me to off her —"

"Regardless, you were unaware of this, and failed," Mr. Peabody responded. "Double-check the length of the train. Ensure that there are no stowaways. From this point on, we will not take on so much as a molecule of unnecessary risk."

The assassin scoffed, but obeyed. As he slipped away, Mr. Peabody sighed and sat down besides Snips.

"You must understand," he said, words heavy with regret. "It was never my desire to see anyone hurt."

"Mmph."

"Of course, I have killed. Mr. Copper was not the first, and he has certainly not been the last," Mr. Peabody explained. "Mr. Eddington became a liability. As did Count Orwick himself."

"Mmphmph."

"Yes, Miss Snips. *You* have been a particularly difficult liability," Mr. Peabody said, folding his arms over his chest. "Nevertheless, I am currently under an agreement which prevents me from killing you."

"Mmph."

"If I had known that you were Nigel Arcanum's daughter, I

certainly would not have sent a mere assassin after you. I would have dealt with you personally."

"Mmnphmph."

"Do you know why the Society was originally founded, Miss Snips? I assume you must, being the daughter of one of its most prestigious members." Mr. Peabody stood, walking towards Snips. "You must understand our goal, our burden. We are not monsters, Arcadia. We only wish to save you from yourselves." He removed the gag.

Snips instantly spat at him.

It caught Mr. Peabody between the eyes. He grimaced, withdrawing a handkerchief from his pocket and dabbing at it carefully. "I suppose," he admitted, "that I should have expected that."

"Hat," Snips snarled.

"Oh, yes. Your precious hat." Mr. Peabody turned and walked towards his seat, where the hat lay. "I think I'll keep it. A token of our meeting."

"Fine. Your funeral," Snips said. "Tell me why you killed him."

"Who? I've killed so many," Mr. Peabody said. "You'll have to be specific."

"Copper," Snips said. "Why did you kill Copper?"

"I sent Mr. Montgomery after him because he obstinately refused to allow Professor Daffodil's technology to be suppressed by the Steamwork. He thought it important enough to seek outside investment. He was an idealist; he either would not or could not understand the danger that the technology posed."

"What danger? Banks can send other banks messages, big deal."

"Financial institutions would only be the beginning. In time, his 'telegraph' would spread across borders and even oceans —reducing the distance between all countries of the earth."

"So?"

Mr. Peabody smiled. It was a grim and depressed thing, absent of all pleasure. "What do you think would happen, Miss Snips? What would happen the moment the nations of the world could speak with one another? Do you think all our differences and quibbles would suddenly vanish?"

Snips opened her mouth to reply, but quickly closed it. She knew the answer Daffodil would probably give; some long-winded speech concerning how it would eventually bring the world together and could only ultimately be a good thing. But Snips knew better.

"No. People would just get to argue faster," Snips said. "And louder."

Mr. Peabody's smile grew. "Indeed. Imagine, if you will, a world where war can be declared in an instant—troops deployed on no more than a whimsical tantrum. Imagine a world where the leaders of nations may talk immediately and without delay—and rediscover just how much it is they loathe one another."

"Yet another step toward a great and terrible war," Snips said.

"A war to end all others," he agreed.

"Is that why you let Eddington keep all the technology under the Steamwork? Because he was suppressing it? Because it slowed down progress?"

"Yes. Mr. Eddington proved quite sufficient for this task, although I'm afraid his usefulness is now at an end. The poor fool thought we intended to profit by collapsing every engine but his own; he remained oblivious to our true intentions until the very end. We've found another means to prevent the coming of the Great War," Mr. Peabody said.

Snips narrowed her eyes. "What have you done?"

"We have refined our approach, Miss Snips. Iron and steel may be what governs the present, but in the future it will be mathematics that will make and break nations," Mr. Peabody said. "And we intend to break this one."

"But Hemlock's equations were annoying, not dangerous," Snips said. "Unless—"

"Your assignment to this case forced my hand, Miss Snips. I realized that there was a chance, however small, that you could unearth my plot. Orwick was a dinosaur, but he was brilliant nevertheless; he foresaw your potential success. It is why I sought your demise and consigned both he and my other associates to the dustbins of history—my plan to topple Aberwick's banks had to be quickened."

"But you can't topple a bank in a few days," Snips said. "...can you?"

"Each of my equations that Mr. Eddington so helpfully inserted inside of the banks was part of a grander plot which I intended to unleash in the distant future," Mr. Peabody explained. "However, when I realized that I could be discovered, I merely hastened my pace. My associates inserted 'trigger' account exploits into each of Aberwick's six banks, activating my mathematical time-bombs. By the end of Aberwick's business hours, each and every bank account will be reset to zero."

Snips stared. "You can't be serious. Aberwick is the financial capital of the Isle, Mr. Peabody. If you bring that down..."

"Oh, yes. It will bring about a financial crisis of unheard proportions," Mr. Peabody agreed. "And it will buy the Society a decade—perhaps more—to prepare our plans to prevent the war."

"Governments will collapse. Businesses will fail. People will *starve*," Snips said, barely able to contain her ire.

"All for the greater good, Miss Snips. All to prevent a cataclysm of unspeakable proportions."

Snips grew quiet and morose. Thinking that he had subdued her, Mr. Peabody rose to leave; suddenly, Snips spoke. Her voice had a quiet quality of command to it that gave him pause despite the fact that she was well beyond any possibility of escape.

"Mr. Peabody?"

"Yes, Miss Snips?"

"I want you to know something. I want you to know that I'm going to escape. And I'm going to find you." Snips clenched her teeth. "And then? I'm going to take my hat back."

"I'm sure," Mr. Peabody said, laughing. He picked her hat up, setting it on his head. "I'll even keep it warm for you."

He left Snips to hang.

~*~

CHAPTER 28: IN WHICH A DARING RESCUE IS HATCHED, RAILS ARE PROVEN UNNECESSARY, PIGEONS ARE UNLEASHED, AND MR. CHEEK MAKES A MISTAKE OF THE SECOND TYPE

~*~

Beneath the Steamwork, scraps of heated metal smoldered. The scene was one of devastation. Cracked cogs and smoking gears littered the floor like the shattered remnants of broken tinker toys. Sheets of iron had been bent beneath the concussive force, twisted into gnarled shapes. A choking cloud of suffocating smoke swirled through the chamber.

Miss Primrose stood up from beneath a pile of molten shrapnel.

Her face was covered in soot and her clothes were charred. The sound of the explosion that had ripped through the calculation engine still rang in her ears. She reached down and rummaged in the pile next to her until she found a mop of fair hair. She tangled her fingers into it and seized William by the roots, pulling the spluttering mathematician out of the heap of ash.

William cried out. "What happened?!"

"He destroyed it," Miss Primrose said, sighing. "The villain destroyed it."

"Who?!"

"Who was it who took Miss Snips?" she asked. "Who was it who confiscated all the bank's paperwork?"

"Who else? Count Orwick," William said, and Miss Primrose nodded. "Wait, no," he added, frowning. "He said he worked for Count Orwick, but I never actually saw the Count. I think he called himself—Limebody? Peaman? No, it was—"

"Peabody," Miss Primrose said, shocked.

"Ah! Yes, that's it. It was Mr. Peabody."

"It is over," she said, slumping back against the wall in surrender. "It is all over."

"I don't understand—" William started.

"He outsmarted us," she said. "All of us. Myself, Miss Snips—even Count Orwick, assuming he was not in on it from the start."

"But why? Why would he want to bring all the banks crashing down? "

"Who could know? Perhaps it was some villainous plan involving money," Miss Primrose said. "Perhaps he had some scheme to extort the banks of Aberwick. Or perhaps he's merely mad."

"We need to get Miss Snips—"

"It does not matter," Miss Primrose said, shaking her head. "You stated that Miss Snips was taken by Orwick's men—she is either with them now, or—" Miss Primrose grew pale and sighed. "And if Mr. Peabody is as half as clever as he's shown himself to be, he will be half-way out of the city by now. On top of it all, we have only a few hours before the banks come crashing down. We have lost, Mr. Daffodil."

"We have to do something," William said. "We can notify the banks—"

"I assume that we cannot use your pneumatic pipes in their current state," Miss Primrose said, gesturing to the remains of the pipes; they had been fused shut by the heat of the explosion. "We could not contact more than a few before the close of business hours on foot. And without Orwick's word, they would never believe us."

"There must be something!"

Miss Primrose slumped down. "This is not a penny dreadful, Mr. Daffodil. The clever hero does not think up a last-minute plan to save the day."

"If only we had a way to get about quickly enough," William said. "If only we had some means to move about the city fast enough to notify the banks—"

Someone cleared their throat. William and Miss Primrose turned, finding themselves facing Dunnigan; the old janitor had just emerged from one of the doorways leading into the room, peering at the destruction with a rather perturbed expression.

"All right," Dunnigan said. "First off, I *ain't* cleanin' this up."

"Mr. McGee—"

"Second off, I sure as hell don't know what's goin' on, but I 'eard you sayin' you need a way to get around fast, and I think I might be able to do somethin' for you on that note," he quickly added. "Assumin' you don't mind waiting here while I go fetch you an antique."

~*~

"Explain this to me again," Miss Primrose said. "Specifically, the part about why I am not terrified for my life."

"It's quite simple," William replied, slipping into the strange contraption's seat. "It functions on a principle of balance via motion."

"It is a giant doughnut," Miss Primrose shot back. "A giant doughnut with a steam-engine inside." She eyed the device warily, keeping her distance.

"I don't know where Mr. Dunnigan dug it up, but it seems quite serviceable," William said. "A bit old, but the design is quite sound. I remember testing a machine built on a similar theory some time ago. Hopefully, this one works better."

"Works better?" Miss Primrose asked.

"Well," William began, shrugging. "It was just a small tinker toy I built when I was a little boy. It used the same principle of balance via velocity, using one wheel…"

"What happened to it?"

"Oh, it didn't work."

"I see."

"And caught fire," he added. "And then exploded. But don't worry. This version looks *far* more stable."

Dunnigan had rolled the monocycle up from somewhere deep in the Steamwork's storage. It sat at the Steamwork's front entrance, still wearing a fresh layer of grit. The whole thing looked like some sort of engineering impossibility; William sat in the driver's seat, a scarf around his neck and his goggles dangling below his throat.

"It is as if its creator designed it with the explicit purpose of crashing," Miss Primrose said. "It has only *one* wheel. Why not three, or at least two? Did he have something against wheels?"

"Stop complaining," William said. "It will work! Just get on."

"But how will this stop the banks from going bottom up?"

William held up a sheet of folded paper. "I've written a little something that will cause their calculation engines to choke on numbers—it isn't a permanent solution, but it will stall the engines long enough to prevent their accounts from being wiped. However, we do have one problem."

"One problem? You believe we have *one* problem?"

"Though I think this invention is fast enough to deliver this note to all of Aberwick's banks or catch up with Count Orwick's train, I doubt it is fast enough to do both," William said. "I'll drop you off along the way, and you'll have to deliver the account exploit to as many banks as you can while I go after Miss Snips."

Miss Primrose frowned. "Miss Snips may not still be alive —"

"Maybe not. But I must try, Miss Primrose."

Something drew Miss Primrose's attention skyward. The explosion that had ripped through the basement of the Steamwork had cracked open yet another hole in its roof; a shaft of sunlight spilled down atop a filthy pigeon that had fluttered in to perch atop a piece of twisted iron. Slowly, a thought began to gestate.

"Perhaps we can do both, Mr. Daffodil. Can we make one stop on our way to Miss Snips' train?"

"If it isn't too far," William agreed.

"It is not. I will explain on the way," she said.

The machine rumbled to life; Miss Primrose grimaced and prepared herself for imminent destruction. But as William leaned forward over the levers, another thought occurred to her:

"William? How will we get anywhere if we don't get this miniature train up on the rail?"

William grinned. "Rails?" He reached down, pulling the goggles up over his eyes. "Where we're going, we don't need rails."

He pushed the levers forward. The monocycle's engine gave out a shrill shriek, propelling the two of them up the ramp and out of the Steamwork.

~*~

It was scarcely half an hour after Miss Primrose's epiphany that she arrived at Jacob Watts' doorstep.

The gentleman of leisure was entertaining several of his favored pigeons when the woman stepped forward and handed him the letter. He plucked it out of her hands, opened it with a twist of his knife, listened to her rushed explanation as he perused its contents, and then assumed an expression of grim duty. He watched as she ran off to rejoin William, riding off into the distance.

Only a minute later, he emerged from the back door of his house in full military regalia, complete with an iron spear-headed helmet.

"Gentlemen," he addressed the legions of birds, arms folded neatly behind his back. "It has once again fallen upon our shoulders to serve queen and country." He paused for emphasis, tapping his riding crop against the side of his hip; when several pigeons fluttered with impatience, he continued.

"The burden you have carried in the past has been heavy, and your losses high. The risks are many—there has been an unquestionable increase in feline hostilities, and hawks remain an ever-present threat. Nevertheless, the task set before you is one of utmost importance. Everything we hold dear stands in the balance."

"My fellow countrymen," he said, holding the message high over his head. "Once again, the mail *must go through*."

A hundred or more pigeons began to coo.

"Corporal Squawkers!" Jacob Watts cried. "Ready your men!"

~*~

Mr. Cheek and Mr. Tongue paused in their discussion long enough to throw their eyes railward; they watched as the railway swept out beneath them, the two stalwart thugs manning the back of the train. What they saw there was odd enough to give them both meaning for pause; after all, it wasn't every day that you saw a steam-driven monocycle riding up the rail.

"Ughungh."

"Aye," Mr. Cheek agreed, narrowing his one good eye. "I agree. This is a most troublesome bleedin' development."

"Ughunuhgh?"

"Naw, I doubt they'd be that bleedin' stupid," Mr. Cheek said. "How the bleedin' hells do they figure to get on the bleedin' train, anyway?"

"Ughungh."

"Huh. Aye, I suppose it is a little bleedin' strange that they haven't slowed the bleedin' hell down—"

The window exploded inwards, sending a shower of glass through the room. The monocycle's wheel shrieked across the cabin's floor, snarling as William brought it to a screeching halt; Mr. Tongue and Mr. Cheek were sent catapulting to the far wall, cracking hard against it.

As soon as the engine was idling, William proceeded to roar. "Oh *yes!* In your *face*, gravity! Oh, dear, I cannot believe I just did that. Did anyone see that? I hope someone saw that, because that was probably the maddest thing anyone has ever successfully done in the whole history of successful madness—"

"Enough," Miss Primrose exclaimed, cutting him off. She stepped off the monocycle, still shaking. "I do hope you'll show a bit more sense in the future, William. That was a rather foolhardy stunt to pull."

"Oh, *come on!* Did you see what I just did?" William asked.

"We have company," Miss Primrose noted.

William turned; Mr. Tongue and Mr. Cheek now loomed over them both, eyes narrowed, freshly bruised and peppered with cuts from the spray of glass.

"Unguh," Mr. Tongue said.

"I agree," said Mr. Cheek, cracking his bolted neck to the side. "A bleedin' pair of punchin' bags. Just what we need."

"Gentlemen," Miss Primrose began. "I beg you to listen to reason. We are here to save a dear friend, and there is absolutely no need for any gratuitous displays of violence—"

"Ughungh!"

"Aye, she's a noisy suffragette, ain't she?" Mr. Cheek agreed.

Miss Primrose's expression wavered. "I beg your pardon?"

"My bleedin' associate here," Mr. Cheek explained, "Was just mentionin' how he can't stand loudmouth suffragettes. Such as yerself."

Deep beneath the layers of the brain that concern themselves with rational thought and what color tie would go best with that shirt, there exists a primordial knot of nerve endings that would be best described as a shiny button labeled 'PANIC'. The tone Miss Primrose used drilled straight down to that button and perched atop of it with an impressive looking sledge hammer.

"Would you care to describe your view on woman's suffrage in detail, sir?" she said, her voice low and dreadfully quiet.

Sensing danger, William took a large step backward.

"You mean women gettin' to vote?" Mr. Cheek asked, oblivious to the danger. "It's th'most absurd bleedin' notion I ever 'eard of. Like a girl could ever make a rational bleedin' decision—"

Miss Primrose cracked her knuckles.

~*~

CHAPTER 29: IN WHICH CALCULATION ENGINES STALL, OUR TITULAR PROTAGONIST PERFORMS A DARING FEAT, AND MISS PRIMROSE FACES A MOST DAUNTING FOE

~*~

Those few denizens of Aberwick who bothered to look skyward were greeted by a perplexing sight—a horde of courier pigeons were swooping down across the city, each one with their own spiked helmet and several medals pasted to their chests. Each flew through the cityscape, fluttering past pipes and railways as they carried their messages in small cigarette-shaped packages fastened to their legs.

When the first pigeon arrived, it was met with a combination of surprise and disbelief—the pigeon coop at the Eastern Crown Bank hadn't been used for over a year. But the employee who noticed the scarred little soldier tapping at the doorway recognized the seal as that of Jacob Watts—a highly respected and valued client. The message was rushed to the front desk immediately, and despite the rather odd nature of the requested account, it was entered into the engine without delay.

And so this scenario was repeated, again and again.

~*~

Snips rolled her shoulders back with a wretched pop; she closed her eyes and wriggled about like a snake working to escape from its skin.

She lurched back and forth, swinging herself over the trapdoor below her; every twist of her body threw her closer to its edge as she began to ease herself out of the last of her bindings.

When she finally managed to slip the straitjacket off over her head, she had enough momentum to fling it beyond the trap door and to the side of the room. By then, it was a simple matter to reach up and untie the bindings around her ankles, swinging her way over the trap and down to the train's carpet. She grimaced as she slammed each shoulder against the wall in turn, popping the joints back into their sockets.

Just as she was rubbing the soreness out of one shoulder, the door to the compartment burst open.

Mr. Tongue and Mr. Cheek rushed in, looking as if they had just seen a ghost. Both were sporting an array of fresh bruises, their suits ragged and torn; they scrambled across the floor towards Snips, throwing terrified glances back over their shoulders.

"Hey, you two," Snips began. "You don't know where Mr. Peabody is, do you?"

"Quickly," Mr. Cheek snarled. "What are your bleedin' views on women's suffrage?"

"Huh? You mean the right to vote?" Snips blinked. "What do I care? I'm a felon. I can't vote."

"Bleedin' perfect," Mr. Cheek said with a grin. He and his companion moved with a newfound confidence, stepping forward to where Snips had been dangling.

Snips reached forward to one of the lockers besides her and plucked out a packed parachute. She threw it to Mr. Cheek, who caught it with a bewildered blink.

"Hope you boys know how to share," Snips said, before stomping down on the trap door and stepping back.

~*~

"Mr. Caddleberry?"

The bank manager sighed, glaring at the secretary. "What is it? I'm busy with—"

"There's a problem with the calculation engine," she said.

At once, all other issues were dismissed; the threat of another attack at the hands of Professor Hemlock had every bank in the city on high alert. He marched straight down into the basement, shoving his way past the engineers and accountants who were scratching their heads in puzzlement.

The bank's engine occupied a relatively large space; the lumbering monstrosity was nearly the size of a house, churning and rumbling as it gnawed over the bank's equations. Mr. Caddleberry instantly scanned the dials on the front panel, eyeing the numbers as they flew past in a series of clicks. "What exactly is the problem?" He asked.

"There seems to be something—something wrong with one of the accounts," one of the mathematicians said.

"Are we under attack?" The thought gave Mr. Caddleberry a terrible fright; he'd have to explain to the creditors why the machine was down for the second time this week. Time was money, and every moment that the calculation engine was down was money lost.

"Oh, God," he said, watching the dials beginning to spin. "Is it—please tell me it isn't dividing by zero."

"No, sir," one of the engineers said, looking quite perplexed. "It's definitely not dividing by zero."

"Thank God."

"It's multiplying by Snips."

"It's—what? What the hell is a Snips?!" Caddleberry shouted.

"I don't know!"

The machine released a sound not unlike a mechanized burp. With an exhausted and dying splutter, it locked down.

~*~

Snips, William, and Miss Primrose met each other between compartments of the train.

"Miss Snips!" William cried. "You're all right—"

"Mr. Peabody isn't that way, I assume," Snips said, hatless and somber.

"No, he is not," Miss Primrose quickly agreed. "William has discovered that the banks are going to—"

"Collapse. I know." Snips looked back over her shoulder to the front-most compartment. "He must be up there."

"The banks are safe," William said. "We took care of it. An equation we entered into the banks will cause the engines will shut down, but the accounts won't be erased. All that's left is to retrieve

Mr. Peabody."

"All right. I'll handle it, then. I don't need anyone slowing me down," Snips replied, turning toward the compartment.

"Miss Snips—" William began.

Steam burst from every side of the train at once. The roof above the front-most compartment snapped off, flying away and tumbling down to the city below. A cloth bag began to swell up over it, growing like a pulsing blister—Miss Primrose and William balked.

"What on earth—" Miss Primrose began.

"An airship!" William cried with surprise. "It's turning into an airship!"

"No," Snips hissed, springing forward and rushing toward the back-end of the compartment.

The cloth bag atop the compartment was growing by leaps and bounds; already, it eclipsed the size of the carriage below it. The wheels beneath the compartment groaned as they detached with a clang, the airship abandoning its own floor; it began to float slowly upwards, curving away from the rails.

"No!" Snips roared, lunging up in an attempt to catch the edge of the floating airship. William jogged up next to her.

They were standing on the front compartment's abandoned floor, the city rushing past them on all sides; the sound of the wind deafened them, forcing them to shout over the noise.

"Miss Snips, we can't reach him—"

"Give me your umbrella," Snips said, her voice cleaving through William's.

"Miss Snips—"

"Now," Snips said.

William hesitated, but complied. He pulled his umbrella out from his belt hoop, handing it over to Snips. She quickly snatched up a length of rope, fastening it about her waist; she tied the other end to the compartment's external railing. Then, she hefted the umbrella high above her head, pointing it at the airship as it rapidly fell behind the train.

William's eyes widened with realization. "Miss Snips, wait —"

"He's got my hat," Snips said. "I'll be right back."
She opened the umbrella and soared.

~*~

Miss Primrose had moved to the back compartment in hopes of finding some way to stop the train; instead, she found a murderer lying in wait.

"Good evening, Madame," the assassin said, slipping out of the shadows behind the compartment door with a mocking bow.

Miss Primrose lost all her color as she turned about to face her aggressor. She knew at once her chances were slim to none; the assassin had previously demonstrated the ability to move through space like a hot buzz-saw through warm butter.

He stepped forward, spreading his hands out apologetically. "I'm afraid I left my pistols in the front compartment," he told her, before folding both hands into a bird, flapping his fingers like wings and whistling. "Gone, gone. So I'm going to have to do this the way God originally intended—bare handed."

"You don't say," Miss Primrose said, stepping back.

The assassin grinned, cracking his knuckles. "Mm."

Miss Primrose licked her lips, putting more distance between herself and the murderer. Her medical bag was behind her feet, stashed in the monocycle; if she could buy herself just a precious few moments, she could retrieve the pistol inside. "I see," she said, mind racing for some plan. "But certainly, you would never stoop to harming a woman," she said; no sooner had these words left her mouth then did she step over the bag, looping her toe through the handle and kicking it up to her hands.

He was there in an instant. The bag was twisted from her grip as if it was a toy in the hands of a small child, followed by a savage head-butt straight to her temple. She staggered back, blinking in a daze. A trickle of blood emerged from the split above her left eyebrow.

He tossed the bag far past her, out the shattered window. "Sorry, sweetheart. That one doesn't work on me. I'm an equal opportunity sociopath."

She scrambled down to the floor for something to fend him off; her fingers coiled around a length of pipe, struggling to bring it between her and him. The assassin snickered, shaking his head.

"Seriously, now," he told her. "You couldn't take me on my worst day, lady." His mirth slipped away, replaced by a frigid hate. "And this? Not my worst day."

Again, he was a blur. He flickered into existence beside her, delivering a blow to her stomach that forced her to drop the pipe and crumple over.

"Really," he told her, throwing her against the wall, "you should be thanking me. I don't discriminate; I'm a very progressive sort of monster. Men, women, children—I'll stomp a basket full of kittens for the right price."

Miss Primrose wheezed; she felt his hand engulf her narrow throat. Struggling to rake in a precious shred of oxygen, she noticed something gleaming inside of his coat.

He opened his mouth to say something else; Miss Primrose wadded up what saliva she could and spat it straight into his one remaining eye.

"Agh!" he cried, losing control for only an instant; only an instant is exactly how much time she needed. Miss Primrose jerked her head forward and bit at his chest, catching a hard bit of metal in her teeth. Pulling back, she thrust her knee into his stomach and shoved him as hard as she could.

The two stumbled apart; the assassin stood in front of the shattered remnants of the window as Miss Primrose ran for the door. Her palm had just wrapped around the knob when something buried itself into the door's surface, landing mere inches from her head.

"Oh," the assassin said, standing up with a cough. "I completely forgot about my throwing knives."

Miss Primrose slowly turned; the assassin produced another knife, giving her a wry smile.

"You made a good run of it," he told her. "Bravo."

Miss Primrose returned his smile with one of her own.

"Eh?" The assassin tilted his head. "Oh, do you have something to say? Some amusing anecdote, perhaps? Please, by all means. I'm in need of some entertainment. But keep in mind," he added, tossing the knife from one hand to the next, "that nothing on the tip of that little tongue will stop this knife from burying itself in your heart."

Miss Primrose spat out the metal pin, letting it clatter to the compartment's floor.

The assassin blinked and looked down to his chest. Several of his explosive glass spheres were still secreted away along the lining of his coat; one of them was now missing its pin.

He looked back up at Miss Primrose.

"By the way," she said. "Has anyone ever mentioned that you look like that Von Grimskull character?"

The assassin scowled. "Oh, do bugger off."

~*~

CHAPTER 30: IN WHICH OUR TITULAR PROTAGONIST FACES THE GRIM ANTAGONIST AND ATTEMPTS TO AVERT DISASTER, AND THE DAFFODIL SCION VISITS A PLACE LOST TO TIME

~*~

Never before had Snips been more thankful for the feel of something solid against her feet.

In the end, the only thing that saved her was a helping of raw, mad luck. Snips swooped between the airship and its balloon, her feet stumbling over the deck. She snapped the umbrella shut just as she slipped out of the rope, rolling to a halt.

She straightened, rose, and turned.

Mr. Peabody stared at her, wearing her hat on top his head. "Has anyone ever told you that you are mad, Miss Snips?"

"Once or twice," Snips said.

"Cease this absurdity," he told her. "I've already seen to the collapse of Aberwick's banks—you're finished. There's nothing left to accomplish."

"Nothing's finished," Snips told him. "William figured out your plan on his own. He's locked the banks down. No one will lose a penny."

Mr. Peabody was immediately seized by a paralyzing shock. "...what?"

"Yeah, you heard me," Snips said, holding out her hand. "Now give me my hat. Before I come over and take it."

"You are bluffing," he said. "There is no way Daffodil could have shut down the calculation engines."

"He entered an equation of his own. They're down, Mr. Peabody. So sorry that we broke your master plan, but it was stupid. Deal with it. Hat, now."

Mr. Peabody's eyes grew dark; his voice was infused with fearful trembling. "No—you idiots! Do you have any idea what you've done? What you've caused? This was the path of *least* harm! All the years I invested—to stem the loss of life that the alternative would bring about!"

"I've heard enough about your war," Snips said.

"I'm not talking about the war," Mr. Peabody snapped, and then he threw a switch.

The airship shuddered; an ancient groan swelled up from its engine as beams of wood splintered. A thick gout of steam surged up through the cracks, engulfing the deck in a hot and choking fog. Snips coughed and threw herself to the floor. Mr. Peabody gripped the wheel and began to turn the ship back towards the center of Aberwick.

"Where are you doing?" Snips asked, fighting for breath through the dissolving cloud of steam.

"Back," Mr. Peabody said. "Back to finish the job I started, in a way I prayed I never would have to."

Snips drew herself to her feet, realization hitting her. "You don't mean—"

"Though we prefer the more subtle tools, the Society has never been above using violence to attain our ends," Mr. Peabody shouted above the roar of engines. "Especially when the stakes are so extraordinarily high!"

"No!" Snips cried out. "You have no idea what the hell you're doing!"

"I know precisely what I am doing," Mr. Peabody said. "You have forced my hands, Miss Snips. I am left with no alternative. Arcanum's device has already been activated."

Snips charged, but the ship was rocky; Mr. Peabody was able to intercept her while she was still wobbly on her feet. He struck her across the side of her head with the butt of his pistol, sending her down to the deck. Looming over her, he held the ship's wheel in one hand and brought the barrel down to her temple with the other.

"For the war to stop, Aberwick must die, Miss Snips. Either by maths or by fire, it will not survive this night."

"You don't know what it can do," she said. "No one does."

"Tonight, we will find out," Mr. Peabody said.

"I won't let you—"

"So much as twitch and you'll be dead," he added. "Stand still, and I'll allow you to behold the horror you have brought about."

"If you think I'm just going to sit here, you're sorely mistaken," Snips hissed.

Mr. Peabody's eyes swept out to the city before him. "It does not matter. Nothing will save Aberwick. Not this time. No last second reprieve, no manna from heaven. No knight clad in vestments of white riding upon a valiant steed—"

The roar of the second airship was deafening. Snips' hat was thrown from Mr. Peabody's head; he turned, staring at shock as the second compartment speared up through the air and slammed into the side of his ship, sending both he and Snips tumbling.

Snips snatched the rim of her hat in one hand and drew her crowbar out from her belt with the other. When the ship righted itself, she leapt to her feet and brought the weapon down in a savage blow across Mr. Peabody's wrist, forcing him to release the pistol.

"Tell me how to turn the bomb off!" Snips roared, kicking the pistol off the deck.

Mr. Peabody stumbled back, nursing his injured wrist. "It can't be deactivated," he said, grinning. "Good day and good night, Miss Snips."

William sprang out from the second ship's mast, leaping down to the deck where Snips now struggled with Mr. Peabody. Though the Society initiate was no stranger to violence, Snips had been trained to fight on the streets—she kicked, spat, and clawed, snarling like an unleashed wildcat. Mr. Peabody was forced back further and further.

"Miss Snips!" William cried out from the other side of the deck. "The whole ship's shaking!"

Snips turned; Mr. Peabody leapt at the opportunity and seized the crowbar in Snips' grip. The two of them briefly struggled as the ship quivered beneath them. With a violent curse, Snips struck Mr. Peabody in the stomach with her knee, releasing the crowbar and shoving him off the ship's back end. The Society initiate flailed as he was flipped over the railing, falling into the city below with Snips' tool held in hand.

She spat over the side after him. "Burn in hell."

"Miss Snips!" William repeated, reaching her at last. "What on earth is happening?"

Snips straightened and sighed. "It's too late," she said. "He activated the bomb."

"The bomb?" William asked.

"It was what nearly destroyed the city over ten years ago," Snips said. "A weapon to end all weapons. The Society's first attempt to prevent the war—by annihilating an entire city."

"My father's experiment," William said, aghast.

"No," Snips corrected him. "My father."

William stared at her. "What—"

"He was one of the founding members of the Society, along with Professor Daffodil and your mother," she told him. "Nigel tried to stop the war by destroying the city. Your parents stopped him."

William shook his head, finding himself confronted with more information than he could readily absorb. "How large will the explosion be?" he asked.

"I don't know. No one does," Snips said. "It just explodes, and explodes, and keeps exploding more, spreading out farther and farther—"

"How is such a diabolical engine even possible?"

"I don't know," Snips said. "I think someone in your family designed the original; Nigel stole the blueprints and built two of his own." .

"But Miss Snips," William said. "The last explosion *didn't* destroy the city."

"No," Snips agreed. "Your parents stopped it, somehow. But I don't know how."

"But the Heap is still burning, is it not?"

"At the center," Snips said. "The fire is still going on, and on. No one can even approach it without getting burnt—"

"Still exploding."

Snips paused. "What are you thinking?"

"Perhaps my parents found a way not to nullify the explosion, but to contain it. Perhaps if we take the airship there, we can do the same."

"Better than nothing," Snips said. "Do you know how to fly one of these things?"

"I was conceived in the belly of an armored dirigible," William said. "I am familiar with its operation."

"Then aim us for the Heap," she told him.

~*~

The center of the Heap was aglow in the mid-day; it still burned, tendrils of flame swelling out from a pillar of smoke. It resembled a tornado of fire and ash, writhing in endless hunger for more fuel.

William finished the last adjustments to the airship's controls, stepping back. "That's it," he told her. "It's set to carry the ship straight into the heart of it. If my parents managed to contain the first explosion, it is reasonable to assume that their solution can contain a second."

"We don't even know how this works," Snips said, watching the burning column.

"We have no alternatives, Miss Snips. If it doesn't work, we shall soon know." Despite himself, William snorted and shook his head; Snips looked at him with a raised eyebrow.

"Are you all right?"

"It just occurred to me," he said, trying to stifle his laughter. "We're on top of an armored dirigible, poised to rain down destruction on the city beneath me. I'm fairly sure I was determined to avoid this very sort of thing."

Snips slapped him on the back and handed him his umbrella.

"All right," she said. "Go."

"Funny," William replied. "I don't recall you having ever possessed the power of flight."

Snips glared.

"I mean, it certainly seems like something I'd remember,"

William continued. "'Oh yes, she can fly, silly me'. Or something like that."

"I'm not going," Snips said, turning back to the heart of the Heap.

"Yes, you are."

"No, I'm not," Snips said, shaking her head. "It's too risky. If the ship doesn't stay steady—if the winds pick up—if *anything* happens, it could shift the airship off and cause it to miss its target. Someone needs to stay and make sure it stays on course."

"No, someone does not," William said. "I did the math, Miss Snips. It will not miss."

"You don't know that."

"I know it well enough."

"There are too many lives at stake."

"Stop trying to go out in a blaze of glory."

Snips stopped, her throat squeezing around her words. "I don't need your help."

"Then help me instead," he told her. "For I have no intention of leaving this place without you, Arcadia."

She turned away from the Heap, facing William. And then, with a gradually melting reluctance, she placed her hand into his.

~*~

Together, William and Snips floated above Aberwick. They clutched at one another desperately, holding on for dear life; beneath them, Mr. Peabody's fiendish contraptions sank toward the swirling inferno that lay at the heart of the Heap.

As they drifted, a cold stillness seized the air about them. William frowned; Snips shivered.

"Did the wind just stop?" she asked.

"I think so," William said. "I think—I think it is about to happen again."

"Huh? What's going to happen again?"

But William did not answer; instead, he searched the cityscape for the familiar face of a clock

"Why did everything get so quiet? I can't even hear the

wind. It's like—" Snips stopped. They passed a sparrow, its wings spread; it was frozen stiff, hanging in the air like a Christmas ornament. "Uh."

"You can see it," William said. "Thank God. I thought I might be mad."

"What the hell is happening?"

William struggled to maintain his grip on Snips with one hand and pulled his pocket watch out with the other. He showed it to her; the second hand was stuck on six. "Time," he said. "Time is —I think that it is trying to go backwards."

"Wait, what?"

"I know that it sounds absurd," William said. "But it has done this before. This is the third time—ever since this whole affair started. I think that—"

The hand jumped back a second.

"That's what happened last time," William said.

Then it jumped back another second.

"Er," he said.

And then it jumped back ten seconds.

"All right, this is new," William admitted.

The hand spun backwards, becoming no more than a blur; the minute hand stirred to life, cranking back the hour. And as they watched, the hour hand began to move.

Above them, the sun slowly swung from one horizon to the next, its burning glow fading behind the city in an orange blossom of flame. Night came, then passed back into day; the sun now accelerated, blinking by in a streak of golden brilliance. Around them, buildings shrank and changed—blurring shapes of men speedily erected scaffolding, took down rooftops and walls, then pulled the scaffolding apart and left for home. Machines trudged back to their workshops to be disassembled, their parts distributed across the city; merchants traded money back for their goods. Muggers and thieves sprang out of alleyways to hand their victims bulging wallets at knife-point.

In only minutes, days became weeks and weeks became months. They watched the ebb and flow of the city, traveling back to the final instants before the fire that devastated the Heap. Smoke was pulled from the sky and drawn in by flames that fell away, leaving the buildings pristine and untouched. The healing inferno crept to the center, back to where the explosion had first began— and then the world began to shiver and break.

"Hold on," William said, but his voice was distant and warped; color bled out of everything, and the universe around them began to unravel, and then...

He was standing on solid ground.

The Heap was gone. In its place was a geometrical impossibility; a sight that defied everything that William understood about the world.

Immense glaciers were suspended in a starless sky, the sound of crumbling ice surrounding him as they scraped across each other in a slow and graceful waltz. Beneath his feet was a layer of flattened frost; across from him was a bridge that lead to another glacier—and on top of it was a gazebo. Inside the gazebo was a chair and table, at which sat a man.

The man was drinking tea.

"Snips?" William called out, but his voice was lost among howling winds and echoes of snapping ice. He turned about frantically, searching for any sign of her; every way he looked, there was nothing but frost. "Arcadia!"

"Relax," the man in the gazebo said. "She's fine."

William turned, pointing the tip of the umbrella at him. "Who are you? Where am I? What's happened to the Heap—what's happened to—"

"I fear that this is a bit complicated," the man said, "and I am somewhat out of practice when it comes to complicated explanations."

William noticed now that the man was old and haggard; he wore a dusty suit and had a long, shaggy beard.

"All right," William said. "If Snips is all right, where is she?"

"I think you mean when," the man said.

"Now!" William cried.

"Precisely," the man replied, and then he smiled. "Have a seat, William."

William Daffodil visits a place lost to time.

"How do you know my name?"

"We've met before. Here."

"No we haven't!" William said. "I've never met you before in my life. I would certainly remember visiting such a strange, wretched place." He waved his umbrella about.

"Well, you haven't met me yet in your timeline," the man said. "But we've met in mine. Here, anyway," he added.

"What?"

The old man sighed. "I said it was complicated. Sit down."

William relented, walking across the small bridge of ice. He used the umbrella as a cane, making sure not to trip on the slick ground; when he sat down, he was surprised to find that the tea was quite hot and accompanied by fresh, warm biscuits.

"Feel free to have one," the old man said, but William only shook his head.

"I want to see Arcadia."

"You will. In the meanwhile, please, relax. Let's talk for a while. Although this is the first time you have met me, it will be the last time I see you. I would like to enjoy it, if I may."

William hesitated, then reached for one of the biscuits. He took it and tasted it; it was quite delicious. A moment after taking the bite, he ventured a question: "Where did you get this food? I do not see an oven..."

"You brought it to me," the old man said, and William choked.

"Will you stop with that? It's confusing," William said. "I haven't brought you anything."

"You will," the old man pointed out. "In your future, and my past. Like I said, it's complicated."

William paused, half-eaten biscuit in hand. "Are you—are you—"

"Yes?"

"Are you my father?"

The old man laughed. "Oh, goodness me, no. No, most certainly not."

William's shoulders slumped. "Oh. I thought, perhaps—"

"I'm your grandfather. Jerome Daffodil."

William snapped to attention. "I—I'm sorry, I beg your pardon?"

"This place," Jerome said, gesturing around him, "is a place outside of your timeline. Rather than traveling forward, it travels backward. For me, this is the last time we'll meet; for you, it is our first time."

"You're saying—you're saying I've been here before? In my future?"

"And in my past," Jerome said, agreeing.

"Really, now," William said, finishing the biscuit and dabbing his fingers on a napkin. "Are you the one responsible for that sordid business with the clocks?"

"Yes," Jerome said. "I've tried to bring you here on several occasions. It's a tricky thing to do, and I don't always get the timing right. Sometimes I try too soon, sometimes I try too late. I hope it didn't cause you too much trouble."

"You terrified me out of my wits!" William fumed. "I thought I was going mad!"

"That seems to be a running theme with our family," Jerome pointed out.

"Fair enough," William said. "How does this place even exist?"

"Your parents created it by accident, when they attempted to stop the first bomb from detonating," Jerome said. "They used my time machine to steal an hour of time and tried to keep the explosion isolated there."

"It didn't work," William said.

"Not completely," Jerome agreed. "They were nearly too late; some of the explosion escaped. Although that isn't their fault. The time machine was never very reliable."

"What about the bomb that Arcadia and I directed to the center of the Heap?"

"It's temporally displaced, just like the first one," Jerome said. "Trapped in an hour lost to time."

"I have so many questions," William said. "So many things I want to ask you."

"And I'm afraid we don't have enough time to go through

them," he said.

"You said this is the last time we'll meet," William said. "What happens to you, then? Is there anything I can do for you? Can you come back with me?"

"No," Jerome said, "I have to stay. And you have to look after Arcadia."

"Miss Snips?" William asked. "How do you even know her name?"

"You told me it. As you told me about her," Jerome explained. "She's the key to this whole affair, William. She's— well, like this place, it's complicated."

"Try me."

"She's the coin flip that lands on its side. The one-in-a-million shot you can always count on. She's probability reversed and turned inside out. A madman's curious experiment gone terribly right."

"You mean wrong?"

"I mean right," Jerome said. "And I'm afraid it's time for you to go. You can't stay here very long, or I won't be able to send you and Arcadia back."

"When will I see you again?"

"Soon, soon. In the meanwhile, I have something for you— two somethings, actually," he said. He drew a tarnished silver pocket watch out from his coat pocket; it was heavy and fitted with all manner of mechanisms, including a glass diode and several wires that dangled from its back. "This is—ah, don't tinker with it, not now, at least. It's very dangerous."

William took the watch, peering down at it. "What is it?"

"The time machine."

William looked up at Jerome with a raised eyebrow. "...really?"

"Yes. But it doesn't work. Well, sometimes it does. But never in the way it's supposed to," Jerome said, sighing. "I never quite figured out the bloody thing."

"What am I supposed to do with it?"

"Use it."

"But you said not to—"

"You'll know when," Jerome said. "Just hold on to it. You'll need it."

"You said you had something else for me," William said.

"Yes. A message," Jerome replied. "From you. In the future."

"What was it?" William asked. The world around him was beginning to shift again; the lethargic dance of the glaciers slowed to an halt as color began to drain from everything around him. In front of him, Jerome was smiling. He said:

"Your parents survived."

Once again, the world unraveled.

~*~

"William!"

William Daffodil opened his eyes.

Snips was crouched over him, her eyes dark with concern. He sat up, prompting her to roll back in a crouch besides him; they had landed somewhere in the Heap.

"Everything went mad back there," Snips said. "For a moment, you disappeared, and I was falling. Then, out of no where, I blacked out and woke up here. With you."

William opened his fist. In it was the watch his grandfather had given him.

"Are you all right, William?"

William placed the watch in his pocket, struggling to his feet. "Yes, actually. I think that I am."

~*~

The little boy had stashed himself into a far off corner of the boarding school, far away from the prying eyes of his peers. He nursed his bloody nose in secret, doing his best to suppress the sniffles that fought to swell up into his throat.

When the girl appeared, she gave him a terrible start; the girl's dormitory was kept separate from the boy's dormitory, and he wondered at once how she had managed to sneak past the

*instructors. She wore a ferocious scowl and a fresh black eye,
along with the school's drab uniform. It showed signs of having
been torn and scuffed in a recent struggle.*

*"Here," she growled, shoving the book back into his arms;
it was the small story book that the other boys had violently taken
from him. He looked down to it, then back up to her, trying to
figure out what had happened.*

"Um—"

"It's yours, isn't it?" she said.

William nodded.

*"Then take it," she said, pressing it against his palms. At
last, he did as she said, accepting the book up and pulling it up
against his chest.*

*The girl sank down next to him, leaning against the wall;
William didn't know what to say. He had never talked to girls
before, never mind one like this. He struggled for something
meaningful, but all that he managed to blurt out was the first
thought in his head.*

"Uh, so, what's your favorite color?"

*"Green," she said without thinking, as if she had been
expecting the question all along.*

*He hesitated, then opened his mouth to say something else,
but she cut him off.*

*"My father used to read me that book," she said. "Sir
Gawain and the Green Knight, right?"*

William nodded again.

*"I like it," she said, and then she added: "I heard your
parents died a week ago. I'm sorry. I'm running away to find my
father in the city. Do you want to come with me?"*

*William blinked, at a loss for how to respond. "I'm—I'm
sorry?"*

*"Yes or no," she said, clearly agitated and wanting an
answer. "I'm leaving tonight, so I can't wait around, okay?"*

*"I—I don't know," William said. "Why are you running
away?"*

*"Because I want to see my father again," she said.
"Because I haven't seen him since I was a little girl. Are you*

Arcadia and William meet as children.

coming or not?"

"I can't," William said. "My grandmother will come for me, soon; I'm sure of it."

"Suit yourself," she said, and then she rose back up to her feet. "My father's a very rich and important person, so when I find him, I'm sure we can come back to adopt you."

William watched as she walked off, then turned back to his book. The very next day, the girl was gone; from then on, he could not help but secretly wish he had told her yes.

~*~

EPILOGUE: IN WHICH THESE MATTERS ARE AT LAST BROUGHT TO A TEMPORARY CLOSE

More astute members of the audience (an esteemed group to which *you*, dear reader, undoubtedly belong) may have noticed that until this point, we have talked much about Count Orwick's nature but little of his appearance. This is not without reason. Count Vladimere von Orwick was a scoundrel.

He was a creature of such abhorrent character that, for fear of your health, our censorous editors have banned us from describing him to you. We cannot write a word of his nose (which had caused several persons of weaker constitutions to faint), nor spend a moment dallying upon his eyes (which were under investigation for their involvement in the tragic death of Mr. Penrose). We have been forbidden from so much as even mentioning his mouth (beyond, of course, noting that we shan't mention it).

So when called upon to imagine Count Orwick, we ask you to think instead of an innocent and helpless fruit. In particular, a deliciously ripe, juicy orange—with skin that parts beneath your fingers, sliding away like frost from a window on the first day of spring.

It was an orange that Count Orwick now worked upon, peeling it with great relish. Miss Primrose could not prevent herself from shifting uncomfortably in her chair; the Count had a way of making you pity his breakfast.

"A clever trick," Count Orwick observed, finishing the orange with calm delight. "Disabling the calculation engines to prevent them from resetting."

"Mr. Daffodil was instrumental in both the realization and execution of the plan," Miss Primrose explained. "I have requested in my report that he be recognized for—"

"Done," Count Orwick said, waving his hand dismissively. "Mr. Daffodil will be taking over the Steamwork, filling in for the now-deceased Mr. Eddington. He will be instituting the very same plan that Mr. Copper had proposed—wiring all calculation engines together so we may prevent these sort of financial disasters in the future."

"That brings me no small degree of comfort."

"Of course. The next order of business, please."

"Just a matter of clarification," Miss Primrose said. "We wanted to know exactly where you were during these recent, ah, events."

"Mr. Peabody foresaw my interference and sought to eliminate me as a potential threat. He poisoned me shortly before launching his insidious plan's final stroke," Count Orwick said.

"You were poisoned?" Miss Primrose said. "But then, how did you—"

"Poison is a regular occupational hazard in my profession. I carry several different antidotes on my person at all times," Orwick said. "It was a simple matter to ferret out which poison Mr. Peabody had employed. Although he had done well to hide his true loyalties from me, I knew him enough to realize he would choose his instrument of murder on the basis of absurd irony."

"He poisoned you with hemlock," Miss Primrose said.

Orwick's smile grew several sizes larger. "Indeed."

"But, ah," Miss Primrose said, hesitating. "Sir, there *is* no cure for hemlock."

"Oh, yes," Count Orwick agreed. "That is what those botany books say, isn't it?"

Miss Primrose fell silent for quite a while.

"If that is all, Miss Primrose—your check is, as they say, in the mail."

"That's it, then?"

"There is still the matter of Mr. Peabody's accomplices, and the matter of Professor Hemlock himself, as well as the damage this whole affair has done to our already lagging economy—but yes, Miss Primrose. As far as you are concerned, that is 'it'."

Orwick paused, then added with a wickedly gleeful smile: "Unless, of course, I could interest you in a job. Mr. Peabody did leave a rather unfortunate vacancy."

The speed with which Miss Primrose left Count Orwick's room could not be described with any term besides legendary.

~*~

Snips waited for her outside of Count Orwick's office. Above them, the morning airships swept up into the sky to peddle their wares. Below, marketplaces buzzed with life; steam-driven devices hummed as they trudged down the streets. Over, under, and through it all, the trains began to move—pumping equal parts prosperity and corruption through the city's brass-lined veins.

Miss Primrose noticed a growing pile of discarded bandages at Snips' feet. The thief was unraveling the wrappings that Orwick's men had put on her.

"That is not particularly wise, Miss Snips."

"Probably not."

Miss Primrose stepped forward. Rather than press on with her complaint, she thought it over, and reached to up to unwind the bandage that had been placed over her own forehead.

"Count Orwick could likely have been convinced to grant you some manner of reward," Miss Primrose said as she folded the bandage up. "You have gone above and beyond the call of duty, Miss Snips. Perhaps you should seek audience with him."

"I don't want to encourage him," Snips said. "I hate his type. He wants to control everything. Maybe he's the best person for the job; maybe he *should* control everything. But it still ticks me off."

"Hm. I think that I might be starting to understand your point of view," Miss Primrose admitted.

Snips sighed. "Listen—don't get any wrong ideas. It was fun, but I just wanted to get that devil off my back."

"I see. I imagine, then, that you would never consider coming to work with me."

Snips looked at Miss Primrose. "Huh?"

"I've begun to think that the Watts Detective Agency could do with a little illegitimacy," Miss Primrose admitted. And then she waggled her eyebrows.

"You're—are you serious?"

"Quite."

Snips laughed. "One condition."

"Name it, Miss Snips."

"No more 'Miss'. Just Snips."

"As you wish, Snips." Miss Primrose said. "Don't you have somewhere to be?"

"Yeah," Snips said. "I've got an appointment with a mummy." She made a face.

~*~

William stared with slack-jawed shock at the smoldering wreckage of Napsbury Asylum.

A hole had been torn through the side of the facility; behind it lay a rubble-strewn path occasionally interrupted either by a bruised and groaning asylum inmate or a dazed looking feline dressed in smart formal attire.

William followed the path for as long as he dared; when he realized where it was going, he turned and hunted down the first doctor he could find.

"My grandmother," he said, pinning an elderly physician to the wall. "What did she do?!"

"D-Daffodil?" the gentleman stammered, wheezing. "We couldn't stop her! She was like—she was a demon! She was atop of some monstrous, mechanical thing—"

"But that's impossible," William said. "How could she have powered it?! There's nothing here to run a machine on—nothing but potatoes and—"

He cut himself off as he felt something brush up against his feet. Looking down, he caught sight of Mr. Snugglewuggums; the feline in the tophat and monocle busily purred and shoved his face against William's ankle.

It was then that William noticed the smell of singed fur mixed with fried potatoes. He reached down and touched Mr. Snugglewuggums' head. Immediately, a burst of electricity crackled up from between the cat's ears, shocking William's fingertip.

"It couldn't be," William said. "She couldn't have—"

Sensing his distraction, the doctor used the moment to slip away from William. Rather than pursue the man and continue with his interrogation, William turned back toward the path of destruction and followed it to its source. When he arrived at his grandmother's room, he found the blueprints for the machine underneath her pillow.

The paper described an immense ambulatory engine powered on one side by a cauldron of potatoes and on the other side by a barrel full of static-generating cats. A stick-figured version of Mrs. Daffodil sat at the engine's helm, beside what William assumed was Mr. Brown and Mr. Wanewright.

Mr. Snugglewuggum meowed. William carefully folded up the designs and placed them in his pocket, then reached down and pulled the cat up into his arms. As he carried the feline to the door, William started to twitch.

By the time he left the room, the twitch had become a spasm; by the time he reached the asylum's exit, the spasm had become a giggle.

By the time he was walking down the street, the giggle had become a genuine mad cackle.

~*~

"He has been expecting you," Starkweather said, leading Snips into Nigel's study.

"I bet he has," Snips replied.

Starkweather waited by the door until Nigel waved him away.

"Can I help you, Arcadia?" Nigel asked, pressing his bandage-wrapped hands together.

"You already did."

"I beg your pardon?"

"You meddled," Snips said, her voice like a frost drenched dagger.

Nigel spoke slowly, choosing his words with care. "And exactly how did you reach that conclusion...?"

"Peabody. Even if he hadn't said what he did, there was no

reason for him to keep me alive back on the train. Not unless you cut him a deal."

"I see. And what if I did? My actions may have saved your life."

"Maybe," Snips said. "No, not maybe. Definitely."

"And so you came here to reprimand me, then? For 'meddling'?"

"No," Snips said, her eyes drifting to the jars that lined the shelves of his study—as if the answers to her questions could be found among the preserved remains of extinct species. "No, I didn't come here to reprimand you. But I didn't come here to thank you, either. I'm not sure what I came here for. I just wanted you to know that *I* know. And that it doesn't change anything."

"Why would I think otherwise?"

"I don't know," Snips said, shaking her head. "Look, what do you want from me? Do you want me to to forgive you? On behalf of the thousands upon thousands you've killed? Do you want me to give you a big, warm hug? Put on a dress, act like a 'good daughter'? Do you want me to come back home?"

"Are any of those things on the table, Arcadia?"

"No," she said, and there was a murderous force behind the word. "No. None of those things are on the table."

"Good," Nigel said.

"Good?"

"Good," he repeated. "As for your question, I will answer it, in exchange for you answering one of my own."

Snips glared, but nodded. "Go ahead."

"Why do you hate me?"

"You're a murderer."

Nigel snorted. "Have I killed anyone you knew? Have I killed someone close to you? Your hatred is far too intimate for the callous scorn we heap upon killers and tyrants."

Snips shook her head. "Do you know what it was like, growing up and admiring you? Reading the articles about all the wonderful things you'd done, the wonderful things you built? Hearing all the stories? Wanting to be like you?"

Nigel grew silent.

"And then do you know what happened, Nigel? I ran away to find you. I ran away to meet the man I had read about in newspapers and scientific journals; I ran away to find the kindly, brilliant philanthropist. And do you know what I found?"

Nigel turned his head away.

"I found a man who had murdered thousands in the name of moral righteousness. A man who cloaked himself in shadows and secrets; who manipulated others as if they were mere tokens in a grand game. I went out to find my father. Instead, I found you."

"And that's why I hate you, Nigel. Maybe it's spiteful. Maybe it's unfair. But I really don't care. I hate you because you aren't the man you were supposed to be."

"And so that's what all this is about?" Nigel asked, turning back to Snips. "The cheap hat, the dirty coat, the silver tooth? Just a little girl rebelling against a father who failed to live up to her expectations?"

Snips was upon him in an instant. Her hands seized either of his wrists, pinning them to the chair; Nigel writhed in pain, but did not cry out.

"You know that's not what this is about," Snips hissed, leaning forward into him. "You *damn* well know that."

"Arcadia," Nigel whimpered. "Pl-please—"

Snips released him, stepping back. Nigel coughed, rubbing his wrists.

"What I did with my life has nothing to do with you, Nigel."

Nigel wheezed and straightened back in his chair, slowly recovering. "You answered my question, so I will answer yours. You wanted to know what I want. It is only this: For you to flourish."

"Why?"

"Because you are my daughter."

"No," Snips replied. "I'm not your daughter. And you sure as hell aren't my father." She turned, moving toward the exit.

"Didn't you hear? My father is dead. He died in a fire."

~*~

When she met him at the Steamwork, Snips insisted on going in first; William patiently waited outside of Mr. Eddington's office until he heard her shout out to him.

"All right," she told him. "Come on in."

When he stepped inside, he was confronted with the familiar scene of his previous employer's belongings. But then he noticed that the bookcase on one side of the room had been shifted over, revealing a hidden passageway that dived deep into the Steamwork. Straightening with surprise, he crept forward and peeked down the stairway.

Snips' voice arose from below. "Come on, William," she shouted. "I'm waiting."

William took the stairs one step at a time. As he did so, he felt his throat clench; he did not know why, but he felt as if he was on the verge of something familiar.

The air was heavy and wet, ripe with age; whorls of dust were whipped up with every step. As he reached the bottom of the stairs, he heard a gentle click and electric *hum*; light after light flickered on, revealing to him a sprawling laboratory of marvels long lost to time.

His mouth went dry.

Snips stood behind one of the tables, smiling at him. For the first time that he had seen, she wore the expression without a hint of malice or contempt; it was the smile of someone who was sincerely happy.

"Welcome to your parents' laboratory."

~*~

Starkweather dipped his hands in the basin, washing them clean of blood. His scarf had been removed, leaving the metal bolts in the side of his neck exposed.

"Fascinating," Nigel spoke, leaning forward in his wheel chair to inspect the figure who lay upon the table. "The sheer number of his scars is daunting. And now his missing eye... No wonder the man sought to numb himself with drugs. He must be in

Mr. Starkweather and Nigel Arcanum discuss the current situation while the rescued assassin rests.

constant physical pain."

"I would not think you would find the matter of another's scars to be fascinating," Starkweather coldly rebuffed him, finishing his work at the sink. "In any matter, his wounds have been tended to, and the grafts completed. He will survive."

"Yes, yes," Nigel said, sounding distracted. The assassin was stretched across a slab of iron beneath the Arcanum estate, stripped of his clothing and eyepatch. His injuries had been grievious, but a quick intervention had brought him underneath the cryptozoologist's care. "Your steady hands and my sharp mind have provided a second chance for our little friend."

"I find it surprising that your minions managed to accomplish the task of bringing him here without incident," Starkweather confessed. "So far, they have proven themselves otherwise incompetent."

"I could not disagree more," Nigel said. "Why, armed only with my instructions, Mr. Tongue and Mr. Cheek singlehandedly prevented the collapse of Aberwick's banks while simultaneously maintaining their cover as instruments of Mr. Peabody and the Society."

Starkweather raised an eyebrow, finishing at the sink. "Oh? And yet the newspapers report that it was Mr. Daffodil's quick thinking that accomplished this task."

"As it should be. I will allow the boy his well-deserved accolades; he provided a clever solution to a problem he was unaware had already been addressed," Nigel said. "I knew of what the Society had planned for Aberwick's financial district since I first investigated Hemlock's mysterious attacks against the banks. I sent my dear creations out to each of the banks a day prior, placing account exploits of my own to counter Mr. Peabody's."

Starkweather's never-ending scowl only deepened. "Why did you not inform your daughter of this from the beginning? Why the duplicity?"

"If I had told her that I had plans to diffuse the situation, she would have left the matter alone," Nigel said. "And if I had asked her to investigate it, she would have refused. Instead, I presented her with a mystery and allowed her to draw her own conclusion."

"But why?"

"Because my daughter is immensely resourceful, and a clever investigator. She could discover something I had missed," Nigel said. "And she did. I was unaware that Mr. Peabody had one of my bombs in his possession—never mind that the man was determined enough to attempt and use it."

"Then I assume this matter is closed."

"Not at all, my dear conscience. The account exploits used against the banks were Mr. Peabody's creation, but if your fellow constructs are to be believed—and I am sure they are—he was working under the authority of Professor Hemlock, a man I know nothing of. And I assure you," Nigel added, his voice growing dark, "that a man who can elude my eyes and ears is a dangerous man indeed."

"You have defeated him, however. The bomb is lost," Starkweather pointed out, "and the banks shall soon be rendered immune to attack. The Society can do nothing to bring Aberwick down."

"There is still one bomb left."

"Where? You built a third bomb?"

"In a manner of speaking," Nigel said. "I built three devices in all; two after studying Jeremiah's model, and one with his aid."

Starkweather stiffened. "William's heart."

Nigel slowly nodded. "And that is why we must keep our eyes upon William and Arcadia. For if Hemlock still wishes to destroy the city of Aberwick—and I have every reason to believe he does—surely, he will seek out the clockwork heart."

~*~

The Detective Watts & Sons Agency is back in business!